MEN AND WOMEN; IN A BALCONY; DRAMATIS PERSONAE

Robert Browning

www.General-Books.net

Publication Data:

Title: Men and Women
Subtitle: In a Balcony; Dramatis Personae
Author: Robert Browning
Reprinted: 2010, General Books, Memphis, Tennessee, USA
Publisher: T. Y. Crowell company
Publication date: 1898
Subjects: Drama / General; Drama / American; Drama / Anthologies; Literary Criticism / Drama; Literary Criticism / Poetry; Poetry / English, Irish, Scottish, Welsh
BISAC subject codes: DRA000000, DRA001000, LIT013000, LIT014000, POE005020

MEN AND WOMEN; IN A BALCONY; DRAMATIS PERSONAE

1

MEN AND WOMEN; IN A BALCONY; DRAMATIS PERSONAE

INTRODUCTION.

Thirteen years after the publication, in 1855, of the Poems, in two volumes, entitled " Men and Women," Browning reviewed his work and made an interesting re-classification of it. He separated the simpler pieces of a lyric or epic cast,–such rhymed presentations of an emotional moment, for example, as "Mesmerism" and "A Womans Last Word," or the picturesque rhymed verse telling a story of an experience, such as " Childe Roland" and "The Statue and the Bust,"–from their more complex companions, which were almost altogether in blank verse, and, in general, markedly personified a typical man in his environment, a Cleon or Fra Lippo, a Rudel or a Blougram. These boldly sculptured figures he set apart from the others as the fit components of the more closely related group which ever since has constituted the division now known as " Men and Women."

Possibly the poet took some pleasure in thus bringing to confusion those critics who, beginning first to take any notice of his work after the issue of these volumes of 1855, discovered therein poems they praised chiefly by means of contrasting them with foregoing work they found unnoticeable and later work they declared inscrutable. Their bland discrimination, at any rate, in favor of " Men and Women became henceforth inapplicable, since the poet not only cast out from the division they elected to honor the little lyrical pieces that caught their eye, but also brought to the front, from his earlier neglected work of the same kind as the monologues retained, his Johannes Agricola of 1836, Pictor Ignotus of 1845, and Rudel of 1842. Later criticism, more-over, that even yet assumes to ring the old changes of discrimination against everything but " Men and Women," is made not merely inapplicable by this re-arrangement, but uninformed, a meaningless echo of a borrowed opinion which has had the very ground from under it shifted.

The self-criticism of which this re-arrangement gives a hint is more valuable.

All the shorter poems accumulated up to this period, various as they are in theme and metrical form, are uniform in the fashioning of their contour and color. As soon as this underlying uniformity of make is recognized, it may be seen to be the coloring and relief belonging to any sort of poetic material, whether ordinarily accounted dramatic material or not, which is imaginatively externalized and made concrete. This peculiarity of make Browning early acknowledged in his estimate of his shorter poems as characteristic of his touch, when he called his lyrics and romances dramatic. He became consciously sensitive later to slight variations effected by his manipulation in shape and shade which it yet takes a little thought to discern, even after his own re-division of his work has given the clew to his self-judgments.

Not only events, deeds, and characters,–the usual subject-matter moulded and irradiated by dramatic power,–but thoughts, impressions, experiences, impulses, no matter how spiritualized or complex or mobile, are transfused with the enlivening light of his creative energy in his shorter poems. Perhaps the very path struck out through them by the poet in his re-division may be traced between the leaves silently closing together again behind him if it be noticed that among these poems there are some with footholds firmly rooted in the earth and others whose proper realm is air. These have wings for alighting, for flitting thither and hither, or for pursuing some sudden rapt whirl of flight in Heavens face at fancys bidding. They are certainly not less original than those other solider, earth-fast poems, but they are less unique. Being motived in transient fancy, they are more akin to poems by other hands, and could be classed more readily with them by any observer, despite all differences, as little poetic romances or as a species of lyric.

They were probably first found praiseworthy, not only because they were simpler, but because, being more like work already understood and approved, a less adventurous criticism was needed to taste their quality. The other longer poems in blank verse, graver and more dignified, yet even more vivid, and far more life-encompassing, which bore the rounded impress of the living human being, instead of the shadowy motion of the-lively human fancy,–these are the birth of a process of imaginative brooding upon the development of man by means of individuality throughout the slow, unceasing flow of human history. Browning evidently grew aware that whatever these poems of personality might prove to be worth to the world, these were the ones deserving of a place apart, under the early title of " Men and Women," which he thought especially suited to them, as the more roundly modelled and distinctively colored exemplars of his peculiar faculty.

In his next following collection, under the similar descriptive title of "Dramatis Personje," he added to this class of work, shaping in the mould of blank verse mainly used for " Men and Women " his personifications of the Medium Mr. Sludge, the embryo theologian Caliban, the ripened mystical saint of "A Death in the Desert; " while Abt Vogler, the creative musician, Rabbi ben Ezra, the intuitional philosopher, and the chastened adept in loving, James Lees wife, although held within the embrace of their makers dramatic conception of them, as persons of his stage, were made to pour out their speech in rhyme as Johannes Agricola in the earlier volume uttered his creed and Rudel his love-message, as if the heat of their emotion-moved personality required such an outlet.

Some such general notion as this of the scope of this volume, and of the design of the poet in the construction, classification, and orderly arrangement of so much of his briefer work as is here contained seems to be borne out upon a closer examination.

On the threshold of this new poetic world of personality stands the Poet of the poem significantly called "Transcendentalism," who is speaking to another poet about the too easily obvious, metaphor-bare philosophy of his opus in twelve books. That the admonishing poet is stationed there at the very door-sill of the Gallery of Men and Women is surely not accidental, even if Brownings habit of plotting his groups of poems symmetrically by opening with a prologue-poem sounding the right key, and rounding the theme with an epilogue, did not tend to prove it intentional.

It is an open secret that the last poem in " Men and Women," for instance, is an epilogue of autobio graphical interest, gathering up the foregoing strains of his lyre, for a few last chords, in so intimate a way that the actual fall of the fingers may be felt, the pausing smile seen, as the performer turns towards the one who inspired " One Word More." The appropriateness of "Transcendentalism" as a prologue need be no more of a secret than that of " One Word More" as an epilogue, although it is left to betray itself.

Other poets writing on the poet, Emerson for example, and Tennyson, place the outright plain name of their thought at the head of their verses, without any attempt to make their titles dress their parts and keep as thoroughly true to their roles as the poems themselves. But a complete impersonation of his thought in name and style as well as matter is characteristic of Browning, and his personified poets playing tlieir parts together in "Transcendentalism" combine to exhibit a little masque exemplifying their writers view of the Poet as veritably as if he had named it specifically "The Poet." One poet shows the other, and brings him visibly forward; but even in such a morsel of dramatic workmanship as this, fifty-one lines all told, there is the complexity and involution of life itself, and, as ever in Brownings monologues, over the shoulder of the poet more obviously portrayed peers as livingly the face of the poet portraying him. And this one—the admonishing poet—is set there with his "sudden rose," as if to indicate with that symbol of poetic magic what kind of spell was sought to be exercised by their maker to conjure up in his house of song the figures that people its niches. Could a poem be imagined more cunningly devised to reveal a typical poetic personality, and a typical theory of poetic method, through its way of revealing another? What poet could have composed it but one who himself employed the dramatic method of causing the abstract to be realizable through the concrete image of it, instead of the contrary mode of seeking to divest the objective of its concrete form in order to lay bare its abstract essence? This opposite theory of the poetic function is precisely the Boehme mode, against which the veiled dramatic poet, who is speaking in favor of the Halberstadtian magic, admonishes his brother, while he himself in practical substantiation of his theory of poetics brings bodily in sight the boy-face above the winged harp, vivified and beautiful himself, although his poem is but a shapeless mist.

Not directly, then, but indirectly, as the dramatic poet ever reveals himself, does the sophisticated face of the subtle poet of " Men and Women " appear as the source of power behind both of the poets of this poem, prepossessing the reader of the verity and beauty of the theory of poetic art therein exemplified.

Such an interpretation of " Transcendentalism," and such a conception of it as a key to the art of the volume it opens, chimes in harmoniously with the note sounded in the next following poem, "How it Strikes a Contemporary." Here again a typical poet is personified, not, however, by means of his own poetic way of seeing, but of the prosaic way in which he is seen by a contemporary, the whole, of course, being poetically seen and presented by the over-poet, Browning himself, and in such a manifold way that the reader is enabled to conceive as vividly of the talker and his mental atmosphere and social background–the people and habitudes of the good old town of Valladolid–as of the betalked-of Corregidor himself; while by the totality of these concrete images an impression is conveyed of the dramatic mode of poetic expression which is far more convincing than any explicit theoretic statement of it could be, because so humanly animated.

"Artemis Prologizes seems to have been selected to close this little opening sequence of poems on the poet, because that fragment of a larger projected work could find place here almost as if it were a poets exercise in blank verse. Its smooth and spacious rhythm, flawless and serene as the distant Greek mythos of the hero and the goddess it celebrates, is in striking contrast with the rougher, but brighter and more humanly colloquial blank verse of " Bishop Blougrams Apology," for example, or the stiff carefulness of the "Epistle" of Karshish. It might alone suffice, by comparison with the metrical craftsmanship of the other poems of "Men and Women," to assure the observant reader that never was a good workman more baselessly accused of metrical carelessness than the poet who designedly varies his complicated verse-effects to suit every inner impulse belonging to his dramatic subject. A golden finish being in place in this statuesque, "Hyperion "-like monologue of Artemis, behold here it is, and none the less perfect because not merely the outcome of the desire to produce a polished piece of poetic mechanism.

Browning, perhaps, linked his next poem, "The Strange Medical Experience of Karshish, the Arab Physician," with the calm prologizing of the Hellenic goddess, by association of the "wise pharmacies" of Esculapius, with the inquisitive sagacity of Karshish, "the not-incurious in Gods handiwork." By this ordering of the poems, the reader may now enjoy, at any rate, the contrasts between three historic phases of wisdom in bodily ills; the phase presented in the de pendence of the old Greek healer upon simple physical effects,–soothing "with lavers the torn brow," and laying "the stripes and jagged ends of flesh even once more; and the phases typified, on the one side, by the ingenious Arab, sire of the modern scientist, whose patient correlation of facts and studious, sceptical scrutiny of cause and effect are caught in the bud in the diagnosis transmitted by Karshish to Abib, and, on the other side, by the Nazarene physician, whose inspired secret of summoning out of the believing soul of man the power to control his body, so baffled and fascinated Karshish, drawing his attention in Lazarus to just that connection of the known physical with the unknown psychical nature which is still mystically alluring the curiosity of investigators.

From the childlike, over-idealizing mood of Lazarus toward the God who had succored him, inducing in him so fatalistic an indifference to human concerns, there is but a step to the rapture of absolute theology expressed in the person of Johannes Agricola. Such poems as these put before the cool gaze of the present century the very men of the elder day of religion. Their robes shine with an unearthly light, and their abstracted eyes are hypnotized by the effulgence of their own haloes. Yet the poet never fails to insinuate some naive foible in their personification, a numbness of the heart or an archaism of soul, which reveals the possessed one as but a human brother, after all, shaped by his environment, and embodying the spirit of an historic epoch out of which the current of modern life is still streaming.

The group of art poems which follows similarly presents a dramatic synthesis of the art of the Renaissance as represented by three types of painters. The religious devotion of the monastic painter, whose ecstatic spirit breathes in "Pictor Ignotus," probably gives this poem its place adjoining Agricola and Lazarus. His artists hankering to create that beauty to bless the world with which his soul refrains from grossly satisfying, unites the poem with the two following ones. In the first of these the realistic artist, Fra Lippo, is graphically pictured personally ushering in the high noon of the Italian efflorescence. In the second, the gray of that day of art is silvering the self-painted portrait of the prematurely frigid and facile formalist, Andrea del Sarto. In " Pictor Ignotus " not only the personality of the often unknown and unnamed painting-brother of the monasteries is made clear, but also the nature of his beautiful cold art and the enslavement of both art and personality to ecclesiastical beliefs and ideals. In " Fra Lippo Lippi" not alone the figure of the frolicsome monk appears caught in his pleasure-loving escapade, amid that picturesque knot of alert-witted Florentine guards, ready to appreciate all the good points in his story of his life and the protection the arms of the Church and the favor of the Medici have afforded his genius, but, furthermore, is illustrated the irresistible tendency of the art-impulse to expand beyond the bounds set for it either by laws of Church or art itself, and to find beauty wheresoever in life it chooses to turn the light of its gaze. So, also, in " Andrea del Sarto," the easy cleverness of the unaspiring craftsman is not embodied apart from the abject relationship which made his very soul a bond-slave to the gross mandates of "the Cousins whistle." Yet in all three poems the biographic and historic conditions contributing toward the individualizing of each artist are so unobtrusively epitomized and vitally blended, that, while M. w.–i scarcely any item of specific study of the art and artists of the Renaissance would be out of place in illustrating the essential truth of the portraiture and assisting in the better appreciation of the poem, there is no detail of the workmanship which does not fall into the background as a mere accessory to the dominant figure throueh whose relationship to his art his station in the past is made clear.

This sort of dramatic synthesis of a salient, historical epoch is again strikingly disclosed in the following poem of the Renaissance period, "The Bishop Orders his

Tomb at Saint Praxeds Church." In this, again, the art-connoissearship of the prelacy, so important an element in the Italian movement towards art-expression, is revealed to the life in the beauty-loving personality of the dying bishop. And by means, also, of his social ties with his nephews, called closer than they wish about him now; with her whom " men would have to. be their mother once"; with old Gandolf, whom he fancies leering at him from his onion-stone tomb; and with all those strong desires of the time for the delight of being envied, for marble baths and horses and brown Greek manuscripts and mistresses, the seeds of human decay planted in the plot of Time, known as the Central Renaissance, by the same lingering fleshli-ness and self-destroying self-indulgence as was at home in pagan days, are livingly exposed to the historic sense.

Is the modern prelate portrayed in " Bishop Blougrams Apology," with all his bland subtlety, complex culture, and ripened perceptions, distant as the nineteenth century from the sixteenth, very different at bottom from his Renaissance brother, in respect to his native hankering for the pleasure of estimation above his fellows? Gigadibs is his Gandolf, whom he would craftily overtop. He is the one raised for the time above the commonalty by his criticism of the bishop, to whom the prelate would fain show how little he was to be despised, how far more honored and powerful he was among men. As for Gigadibs, it is to be noticed that Browning quietly makes him do more thin leer enviously at his complacent competitor from a tomb-top. The "sudden healthy vehemence" that struck him and made him start to test his first plough in a new world, and read his last chapter of St. John to better purpose than towards self-glorification beyond his fellows, is a parable of the more profitable life to be found in following the famous injunction of that chapter in Johns Gospel, "Feed my sheep!" than in causing those sheep to motion one, as the bishop would have his obsequious wethers of the flock motion him, to the choice places of the sward.

So, as vivid a picture of the materialism and monopolizing of the present century sowing seeds of decay and self-destruction in the movement of this age toward love of the truth, of the beauty of genuineness in character and earnestness in aim, is portrayed through the realistic personality of the great modern bishop, in his easy-smiling after-dinner talk with Gigadibs, the literary man, as is presented of the Central Renaissance period in the companion picture of the Bishop of Saint Praxeds.

In Cleon, the man of composite art and culture, the last ripe fruitage of Greek development, is personified and brought into contact, at the moment of the dawn of Christianity in Europe, with the ardent impulse the Chiistian ideal of spiritual life supplied to human civilization. How close the wise and broad Greek culture came to being all-sufficing, capable of effecting almost enough of impetus for the aspiring progress of the world, and yet how much it lacked a warmer element essential to be engrafted upon its lofty beauty, the reader, upon whose imaginative vision the personality of Cleon rises, can scarcely help but feel.

The aesthetic and religious or philosophical interests vitally conceived and blended, which link together? o many of the main poems of " Men and Women," close with "Cleon." Rudel, the troubadour, presenting, in the self-abandonment of his offering of love to the Lady of Tripoli, an impersonation of the chivalric love characteristic of the Provencal life of the twelfth century, intervenes, appropriately, last of all, between the preceding poems and the epilogue, which devotes heart and brain of the poet himself, with the creatures of his hand, to his " Moon of Poets."

As these poetic creations now stand, they all seem, upon examination, to incarnate the full-bodied life of distinctive types of men, centred amid their relations with other men within a specific social environment, and fulfilling the possibilities for such unique, dramatic syntheses as were revealed but partially or in embryo here and there among the other shorter poems of this period of the poets growth.

In one important particular the re-arrangement of the " Men and Women" group of poems made its title inappropriate. The graceful presence and love-lit eyes of the many women of the shorter love-poems were withdrawn, and Artemis, Andrea del Sartos wife, the Priors niece,–" Saint Lucy, I would say," as Fra Lippo explains,–and, perhaps, the inspirer of Rudels chivalry, too, the shadowy yet learned and queenly Lady of Tripoli, alone were left to represent the " women " of the title. As for minor inexactitudes, what does it matter that the advantage gained by nicely selecting the poems properly belonging together, both in conception and artistic modelling, was won at the cost of making the reference inaccurate, in the opening lines of " One Word More," to " my fifty men and women, naming me the fifty poems finished "?–Or that the mention of Roland in line 138 is no longer in place with Karshish, Cleon, Lippo, and Andrea, now that the fantastic story of Childe Rolands desperate loyalty is given closer companionship among the varied experiences narrated in the "Dramatic Romances"? While as for the mention of the Norbert of "In a Balcony,"–which was originally included as but one item along with the other contents of "Men and Women,"–that miniature drama, although it stands by itself now, is still near enough at hand in the revised order to account for the allusion. These are all trifles–mere sins against literal accuracy. But the discrepancy in the title occasioned by the absence of women is of more importance. It is of especial interest, in calling attention to the fact that the creator of Pompilia, Balaustion, and the heroine of the "Inn Album"–all central figures, whence radiate the life and spiritual energy of the work they ennoble–had, at this period, created no typical figures of women in any degree corresponding to those of his men.

Constance and the Queen of " In a Balcony," both of them disclosed in their characteristic individuality by means of their relation to Norbert, are the closest approach made in the modelling of women to that dwarfed dramatic mode of showing forth the personality within its social environment, which is peculiar to the monologues of his men. It is as if, in that dramatic brief, the poets pathway could be traced, turning its direction sadly but determinedly away from the free field for the exercise of his humanizing poetic bent, which he sought in the early plays, to the condensed dramatic-portraitures of a central personality within the scope of a prescribed yet representatively broad series of relationships, which his artistic originality invented to be its distinctive poetic empire.

The figures of Norbert and the Queen of " In a Balcony" stand out more boldly, at the first view, than the subtle, shifty Constance; but watch out the inter-play of the three, and it may be seen that both of these more forthright souls are presented as the reagents and solvents of that complexity and double-sightedness in Constance, whose modification, in the evolution of her character which goes on throughout the little drama, is the gist of the happy spiritual plot for the two lovers, although it is consummated in the face of the tragic vengeance of the outraged Queen. Norbert is, as he says of himself, "loves self, and cannot change." The Queen, both in her consciousness of her coldness, before the sudden re-animation of her life by the open acknowledgment of love, and afterward in the unrepressed enjoyment of her starved hearts fervor, is as single-souled and unchangeable as he. What surprises and fluctuations in the plot these two occasion, arise from the superficial influence of Constance upon them. Their individualities are true to themselves throughout the play, asserting their truth, unequivocally, however circumstances temporarily mask them. But Constance is herself in a state of flux, growing away. from her shallower self, through her false and ineffective influence upon these two riper natures, to the level of her possibilities. Her crooked policy of self-sacrifice in love for the sake of considerations really sordid makes all the difficulties against which she struggles. The clearer spiritual perception she gains, at last, flowers at the close of the play in the capability for perfect love unalloyed by any shadow of trick or artifice.

A similar illumination of a life through the development caused by a love-experience, is given through the expression of the personality of a riper woman, who is much more like the Queen than Constance, in "James Lees Wife." The manner of telling the story of this womans development is distinctly new, and, as it was not followed up in later work, is a style of impersonation especially noteworthy. This manner of giving, in sequence, selected glimpses of a love-experience and its spiritual value, through a cycle of lyrics, suiting their scene-setting and symbolism to the stages of the story, relates "James Lees Wife" to the class of the lyrically dramatic poems, from which the greater monologues of this collection, already mentioned as being a direct continuation of their prototypes in "Men and Women," are markedly differentiated. The lesser pieces of " Dramatis Persons," also, place the emphasis, although with slighter artistic elaboration than in "James Lees Wife," upon the lyricism suited to the emotion which in each piece tells the tale of some personal experience, instead of on the dramatic modelling of a central personality.

The great monologues of the poets, the artists, and the musicians, of the prelates and the philosophers, whether saintly as John, or secular as Cleon, or pseudo-spiritualistic as Sludge, remain the marked creations of the poets genius, as shown in the present volume.

Charlotte Porter.

Helen A. Clarke.

MEN AND WOMEN.

184–185–

"TRANSCENDENTALISM: A POEM IN TWELVE BOOKS." v 1855

Stop playing, poet! May a brother speak?

Tis you speak, thats your error. Song s our art:

Whereas you please to speak these naked thoughts

Instead of draping them in sights and sounds.

–True thoughts, good thoughts, thoughts fit to treas-

ure up!

But why such long prolusion and display,
Such turning and adjustment of the harp,
And taking it upon your breast, at length,
Only to speak dry words across its strings?
Stark-naked thought is in request enough: 1 o
  Speak prose and hollo it till Europe hears!
The six-foot Swiss tube, braced about with bark,
Which helps the hunters voice from Alp to Alp–
Exchange our harp for that,–who hinders you?
  But here s your fault; grown men want thought, you think; Thoughts what they
mean by verse, and seek in verse.
  Boys seek for images and melody,
Men must have reason–so, you aim at men.
  M. W.–I
  Quite otherwise! Objects throng our youth, t is true;
  We see and hear and do not wonder much:. 20 If you could tell us what they mean,
indeed!
  As German Boehme never cared for plants
  Until it happed, a-walking in the fields,
  He noticed all at once that plants could speak,
  Nay, turned with loosened tongue to talk with him.
  That day the daisy had an eye indeed–
  Colloquized with the cowslip on such themes!
  We find them extant yet in Jacobs prose.
  But by the time youth slips a stage or two
  While reading prose in that tough book he wrote 30 (Collating and emendating the
same
  And settling on the sense most to our mind),
  We shut the clasps and find lifes summer past.
  Then, who helps more, pray, to repair our loss–
  Another Boehme with a tougher book
  And subtler meanings of what roses say,–
  Or some stout Mage like him of Halberstadt,
  John, who made things Boehme wrote thoughts about?
  He with a "look you!" vents a brace of rhymes,
  And in there breaks the sudden rose herself, 40
  Over us, under, round us every side,
  Nay, in and out the tables and the chairs
  And musty volumes, Boehmes book and all,–
  Buries us with a glory, young once more,
  Pouring heaven into this shut house of life.
  So come, the harp back to your heart again! You are a poem, though your poem s
naught. The best of all you showed before, believe, Was your own boy-face oer the
finer chords Bent, following the cherub at the top 50
  That points to God with his paired half-moon wings.

HOW IT STRIKES A CONTEMPORARY. 1855.

I Only knew one poet in my life:
And this, or something like it, was his way.
You saw go up and down Valladolid,
A man of mark, to know next time you saw.
His very serviceable suit of black
Was courtly once and conscientious still,
And many might have worn it, though none did:
The cloak, that somewhat shone and showed the threads,
Had purpose, and the ruff, significance.
He walked and tapped the pavement with his cane, 10
Scenting the world, looking it full in face,
An old dog, bald and blindish, at his heels.
They turned up, now, the alley by the church,
That leads nowhither; now, they breathed themselves
On the main promenade just at the wrong time:
You d come upon his scrutinizing hai,
Making a peaked shade blacker than itself
Against the single window spared some house
Intact yet with its mouldered Moorish work,–
Or else surprise the ferrel of his stick 20
  Trying the mortars temper tween the chinks
Of some new shop a-building, French and fine.
He stood and watched the cobbler at his trade,
The man who slices lemons into drink,
The coffee-roasters brazier, and the boys
That volunteer to help him turn its winch.
He glanced oer books on stalls with half an eye,
And fly-leaf ballads on the vendors string,
  And broad-edge bold-print posters by the wall.
He took such cognizance of men and things, 30 If any beat a horse, you felt he saw;
If any cursed a woman, he took note;
  Yet stared at nobody,–you stared at him,
  And found, less to your pleasure than surprise,
  He seemed to know you and expect as much.
  So, next time that a neighbors tongue was loosed, It marked the shameful and notorious fact,
  We had among us, not so much a spy,
  As a recording chief-inquisitor,
  The towns true master if the town but knew! 40
  We merely kept a governor for form,
  While this man walked about and took account
  Of all thought, said and acted, then went home,
  And wrote it fully to our Lord the King
  Who has an itch to know things, he knows why,

And reads them in his bedroom of a night.
Oh, you might smile! there wanted not a touch,
A tang of. well, it was not wholly ease
As back into your mind the mans look came.
Stricken in years a little,–such a brow 50
His eyes had to live under!–clear as flint . On either side the formidable nose
Curved, cut and colored like an eagles claw.
. Had he to do with A. s surprising fate?
When altogether old B. disappeared
And young C. got his mistress,–wast our friend.
His letter to the King, that did it all?
What paid the bloodless man for so much pains?
Our Lord the King has favorites manifold,
And shifts his ministry some once a month; 60
Our city gets new governors at whiles,–
But never word or sign, that I could hear,
Notified to this man about the streets
The Kings approval of those letters conned
The last thing duly at the dead of night.
Did the man love his office? Frowned our Lord,
Exhorting when none heard–" Beseech me not!
Too far above my people,—beneath me!
I set the watch,–how should the people know?
Forget them, keep me all the more in mind! " 70
Was some such understanding twixt the two?
I found no truth in one report at least–
That if you tracked him to his home, down lanes
Beyond the Jewry, and as clean to pace,
You found he ate his supper in a room
Blazing with lights, four Titians on the wall,
And twenty naked girls to change his plate!
Poor man, he lived another kind of life
In that new stuccoed third house by the bridge,
Fresh-painted, rather smart than otherwise! 80
The whole street might oerlook him as he sat,
Leg crossing leg, one foot on the dogs back,
Playing a decent cribbage with his maid
(Jacynth, you re sure her name was) oer the cheese
And fruit, three red halves of starved winter-pears,
Or treat of radishes in April. Nine,
Ten, struck the church clock, straight to bed went he.
My father, like the man of sense he was,
Would point him out to me a dozen times;
"St–St," he d whisper, " the Corregidor! " 90
I had been used to think that personage

Was one with lacquered breeches, lustrous belt,
And feathers like a forest in his hat,
Who blew a trumpet and proclaimed the news,
Announced the bull-fights, gave each church its turn,
    And memorized the miracle in vogue!
He had a great observance from us boys;
We were in error; that was not the man.
    I d like now, yet had haply been afraid,
To have just looked, when this man came to die, loo
And seen who lined the clean gay garret-sides
And stood about the neat low truckle-bed,
With the heavenly manner of relieving guard.
Here had been, mark, the general-in-chief,
Thro a whole campaign of the worlds life and death,
    Doing the Kings work all the dim day long,
In his old coat and up to knees in mud,
Smoked like a herring, dining on a crust,–
And, now the day was won, relieved at once!
No further show or need for that old coat, 110
    You are sure, for one thing! Bless us, all the while
How sprucely we are dressed out, you and I!
A second, and the angels alter that.
Well, I could never write a verse,–could you?
Lets to the Prado and make the most of time.
    ARTEMIS PROLOGIZES.
1842.
    I Am a goddess of the ambrosial courts,
And save by Here, Queen of Pride, surpassed
By none whose temples whiten this the world.
Through heaven I roll my lucid moon along;
I shed in hell oer my pale people peace;
On earth I, caring for the creatures, guard
    Each pregnant yellow wolf and fox-bitch sleek,
    And every feathered mothers callow brood,
    And all that love green haunts and loneliness.
    Of men, the chaste adore me, hanging crowns 10
    Of poppies red to blackness, bell and stem,
    Upon my image at Athenai here;
    And this dead Youth, Asclepios bends above,
    Was dearest to me. He, my buskined step
    To follow through the wild-wood leafy ways,
    And chase the panting stag, or swift with darts
    Scop the swift ounce, or lay the leopard low,
    Neglected homage to another god:
    Whence Aphrodite, by no midnight smoke

Of tapers lulled, in jealousy despatched 20
A noisome lust that, as the gadbee stings,
Possessed his stepdame Phaidra for himself
The son of Theseus her great absent spouse.
Htppolutos exclaiming in his rage
Against the fury of the Queen, she judged
Life insupportable; and, pricked at heart
An Amazonian strangers race should dare
To scorn her, perished by the murderous cord:
Yet, ere she perished, blasted in a scroll
The fame of him her swerving made not swerve. 30
And Theseus, read, returning, and believed,
And exiled, in the blindness of his wrath,
The man without a crime who, last as first,
Loyal, divulged not to his sire the truth.
Now Theseus from Poseidon had obtained
That of his wishes should be granted three,
And one he imprecated straight–" Alive
May neer Hippolutos reach other lands!"
Poseidon heard, ai ai! And scarce the prince
Had stepped into the fixed boots of the car 40 That give the feet a stay against the strength
Of the Henetian horses, and around
His body flung the rein, and urged their speed
Along the rocks and shingles of the shore,
When from the gaping wave a monster flung
His obscene body in the coursers path.
These, mad with terror, as the sea-bull sprawled
Wallowing about their feet, lost care of him
That reared them; and the master-chariot-pole
Snapping beneath their plunges like a reed, 50
Hippolutos, whose feet were trammelled fast,
Was yet dragged forward by the circling rein
Which either hand directed; nor they quenched
The frenzy of their flight before each trace,
Wheel-spoke and splinter of the woful car,
Each boulder-stone, sharp stub and spiny shell,
Huge fish-bone wrecked and wreathed amid the sands
On that detested beach, was bright with blood
And morsels of his flesh: then fell the steeds
Head foremost, crashing in their mooned fronts, 60
Shivering with sweat, each white eye horror-fixed.
His people, who had witnessed all afar,
Bore back the ruins of Hippolutos.
But when his sire, too swoln with pride, rejoiced

(Indomitable as a man foredoomed)
That vast Poseidon had fulfilled his prayer,
I, in a flood of glory visible,
Stood oer my dying votary and, deed
By deed, revealed, as all took place, the truth.
Then Theseus lay the wofullest of men, 70
    And worthily; but ere the death-veils hid
His face, the murdered prince full pardon breathed
To his rash sire. Whereat Athenai wails.
    So I, who neer forsake my votaries,
Lest in the cross-way none the honey-cake
Should tender, nor pour out the dogs hot life;
Lest at my fane the priests disconsolate
Should dress my image with some faded poor
Few crowns, made favors of, nor dare object
Such slackness to my worshippers who turn 80
    Elsewhere the trusting heart and loaded hand,
As they had climbed Olumpos to report
Of Artemis and nowhere found her throne–
I interposed: and, this eventful night,–
(While round the funeral pyre the populace
Stood with fierce light on their black robes which bound
Each sobbing head, while yet their hair they clipped
Oer the dead body of their withered prince,
And, in his palace, Theseus prostrated
On the cold hearth, his brow cold as the slab 90
    T was bruised on, groaned away the heavy grief–
As the pyre fell, and down the cross logs crashed
Sending a crowd of sparkles through the night,
And the gay fire, elate with mastery,
Towered like a serpent oer the clotted jars
Of wine, dissolving oils and frankincense,
And splendid gums like gold),–my potency
Conveyed the perished man to my retreat
In the thrice-venerable forest here.
And this white-bearded sage who squeezes now 100
The berried plant, is Phoibos son of fame,
Asclepios, whom my radiant brother taught
The doctrine of each herb and flower and root,
To know their secretst virtue and express
The saving soul of all: who so has soothed
With lavers the torn brow and murdered cheeks,
Composed the hair and brought its gloss again,
    And called the red bloom to the pale skin back,
    And laid the strips and jagged ends of flesh

Even once more, and slacked the sinews knot no
Of every tortured limb–that now he lies
As if mere sleep possessed him underneath
These interwoven oaks and pines. Oh cheer,
Divine presenter of the healing rod,
Thy snake, with ardent throat and lulling eye,
Twines his lithe spires around! I say, much cheer!
Proceed thou with thy wisest pharmacies!
And ye, white crowd of woodland sister-nymphs,
Ply, as the sage directs, these buds and leaves
That strew the turf around the twain! While I 1 zo
Await, in fitting silence, the event.

AN EPISTLE
CONTAINING THE STRANGE MEDICAL ExpERIENCE OF KARSHISH,
THE ARAB PHYSICIAN.
1855.
Karsh1sh, the picker-up of learnings crumbs,
The not-incurious in Gods handiwork (This mans-flesh he hath admirably made,
Blown like a bubble, kneaded like a paste,
To coop up and keep down on earth a space
That puff of vapor from his mouth, mans soul) –To Abib, all-sagacious in our art,
Breeder in me of what poor skill I boast,
Like me inquisitive how pricks and cracks
Befall the flesh through too much stress and strain, lo
Whereby the wily vapor fain would slip
Back and rejoin its source before the term,—
And aptest in contrivance (under God)
To baffle it by deftly stopping such:–
The vagrant Scholar to his Sage at home
Sends greeting (health and knowledge, fame with peace)
Three samples of true snake stone–rarer still,
One of the other sort, the melon-shaped,
(But fitter, pounded fine, for charms than drugs)
And writeth now the twenty-second time. 20
My journeyings were brought to Jericho:
Thus I resume. Who studious in our art
Shall count a little labor unrepaid?
I have shed sweat enough, left flesh and bone
On many a flinty furlong of this land.
Also, the country-side is all on fire
With rumors of a marching hitherward:
Some say Vespasian cometh, some, his son.
A black lynx snarled and pricked a tufted ear;
Lust of my blood inflamed his yellow balls: 30 I cried and threw my staff and he was
gone.

Twice have the robbers stripped and beaten me,
And once a town declared me for a spy;
But at the end, I reach Jerusalem,
Since this poor covert where I pass the night,
This Bethany, lies scarce the distance thence
A man with plague-sores at the third degree
Runs till he drops down dead. Thou laughest here!
Sooth, it elates me, thus reposed and safe,
To void the stuffing of my travel-scrip 40
    And share with thee whatever Jewry yields.
A viscid choler is observable
In tertians, I was nearly bold to say;
    And falling-sickness hath a happier cure
    Than our school wots of: there s a spider here
    Weaves no web, watches on the ledge of tombs,
    Sprinkled with mottles on an ash-gray back;
    Take five and drop them. but who knows his mind,
    The Syrian runagate I trust this to?
His service payeth me a sublimate 50
Blown up his nose to help the ailing eye.
Best wait: I reach Jerusalem at morn,
There set in order my experiences,
Gather what most deserves, and give thee all—
Or I might add, Judaeas gum-tragacanth
Scales off in purer flakes, shines clearer-grained,
Cracks twixt the pestle and the porphyry, In fine exceeds our produce. Scalp-disease
Confounds me, crossing so with leprosy—
Thou hadst admired one sort I gained at Zoar—60
But zeal outruns discretion. Here I end.
    Yet stay: my Syrian blinketh gratefully, Protesteth his devotion is my price—Suppose I write what harms not, though he steal? I half resolve to tell thee, yet I blush, What set me offa-writing first of all. An itch I had, a sting to write, a tang For, be it this towns barrenness—or else The Man had something in the look of him—His case has struck me far more than t is worth. 70 So, pardon if—(lest presently I lose In the great press of novelty at hand The care and pains this somehow stole from me) I bid thee take the thing while fresh in mind, Almost in sight—for, wilt thou have the truth? The very man is gone from me but now,
    Whose ailment is the subject of discourse.
Thus then, and let thy better wit help all!
    Tis but a case of mania—subinduced
By epilepsy, at the turning-point 80
    Of trance prolonged unduly some three days:
When, by the exhibition of some drug
Or spell, exorcisation, stroke of art
Unknown to me and which t were well to know,

The evil thing (Jut-breaking all at once
Left the man whole and sound of body indeed,–
But, flinging (so to speak) lifes gates too wide,
Making a clear house of it too suddenly,
The first conceit that entered might inscribe
Whatever it was minded on the wall 90
    So plainly at that vantage, as it were,
(First come, first served) that nothing subsequent
Attaineth to erase those fancy-scrawls
The just-returned and new-established soul
Hath gotten now so thoroughly by heart
That henceforth she will read or these or none.
And first–the mans own firm conviction rests
That he was dead (in fact they buried him) –That he was dead and then restored to life
    By a Nazarene physician of his tribe: 100 –Sayeth, the same bade " Rise," and he
did rise. " Such cases are diurnal," thou wilt cry.
    Not so this figment!–not, that such a fume,
Instead of giving way to time and health,
Should eat itself into the life of life,
As saffron tingeth flesh, blood, bones and all!
For see, how he takes up the after-life.
The man–it is one Lazarus a Jew,
Sanguine, proportioned, fifty years of age,
    The bodys habit wholly laudable, no
As much, indeed, beyond the common health
As he were made and put aside to show.
Think, could we penetrate by any drug
And bathe the wearied soul and worried flesh,
And bring it clear and fair, by three days sleep!
Whence has the man the balm that brightens all?
This grown man eyes the world now like a child.
Some elders of his tribe, I should premise,
Led in their friend, obedient as a sheep,
To bear my inquisition. While they spoke, 120
Now sharply, now with sorrow,–told the case,–
He listened not except I spoke to him,
But folded his two hands and let them talk,
Watching the flies that buzzed: and yet no fool.
And thats a sample how his years must go.
Look, if a beggar, in fixed middle-life,
Should find a treasure,–can he use the same
With straitened habits and with tastes starved small,
And take at once to his impoverished brain
The sudden element that changes things, 130
That sets the undreamed-of rapture at his hand

And puts the cheap old joy in the scorned dust?
Is he not such an one as moves to mirth–
Warily parsimonious, when no need,
Wasteful as drunkenness at undue times?
All prudent counsel as to what befits
The golden mean, is lost on such an one:
The mans fantastic will is the mans law.
So here–we call the treasure knowledge) say, Increased beyond the fleshly faculty–
140
Heaven opened to a soul while yet on earth,
Earth forced on a souls use while seeing heaven:
The man is witless of the size, the sum,
The value in proportion of all things,
Or whether it be little or be much.
Discourse to him of prodigious armament
Assembled to besiege his city now,
And of the passing of a mule with gourds–
T is one! Then take it on the other side,
Speak of some trifling fact,–he will gaze rapt 150
With stupor at its very littleness, (Far as I see) as if in that indeed
He caught prodigious import, whole results;
And so will turn to us the bystanders In ever the same stupor (note this point)
That we too see not with his opened eyes.
Wonder and doubt come wrongly into play,
Preposterously, at cross purposes.
Should his child sicken unto death,–why, look
For scarce abatement of his cheerfulness, 160
Or pretermission of the daily craft!
While a word, gesture, glance from that same child
At play or in the school or laid asleep,
Will startle him to an agony of fear,
Exasperation, just as like. Demand
The reason why–" t is but a word," object–
"A gesture "–he regards thee as our lord
Who lived there in the pyramid alone,
Looked at us (dost thou mind?) when, being young,
We both would unadvisedly recite 170
Some charms beginning, from that book of his,
Able to bid the sun throb wide and burst
All into stars, as suns grown old are wont.
Thou and the child have each a veil alike
Thrown oer your heads, from under which ye both
Stretch your blind hands and trifle with a match
Over a mine of Greek fire, did ve know!

He holds on firmly to some thread of life—
(It is the life to lead perforcedly)
Which runs across some vast distracting orb 180
    Of glory on either side that meagre thread,
Which, conscious of, he must not enter yet—
, The spiritual life around the earthly life:
The law of that is known to him as this,
His heart and brain move there, his feet stay here.
So is the man perplext with impulses
Sudden to start off crosswise, not straight on,
Proclaiming what is right and wrong across,
And not along, this black thread through the blaze—
"It should be " balked by " here it cannot be." 190
And oft the mans soul springs into his face
As if he saw again and heard again
His sage that bade him " Rise " and he did rise.
Something, a word, a tick o the blood within
Admonishes: then back he sinks at once
To ashes, who was very fire before,
In sedulous recurrence to his trade
Whereby he earneth him the daily bread;
And studiously the humbler for that pride,
Professedly the faultier that he knows 200
    Gods secret, while he holds the thread of life.
Indeed the especial marking of the man
Is prone submission to the heavenly will—
Seeing it, what it is, and why it is.
Sayeth, he will wait patient to the last
For that same death which must restore his being
To equilibrium, body loosening soul
Divorced even now by premature full growth:
He will live, nay, it pleaseth him to live
So long as God please, and just how God please. 210
He even seeketh not to please God more (Which meaneth, otherwise) than as God
please.
    Hence, I perceive not he affects to preach
    The doctrine of his sect whateer it be,
    Make proselytes as madmen thirst to do:
    How can he give his neighbor the real ground,
    His own conviction? Ardent as he is—
    Call his great truth a lie, why, still the old
    "Be it as God please " reassureth him.
    I probed the sore as thy disciple should: 2 20
    "How, beast," said I, " this stolid carelessness
    Sufficeth thee, when Rome is on her march

To stamp out like a little spark thy town,
Thy tribe, thy crazy tale and thee at once?"
He merely looked with his large eyes on me.
The man is apathetic, you deduce?
Contrariwise, he loves both old and young,
Able and weak, affects the very brutes
And birds–how say I? flowers of the field–
As a wise workman recognizes tools 230 In a masters workshop, loving what they make.
Thus is the man as harmless as a lamb:
Only impatient, let him do his best,
At ignorance and carelessness and sin–
An indignation which is promptly curbed:
As when in certain travel I have feigned
To be an ignoramus in our art
According to some preconceived design,
And happed to hear the lands practitioners
Steeped in conceit sublimed by ignorance, 240
Prattle fantastically on disease, Its cause and cure–and I must hold my peace!
Thou wilt object–Why have I not ere this Sought out the sage himself, the Nazarene
Who wrought this cure, inquiring at the source,
Conferring with the frankness that befits?
Alas! it grieveth me, the learned leech
Perished in a tumult many years ago,
Accused,–our learnings fate,–of wizardry,
Rebellion, to the setting up a rule 250
And creed prodigious as described to me.
His death, which happened when the earthquake fell (Prefiguring, as soon appeared, the loss
To occult learning in our lord the sage
Who lived there in the pyramid alone)
Was wrought by the mad people–thats their wont!
On vain recourse, as I conjecture it,
To his tried virtue, for miraculous help–
How could he stop the earthquake? Thats their way!
The other imputations must be lies; 260
But take one, though I loathe to give it thee,
In mere respect for any good mans fame.
(And after all, our patient Lazarus
Is stark mad; should we count on what he says?
Perhaps not: though in writing to a leech
Tis well to keep back nothing of a case.)
This man so cured regards the curer, then,
As–God forgive me! who but God himself,
Creator and sustainer of the world,

That came and dwelt in flesh on it awhile! 270 —Sayeth that such an one was born and lived,
Taught, healed the sick, broke bread at his own house,
Then died, with Lazarus by, for aught I know,
And yet was. what I said nor choose repeat,
And must have so avouched himself, in feet.
In hearing of this very Lazarus
Who saith—but why all this of what he saith?
   Why write of trivial matters, things of price
Calling at every moment for remark?
I noticed on the margin of a pool 280
   Blue-flowering borage, the Aleppo sort,
Aboundeth, very nitrous. It is strange!
   Thy pardon for this long and tedious ease,
Which, now that I review it, needs must seem
Unduly dwelt on, prolixly set forth!
Nor I myself discern in what is writ
Good cause for the peculiar interest
And awe indeed this man has touched me with.
Perhaps the journeys end, the weariness
Had wrought upon me first. I met him thus: 290
I crossed a ridge of short sharp broken hills
Like an old lions cheek teeth. Out there came
A moon made like a face with certain spots
Multiform, manifold and menacing:
Then a wind rose behind me. So we met
In this ola sleepy town at unaware,
The man and I. I send thee what is writ.
Regard it as a chance, a matter risked
To this ambiguous Syrian—he may lose,
Or steal, or give it thee with equal good. 300
   Jerusalems repose shall make amends
For time this letter wastes, thy time and mine;
Till when, once more thy pardon and farewell!
   The very God! think, Abib; dost thou think?
So, the All-Great, were the All-Loving too—
So, through the thunder comes a human voice
Saying, "O heart I made, a heart beats here!
Face, my hands fashioned, see it in myself!
   Thou hast no power nor mayst conceive of mine,
But love T gave thee, with myself to love, 310
   And thou must love me who have died for thee! "
The madman saith He said so: it is strange.
   JOHANNES AGRICOLA IN
MEDITATION.

1842.

Theres heaven above, and night by night I look right through its gorgeous roof; No suns and moons though eer so bright

Avail to stop me; splendor-proof I keep the broods of stars aloof: For I intend to get to God,

For t is to God I speed so fast, For in Gods breast, my own abode,

Those shoals of dazzling glory, passed.

I lay my spirit down at last. 10 I lie where I have always lain,

God smiles as he has always smiled; Ere suns and moons could wax and wane,

Ere stars were thundergirt, or piled

The heavens, God thought on me his child; Ordained a life for me, arrayed Its circumstances every one To the minutest; ay, God said

This head this hand should rest upon

Thus, ere he fashioned star or sun. 20

And having thus created me,

Thus rooted me, he bade me grow, Guiltless forever, like a tree

That buds and blooms, nor seeks to know

The law by which it prospers so:

But sure that thought and word and deed

All go to swell his love for me,

Me, made because that love had need

Of something irreversibly

Pledged solely its content to be. 30

Yes, yes, a tree which must ascend,

No poison-gourd foredoomed to stoop! I have Gods warrant, could I blend

All hideous sins, as in a cup,

To drink the mingled venoms up; Secure my nature will convert

The draught to blossoming gladness fast: While sweet dews turn to the gourds hurt,

And bloat, and while they bloat it, blast,

As from the first its lot was cast. 40

For as I lie, smiled on, full-fed

By unexhausted power to bless, I gaze below on hells fierce bed,

And those its waves of flame oppress,

Swarming in ghastly wretchedness; Whose life on earth aspired to be

One altar-smoke, so pure!–to win If not love like Gods love for me,

At least to keep his anger in;

And all their striving turned to sin. 50

Priest, doctor, hermit, monk grown white

With prayer, the broken-hearted nun, The martyr, the wan acolyte,

The incense-swinging child,–undone

Before God fashioned star or sun!

God, whom I praise; how could I praise, If such as I might understand,

Make out and reckon on his ways,

And bargain for his love, and stand,

Paying a price, at his right hand? 60

PICTOR IGNOTUS.
FLORENCE, 15–.
1845.

I Could have painted pictures like that youths

Ye praise so. How my soul springs up! No bar Stayed me–ah, thought which saddens while it soothes!

–Never did fate forbid me, star by star, To outburst on your night with all my gift

Of fires from God: nor would my flesh have shrunk From seconding my soul, with eyes uplift

And wide to heaven, or, straight like thunder, sunk To the centre, of an instant; or around

Turned calmly and inquisitive, to scan 10

The license and the limit, space and bound,

Allowed to truth made visible in man. And, like that youth ye praise so, all I saw,

Over the canvas could my hand have flung, Each face obedient to its passions law,

Each passion clear proclaimed without a tongue; Whether Hope rose at once in all the blood,

A-tiptoe for the blessing of embrace,

Or Rapture drooped the eyes, as when her brood

Pull down the nesting doves heart to its place; 20 Or Confidence lit swift the forehead up,

And locked the mouth fast, like a castle braved,–

O human faces, hath it spilt, my cup r

What did ye give me that I have not saved? Nor will I say I have not dreamed (how well!)

Of going–I, in each new picture,–forth, As, making new hearts beat and bosoms swell,

To Pope or Kaiser, East, West, South, or North, Bound for the calmly-satisfied great State,

Or glad aspiring little burgh, it went, 30

Flowers cast upon the car which bore the freight,

Through old streets named afresh from the event, Till it reached home, where learned age should greet

My face, and youth, the star not yet distinct Above his hair, lie learning at my feet!–

Oh, thus to live, I and my picture, linked With love about, and praise, till life should end,

And then not go to heaven, but linger here, Here on my earth, earths every man my friend,–39

The thought grew frightful, t was so wildly dear! But a voice changed it. Glimpses of such sights

Have scared me, like the revels through a door Of some strange house of idols at its rites!

This world seemed not the world it was before: Mixed with my loving trusting ones, there trooped . Who summoned those cold faces that begun To press on me and judge me? Though I stooped

Shrinking, as from the soldiery a nun, They drew me forth, and spite of me. enough!

These buy and sell our pictures, take and give, 50 Count them for garniture and household-stuff,

And where they live needs must our pictures live And see their faces, listen to their prate,

Partakers of their daily pettiness,

Discussed of,–" This I love, or this I hate,

This likes me more, and this affects me less!"

Wherefore I chose my portion. If at whiles

My heart sinks, as monotonous I paint These endless cloisters and eternal aisles

With the same series, Virgin, Babe and Saint, 60 With the same cold calm beautiful regard,–

At least no merchant traffics in my heart; The sanctuarys gloom at least shall ward

Vain tongues from where my pictures stand apart: Only prayer breaks the silence of the shrine

While, blackening in the daily candle-smoke, They moulder on the damp walls travertine,

Mid echoes the light footstep never woke. So, die my pictures! surely, gently die!

O youth, men praise so,–holds their praise its worth? 70

Blown harshly, keeps the trump its golden cry?

Tastes sweet the water with such specks of earth

FRA LIPPO LIPPI.

igjs.

I Am poor brother Lippo, by your leave!

You need not clap your torches to my face.

Zooks, what s to blame? you think you see a monk!

What, tis past midnight, and you go the rounds,

And here you catch me at an alleys end

Where sportive ladies leave their doors ajar?

The Carmine s my cloister: hunt it up,

Do,–harry out, if you must show your zeal,

Whatever rat, there, haps on his wrong hole,

And nip each softling of a wee white mouse, 10

Weke, vieke, thats crept to keep him company!

Aha, you know your betters! Then, you Ml take

Your hand away that s fiddling on my throat,

And please to know me likewise. Who am I?

Why, one, sir, who Is lodging with a friend

Three streets off–he s a certain. how dye call.

Master–a. Cosimo of the Medici, I the house that caps the corner. Boh! you were best!

Remember and tell me, the day you re hanged,

How you affected such a gullets-gripe! 20

But you, sir, it concerns you that your knaves

Pick up a manner nor discredit you:

Zooks, are we pilchards, that they sweep the streets
And count fair prize what comes into their net?
He s Judas to a tittle, that man is!
Just such a face! Why, sir, you make amends.
Lord, I mnot angry! Bid your hangdogs go
Drink out this quarter-florin to the health
Of the munificent House that harbors me (And many more beside, lads! more
beside!) 30
And alls come square again. I d like his face–
His, elbowing on his comrade in the door
With the pike and lantern,–for the slave that holds
John Baptists head a-dangle by the hair
With one hand ("Look you, now," as who should say)
And his weapon in the other, yet unwiped!
Its not your chance to have a bit of chalk,
A wood-coal or the like? or you should see!
Yes, Im the painter, since you style me so.
What, brother Lippos doings, up and down, 40
You know them and they take you? like enough!
I saw the proper twinkle in your eye–
Tell you, I liked your looks at very first.
Lets sit and set things straight now, hip to haunch.
Heres spring come, and the nights one makes up bands
To roam the town and sing out carnival,
And I ve been three weeks shut within my mew,
A-painting for the great man, saints and saints
And saints again. I could not paint all night–
Ouf! I leaned out of window for fresh air. 50
There came a hurry of feet and little feet,
A sweep of lute-strings, laughs, and whifts of song,–.
Flower o the broom,
Take away love, and our earth is a tomb!
Flower the quince, I let Lisa go, and what good in life since?
Flower o the thyme –and so on. Round they went.
Scarce had they turned the corner when a titter
Like the skipping of rabbits by moonlight,–three slim shapes, And a face that
looked up. zooks, sir, flesh and blood, 60
Thats all I m made of! Into shreds it went,
Curtain and counterpane and coverlet,
All the bed-furniture–a dozen knots,
There was a ladder! Down I let myself,
Hands and feet, scrambling somehow, and so dropped,
And after them. I came up with the fun
Hard by Saint Laurence, hail fellow, well met,–

Flower o the rose, If Ive been merry, what matter who knows?
And so as I was stealing back again 70
    To get to bed and have a bit of sleep
Ere I rise up to-morrow and go work
On Jerome knocking at his poor old breast
With his great round stone to subdue the flesh,
You snap me of the sudden. Ah, I see!
Though your eye twinkles still, you shake your head–
    Mines shaved–a monk, you say–the stings in that!
    If Master Cosimo announced himself,
    Mum s the word naturally; but a monk!
    Come, what am I a beast for? tell us, now! 80 I was a baby when my mother died
And father died and left me in the street.
I starved there, God knows how, a year or two
On fig-skins, melon-parings, rinds and shucks,
Refuse and rubbish. One fine frosty day,
My stomach being empty as your hat,
The wind doubled me up and down I went.
Old Aunt Lapaccia trussed me with one hand, (Its fellow was a stinger as I knew)
And so along the wall, over the bridge, go
By the straight cut to the convent. Six words there,
While I stood munching my first bread that month:
"So, boy, youre minded," quoth the good fat father
Wiping his own mouth, t was refection-time,–
"To quit this very miserable world?
Will you renounce". "the mouthful of bread?"
thought I;
    By no means! Brief, they made a monk of me;
I did renounce the world, its pride and greed,
Palace, farm, villa, shop and banking-house,
Trash, such as these poor devils of Medici loo
    Have given their hearts to–all at eight years old.
Well, sir, I found in time, you may be sure,
T was not for nothing–the good bellyful,
The warm serge and the rope that goes all round,
And day-long blessed idleness beside!
"Lets see what the urchins fit for"–that came next.
Not overmuch their way, l must confess.
Such a to-do! They tried me with their books:
    Lord, they d have taught me Latin in pure waste!
    Flower o the clove, 11 o
    All the Latin I construe is, " amo " I love!
    But, mind you, when a boy starves in the streets
    Eight years together, as my fortune was,
    Watching folks faces to know who will fling

The bit of half-stripped grape-bunch he desires,
And who will curse or kick him for his pains,–
Which gentleman processional and fine,
Holding a candle to the Sacrament,
Will wink and let him lift a plate and catch
The droppings of the wax to sell again, i 20
Or holla for the Eight and have him whipped,–
How say I?–nay, which dog bites, which lets drop
His bone from the heap of offal in the street,–
Why, soul and sense of him grow sharp alike,
He learns the look of things, and none the less
For admonition from the hunger-pinch.
I had a store of such remarks, be sure,
Which, after I found leisure, turned to use.
I drew mens faces on my copy-books,
Scrawled them within the antiphonarys marge, 130
Joined legs and arms to the long music-notes,
Found eyes and nose and chin for As and Bs,
And made a string of pictures of the world
Betwixt the ins and outs of verb and noun,
On the wall, the bench, the door. The monks looked black.
"Nay," quoth the Prior, "turn him out, d ye say?
In no wise. Lose a crow and catch a lark.
What if at last we get our man of parts,
We Carmelites, like those Camaldolese
And Preaching Friars, to do our church up fine 140
And put the front on it that ought to be! "
And hereupon he bade me daub away.
Thank you! my head being crammed, the walls a blank,
Never was such prompt disemburdening.
First, every sort of monk, the black and white,
I drew them, fat and lean: then, folk at church,
From good old gossips waiting to confess
Their cribs of barrel-droppings, candle-ends,–
To the breathless fellow at the altar-foot,
Fresh from his murder, safe and sitting there 150
With the little children round him in a row
Of admiration, half for his beard and half
For that white anger of his victims son
Shaking a fist at him with one fierce arm,
Signing himself with the other because of Christ
(Whose sad face on the cross sees only this
After the passion of a thousand years)
Till some poor girl, her apron oer her head,

(Which the intense eyes looked through) came at eve
On tiptoe, said a word, dropped in a loaf, 160
    Her pair of earrings and a bunch of flowers
(The brute took growling), prayed, and so was gone.
I painted all, then cried " T is ask and have;
Choose, for mores ready! "–laid the ladder flat,
And showed my covered bit of cloister-wall.
The monks closed in a circle and praised loud
Till checked, taught what to see and not to see,
Being simple bodies,–" Thats the very man!
Look at the boy who stoops to pat the dog!
That woman s like the Priors niece who comes 170
"To care about his asthma: its the life! "
But there my triumphs straw-fire flared and funked;
Their betters took their turn to see and say:
The Prior and the learned pulled a face
And stopped all that in no time. " How? whats here!
    Quite from the mark of painting, bless us all!
    Faces, "arms, legs and bodies like the true
    As much as pea and pea! its devils-game!
    Your business is not to catch men with show,
    With homage to the perishable clay, 180
    But lift them over it, ignore it all,
    Make them forget there s such a thing as flesh.
    Your business is to paint the souls of men–
    Mans soul, and its a fire, smoke. no, it s not.
    Its vapor done up like a new-born babe– (In that shape when you die it leaves your
mouth) Its. well, what matters talking, its the soul!
    Give us no more of body than shows soul!
    Here s Giotto, with his Saint a-praising God,
    That sets us praising,–why not stop with him? 190
    Why put all thoughts of praise out of our head
    With wonder at lines, colors, and what not?
    Paint the soul, never mind the legs and arms!
    Rub all out, try at it a second time.
    Oh, that white smallish female with the breasts,
    She s just my niece. Herodias, I would say,–
    Who went and danced and got mens heads cut off!
    Have it all out! " Now, is this sense, I ask?
A fine way to paint soul, by painting body
So ill, the eye cant stop there, must go further 200
And cant fare worse! Thus, yellow does for white
When what you put for yellow s simply black,
And any sort of meaning looks intense
When all beside itself means and looks naught.

Why cant a painter lift each foot in turn,
Left foot and right foot, go a double step,
Make his flesh liker and his soul more like,
Both in their order? Take the prettiest face,
The Priors niece. patron-saint–is it so pretty
You cant discover if it means hope, fear, 210
Sorrow or joy? wont beauty go with these?
Suppose Ive made her eyes all right and blue,
Cant I take breath and try to add lifes flash,
And then add soul and heighten them three-fold?
Or say theres beauty with no soul at all– (I never saw it–put the case the same–) If
you get simple beauty and naught else,
    You get about the best thing God invents:
    Thats somewhat: and you ll find the soul you have missed,
    Within yourself, when you return him thanks. 220
"Rub all out! " Well, well, there s my life, in short,
And so the thing has gone on ever since.
I m grown a man no doubt, I ve broken bounds:
You should not take a fellow eight years old
And make him swear to never kiss the girls.
Im my own master, paint now as I please–
Having a friend, you see, in the Corner-house!
Lord, its fast holding by the rings in front–
Those great rings serve more purposes than just
To plant a flag in, or tie up a horse! 230
    And yet the old schooling sticks, the old grave eyes
Are peeping oer my shoulder as I work,
The heads shake still–" Its arts decline, my son!
You re not of the true painters, great and old;
Brother Angelico s the man, you ll find;
Brother Lorenzo stands his single peer:
Fag on at flesh, you ll never make the third! "
Flower o the fine,
Tou keep your mistr.,. manners, and Ill stick to mine! 239 I m not the third, then:
bless us, they must know! Dont you think they re the likeliest to know,
    They with their Latin? So, I swallow my rage,
    Clench my teeth, suck my lips in tight, and paint
    To please them–sometimes do and sometimes dont;
    For, doing most, theres pretty sure to come
    A turn, some warm eve finds me at my saints–
    A laugh, a cry, the business of the world– (Flower o the peach,
    Death for us all, and his own life for each /)
    And my whole soul revolves, the cup runs over, 250
    The world and life s too big to pass for a dream,
    And I do these wild things in sheer despite,

And play the fooleries you catch me at, In pure rage! The old mill-horse, out at grass
    After hard years, throws up his stiff heels so,
    Although the miller does not preach to him
    The only good of grass is to make chaff.
    What would men have? Do they like grass or no—
    May they or may nt they? all I wants the thing
    Settled forever one way. As it is, 260
    You tell too many lies and hurt yourself:
    You dont like what you only like too much,
    You do like what, if given you at your word,
    You find abundantly detestable.
    For me, I think I speak as I was taught; I always see the garden and God there
    A-making mans wife: and, my lesson learned,
    The value and significance of flesh, I cant unlearn ten minutes afterwards,
    You understand me: I m a beast, I know. 270 But see, now—why, I see as certainly
As that the morning-stars about to shine, What will hap some day. We ve a youngster here Comes to our convent, studies what I do.
    Slouches and stares and lets no atom drop:
    His name is Guidi—he ll not mind the monks—
    They call him Hulking Tom, he lets them talk—
    He picks my practice up—hell paint apace, I hope so—though I never live so long, I know whats sure to follow. You be judge! 280
    You speak no Latin more than I, belike;
    However, you re my man, you ve seen the world —The beauty and the wonder and the power,
The shapes of things, their colors, lights and shades,
Changes, surprises,—and God made it all!
    —For what? Do you feel thankful, ay or no,
For this fair towns face, yonder rivers line,
The mountain round it and the sky above,
Much more the figures of man, woman, child,
These are the frame to? Whats it all about? 290
To be passed over, despised? or dwelt upon,
Wondered at? oh, this last of course!—you say.
But why not do as well as say,—paint these
    Just as they are, careless what comes of it?
    Gods works—paint any one, and count it crime
    To let a truth slip. Dont object, "His works
    Are here already; nature is complete:
    Suppose you reproduce her—(which you cant)
    There s no advantage! you must beat her, then."
    For, dont you mark? we re made so that we love 300
    First when we see them painted, things we have passed
    Perhaps a hundred times nor cared to see;

And so they are better, painted–better to us,
Which is the same thing. Art was given for that;
God uses us to help each other so,
Lending our minds out. Have you noticed, now,
Your cullions hanging face? A bit of chalk,
And trust me but you should, though! How much more,
M. W.–3 If I drew higher things with the same truth!
That were to take the Priors pulpit-place, 310 Interpret God to all of you! Oh, oh,
It makes me mad to see what men shall do
And we in our graves! This worlds no blot for us,
Nor blank; it means intensely, and means good:
To find its meaning is my meat and drink.
"Ay, but you dont so instigate to prayer! "
Strikes in the Prior: "when your meanings plain
It does not say to folk–remember matins,
Or, mind you fast next Friday! " Why, for this
What need of art at all? A skull and bones, 3 20
Two bits of stick nailed crosswise, or, whats best,
A bell to chime the hour with, does as well.
I painted a Saint Laurence six months since
At Prato, splashed the fresco in fine style:
"How looks my painting, now the scaffold s down? "
I ask a brother: "Hugely," he returns–
"Already not one phiz of your three slaves
Who turn the Deacon off his toasted side,
Buts scratched and prodded to our hearts content,
The pious people have so eased their own 330
With coming to say prayers there in a rage:
We get on fast to see the bricks beneath.
Expect another job this time next year,
For pity and religion grow i the crowd–
Your painting serves its purpose! " Hang the fools!
–That is–you ll not mistake an idle word
Spoke in a huff by a poor monk, God wot,
Tasting the air this spicy night which turns
The unaccustomed head like Chianti wine! 339
Oh, the church knows! dont misreport me, now!
Its natural a poor monk out of bounds
Should have his apt word to excuse himself:
And hearken how I plot to make amends.
I have bethought me: I shall paint a piece . Theres for you! Give me six months,
then go, see
Something in Sant Ambrogios! Bless the nuns!
They want a cast o my office. I shall paint
God in the midst, Madonna and her babe,

Ringed by a bowery flowery angel-brood,
Lilies and vestments and white faces, sweet 350
    As puff on puff of grated orris-root
When ladies crowd to Church at midsummer.
And then i the front, of course a saint or two–
Saint John, because he saves tlie Florentines,
Saint Ambrose, who puts down in black and white
The convents friends and gives them a long day,
And Job, I must have him there past mistake,
The man of Uz (and Us without the z,
Painters who need his patience). Well, all these
Secured at their devotion, up shall come 360
    Out of a corner when you least expect,
As one by a dark stair into a great light,
Music and talking, who but Lippo! I!–
Mazed, motionless and moonstruck–Im the man!
Back I shrink–what is this I see and hear?
I, caught up with my monks-things by mistake,
My old serge gown and rope that goes all round,
I, in this presence, this pure company!
Wheres a hole, where s a corner for escape?
Then steps a sweet angelic slip of a thing 370
    Forward, puts out a soft palm–" Not so fast! "
–Addresses the celestial presence, "nay–
He made you and devised you, after all,
    Though he s none of you! Could Saint John there draw–
    His camel-hair make up a painting-brush?
We come to brother Lippo for all that,
Isteperfecit opus!" So, all smile–
I shuffle sideways with my blushing face
Under the cover of a hundred wings
Thrown like a spread of kirtles when you re gay 380
And play hot cockles, all the doors being shut,
Till, wholly unexpected, in there pops
The hothead husband! Thus I scuttle off
To some safe bench behind, not letting go
The palm of her, the little lily thing
That spoke the good word for me in the nick,
Like the Priors niece. Saint Lucy, I would say.
And so all s saved for me, and for the church
A pretty picture gained. Go, six months hence!
Your hand, sir, and good-bye: no lights, no lights! 390
The streets hushed, and I know my own way back,
Dont fear me! There s the gray beginning. Zooks!
    ANDREA DEL SARTO.

(called "the Faultless Pa1nter.")
1855.

But do not let us quarrel any more,
No, my Lucrezia; bear with me for once:
Sit down and all shall happen as you wish.
You turn your face, but does it bring your heart?
Ill work then for your friends friend, never fear
Treat his own subject after his own way,
Fix his own time, accept too his own price,
And shut the money into this small hand
When next it takes mine. Will it? tenderly?
Oh, I ll content him,–but to-morrow, Love! 10 I often am much wearier than you think,
This evening more than usual, and it seems
As if–forgive now–should you let me sit
Here by the window with your hand in mine
And look a half-hour forth on Fiesole,
Both of one mind, as married people use,
Quietly, quietly the evening through, I might get up to-morrow to my work
Cheerful and fresh as ever. Let us try.
To-morrow, how you shall be glad for this! 20
Your soft hand is a woman of itself,
And mine the mans bared breast she curls inside.
Dont count the time lost, neither; you must serve
For each of the five pictures we require: It saves a model. So! keep looking so–
My serpentining beauty, rounds on rounds!
–How could you ever prick those perfect ears, Even to put the pearl there! oh, so sweet–My face, my moon, my everybodys moon,
Which everybody looks on and calls his, 30
And, I suppose, is looked on by in turn,
While she looks–no ones: very dear, no less.
You smile? why, there s my picture ready made,
There s what we painters call our harmony!
A common grayness silvers everything,–
All in a twilight, you and I alike –You, at the point of your first pride in me
(Thats gone you know),–but I, at every point;
My youth, my hope, my art, being all toned down
To yonder sober pleasant Fiesole. 40
Theres the bell clinking from the chapel-top;
That length of convent-wall across the way
Holds the trees safer, huddled more inside;
The last monk leaves the garden; days decrease,
And autumn grows, autumn in everything.
Eh? the whole seems to fall into a shape
As if I saw alike my work and self

And all that I was born to be and do,
A twilight-piece. Love, we are in Gods hand.
How strange now, looks the life he makes us lead; 50
So free we seem, so fettered fast we are!
I feel he laid the fetter: let it lie!
This chamber for example–turn your head–
All thats behind us! You dont understand
Nor care to understand about my art,
But you can hear at least when people speak:
And that cartoon, the second from the door –It is the thing, Love! so such things should be–Behold Madonna!–I am bold to say.
I can do with my pencil what I know, 6c
What I see, what at bottom of my heart I wish for, if I ever wish so deep–
Do easily, too–when I say, perfectly, I do not boast, perhaps: yourself are judge,
Who listened to the Legates talk last week.
And just as much they used to say in France.
At any rate t is easy, all of it!
No sketches first, no studies, thats long past: I do what many dream of, all their lives, –Dream? strive to do, and agonize to do, 70 And fail in doing. I could count twenty such
On twice your fingers, and not leave this town, Who strive–you dont know how the others strive To paint a little thing like that you smeared
Carelessly passing with your robes afloat,–
Yet do much less, so much less, Someone says, (I know his name, no matter)–so much less!
Well, less is more, Lucrezia: I am judged.
There burns a truer light of God in them, In their vexed beating stuffed and stopped-up brain, 80
Heart, or whateer else, than goes on to prompt
This low-pulsed forthright craftsmans hand of mine.
Their works drop groundward, but themselves, I know,
Reach many a time a heaven thats shut to me,
Enter and take their place there sure enough,
Though they come back and cannot tell the world.
My works are nearer heaven, but I sit here.
The sudden blood of these men! at a word–
Praise them, it boils, or blame them, it boils too.
I, painting from myself and to myself, 90
Know what I do, am unmoved by mens blame
Or their praise either. Somebody remarks
Morellos outline there is wrongly traced,
His hue mistaken; what of that? or else,
Rightly traced and well ordered; what of that?
Speak as they please, what does the mountain care?
Ah, but a mans reach should exceed his grasp,

Or whats a heaven for? All is silver-gray
Placid and perfect with my art: the worse!
I know both what I want and what might gain, 100
And yet how profitless to know, to sigh
"Had I been two, another and myself,
Our head would have oerlooked the world! " No doubt.
Yonders a work now, of that famous youth
The Urbinate who died five years ago.
(Tis copied, George Vasari sent it me.)
Well, I can fancy how he did it all,
Pouring his soul, with kings and popes to see,
Reaching, that heaven might so replenish him,
Above and through his art—for it gives way; 11 a
That arm is wrongly put—and there again—
A fault to pardon in the drawings lines, Its body, so to speak: its soul is right,
He means right—that, a child may understand.
Still, what an arm! and I could alter it:
But all the play, the insight and the stretch—
Out of me, out of me! And wherefore out?
Had you enjoined them on me, given me soul,
We might have risen to Rafael, I and you!
Nay, Love, you did give all I asked, I think—I zo
More than I merit, yes, by many times.
But had you—oh, with the same perfect brow,
And perfect eyes, and more than perfect mouth,
And the low voice my soul hears, as a bird
The fowlers pipe, and follows to the snare—
Had you, with these the same, but brought a mind!
Some women do so. Had the mouth there urged
"God and the glory! never care for gain.
The present by the future, what is that?
Live for fame, side by side with Agnolo! 130
Rafael is waiting: up to God, all three!"
I might have done it for you. So it seems:
Perhaps not. All is as God over-rules.
Beside, incentives come from the souls self;
The rest avail not. Why do I need you?
What wife had Rafael, or has Agnolo?
In this world, who can do a thing, will not;
And who would do it, cannot, I perceive:
Yet the wills somewhat—somewhat, too, the power—And thus we half-men struggle.
At the end, 140 God, I conclude, compensates, punishes.
T is safer for me, if the award be strict,
That I am something underrated here,
Poor this long while, despised, to speak the truth.

I dared not, do you know, leave home all day,
For fear of chancing on the Paris lords.
The best is when they pass and look aside;
But they speak sometimes; I must bear it all.
Well may they speak! That Francis, that first time,
And that long festal year at Fontainebleau! 150 I surely then could sometimes leave the ground,
Put on the glory, Rafaels daily wear, In that humane great monarchs golden look,–
One finger in his beard or twisted curl
Over his mouths good mark that made the smile,
One arm about my shoulder, round my neck,
The jingle of his gold chain in my ear, I painting proudly with his breath on me,
All his court round him, seeing with his eyes,
Such frank French eyes, and such a fire of souls 160
Profuse, my hand kept plying by those hearts,–
And, best of all, this, this, this face beyond,
This in the background, waiting on my work,
To crown the issue with a last reward!
A good time, was it not, my kingly days?
And had you not grown restless. but I know–
T is done and past; twas right, my instinct said;
Too live the life grew, golden and not gray,
And I m the weak-eyed bat no sun should tempt 169
Out of the grange whose four walls make his world.
How could it end in any other way?
You called me, and I came home to your heart.
The triumph was–to reach and stay there; since I reached it ere the triumph, what is lost?
Let my hands frame your face in your hairs gold,
You beautiful Lucrezia that are mine!
"Rafael did this, Andrea painted that;
The Romans is the better when you pray,
But still the others Virgin was his wife–"
Men will excuse me. I am glad to judge r 80
Both pictures in your presence; clearer grows
My better fortune, I resolve to think.
For, do you know, Lucrezia, as God lives,
Said one day Agnolo, his very self,
To Rafael. I have known it all these years.
(When the young man was flaming out his thoughts
Upon a palace-wall for Rome to see,
Too lifted up in heart because of it)
"Friend, there s a certain sorry little scrub 189
Goes up and down our Florence, none cares how,
Who, were he set to plan and execute

As you are, pricked on by your popes and kings,
Would bring the sweat into that brow of yours!"
To Rafaels!–And indeed the arm is wrong.
I hardly dare. yet, only you to see,
Give the chalk here–quick, thus the line should go I
Ay, but the soul! he s Rafael! rub it out!
Still, all I care for, if he spoke the truth, (What he? why, who but Michel Agnolo?
Do you forget already words like those?) 200 If really there was such a chance,
so lost,– Is, whether you re–not grateful–but more pleased.
Well, let me think so. And you smile indeed!
This hour has been an hour! Another smile?
If you would sit thus by me every night I should work better, do you comprehend?
I mean that I should earn more, give you more.
See, it is settled dusk now; there s a star;
Morello s gone, the watch-lights show the wall,
The cue-owls speak the name we call them by. 210
Come from the window, love,–come in, at last, Inside the melancholy little house
We built to be so gay with. God is just.
King Francis may forgive me: oft at nights
When I look up from painting, eyes tired out,
The walls become illumined, brick from brick
Distinct, instead of mortar, fierce bright gold,
That gold of his I did cement them with!
Let us but love each other. Must you go?
That Cousin here again? he waits outside? 220
Must see you–you, and not with me? Those loans?
More gaming debts to pay? you smiled for that?
Well, let smiles buy me! have you more to spend?
While hand and eye and something of a heart
Are left me, work s my ware, and whats it worth?
I ll pay my fancy. Only let me sit
The gray remainder of the evening out,
Idle, you call it, and muse perfectly
How I could paint, were I but back in France,
One picture, just one more–the Virgins face, 230
Not yours this time! I want you at my side
To hear them–that is, Michel Agnolo–
Judge all I do and tell you of its worth.
Will you? To-morrow, satisfy your friend.
I take the subjects for his corridor,
Finish the portrait out of hand–there, there,
And throw him in another thing or two
If he demurs; the whole should prove enough
To pay for this same Cousins freak. Beside,
Whats better and whats all I care about, 240

Get you the thirteen scudi for the ruff!
Love, does that please you? Ah, but what does he, The Cousin! what does he to
please you more?
I am grown peaceful as old age to-night.
I regret little, I would change still less.
Since there my past life lies, why alter it?
The very wrong to Francis!–it is true
I took his coin, was tempted and complied,
And built this house and sinned, and all is said.
My father and my mother died of want. 250
Well, had I riches of my own? you see
How one gets rich! Let each one bear his lot.
They were born poor, lived poor, and poor they died:
And I have labored somewhat in my time
And not been paid profusely. Some good son
Paint my two hundred pictures–let him try!
No doubt, there s something strikes a balance. Yes,
You loved me quite enough, it seems to-night.
This must suffice me here. What would one have?
In heaven, perhaps, new chances, one more chance–
Four great walls in the New Jerusalem, 261
Meted on each side by the angels reed,
For Leonard, Rafael, Agnolo and me
To cover–the three first without a wife,
While I have mine! So–still they overcome
Because theres still Lucrezia,–as I choose.
Again the Cousins whistle! Go, my Love.

THE BISHOP ORDERS HIS TOMB AT SAINT PRAXEDS CHURCH.

ROME, 15–.
1845.

Van1ty, saith the preacher, vanity!
Draw round my bed: is Anselm keeping back?
Nephews–sons mine. ah God, I know not!
Well–
She, men would have to be your mother once,
Old Gandolf envied me, so fair she was!
Whats done is done, and she is dead beside,
Dead long ago, and I am Bishop since,
And as she died so must we die ourselves,
And thence ye may perceive the world s a dream.
Life, how and what is it? As here I lie 1 o In this state-chamber, dying by degrees,
Hours and long hours in the dead night, I ask
"Do I live, am I dead? " Peace, peace seems all.
Saint Praxeds ever was the church for peace;

And so, about this tomb of mine. I fought
With tooth and nail to save my niche, ye know:
—Old Gandolf cozened me, despite my care;
Shrewd was that snatch from out the corner South
He graced his carrion with, God curse the same!
Yet still my niche is not so cramped but thence 20
One sees the pulpit o the epistle-side,
And somewhat of the choir, those silent seats,
And up into the aery dome where live
The angels, and a sunbeam s sure to lurk:
And I shall fill my slab of basalt there,
    And neath my tabernacle take my rest,
    With those nine columns round me, two and two,
    The odd one at my feet where Anselm stands:
    Peach-blossom marble all, the rare, the ripe
    As fresh-poured red wine of a mighty pulse. 30 —Old Gandolf with his paltry onion-stone,
    Put me where I may look at him! True peach,
Rosy and flawless: how I earned the prize!
Draw close: that conflagration of my church —What then? So much was saved if aught were missed!
    My sons, ye would not be my death? Go dig
The white-grape vineyard where the oil-press stood,
Drop water gently till the surface sink,
And if ye find. Ah God, I know not, I!.
Bedded in store of rotten fig-leaves soft, 4.0
    And corded up in a tight olive-frail,
Some lump, ah God, of lapis lazuli,
Big as a Jews head cut off at the nape,
Blue as a vein oer the Madonnas breast.
Sons, all have I bequeathed you, villas, all,
That brave Frascati villa with its bath,
So, let the blue lump poise between my knees,
Like God the Fathers globe on both his hands
Ye worship in the Jesu Church so gay,
For Gandolf shall not choose but see and burst! 50
Swift as a weavers shuttle fleet our years:
Man goeth to the grave, and where is he?
Did I say basalt for my slab, sons? Black—
Twas ever antique-black I meant! How else
Shall ye contrast my frieze to come beneath?
The bas-relief in bronze ye promised me,
Those Pans and Nymphs ye wot of, and perchance
Some tripod, thyrsus, with a vase or so,
    The Saviour at his sermon on the mount,

Saint Praxed in a glory, and one Pan 60
Ready to twitch the Nymphs last garment off,
And Moses with the tables. but I know
Ye mark me not! What do they whisper thee,
Child of my bowels, Anselm? Ah, ye hope
To revel down my villas while I gasp
Bricked oer with beggars mouldy travertine
Which Gandolf from his tomb-top chuckles at!
Nay, boys, ye love me—all of jasper, then!
T is jasper ye stand pledged to, lest I grieve.
My bath must needs be left behind, alas! 70
One block, pure green as a pistachio-nut,
Theres plenty jasper somewhere in the world—
And have I not Saint Praxeds ear to pray
Horses for ye, and brown Greek manuscripts,
And mistresses with great smooth marbly limbs?
—Thats if ye carve my epitaph aright,
Choice Latin, picked phrase, Tullys every word,
No gaudy ware like Gandolfs second line—
Tully, my masters? Ulpian serves his need!
And then how I shall lie through centuries, 80
And hear the blessed mutter of the mass,
And see God made and eaten all day long,
And feel the steady candle-flame, and taste
Good strong thick stupefying incense-smoke!
For as I lie here, hours of the dead night,
Dying in state and by such slow degrees, I fold my arms as if they clasped a crook,
And stretch my feet forth straight as stone can point,
And let the bedclothes, for a mortcloth, drop Into great laps and folds of sculptors-work: 90
And as yon tapers dwindle, and strange thoughts
Grow, with a certain humming in my ears,
About the life before I lived this life,
And this life too, popes, cardinals and priests,
Saint Praxed at his sermon on the mount,
Your tall pale mother with her talking eyes,
And new-found agate urns as fresh as day,
And marbles language, Latin pure, discreet, —Aha, Elucescebat quoth our friend?
No Tully, said I, Ulpian at the best! 1 oo
Evil and brief hath been my pilgrimage.
All lapis, all, sons! Else I give the Pope
My villas! Will ye ever eat my heart 1
Ever your eyes were as a lizards quick,
They glitter like your mothers for my soul,
Or ye would heighten my impoverished frieze,

Piece out its starved design, and fill my vase
With grapes, and add a vizor and a Term,
And to the tripod, ye would tie a lynx
That in his struggle throws the thyrsus down, 110
To comfort me on my entablature
Whereon I am to lie till I must ask
"Do I live, am I dead?" There, leave me, there!
For ye have stabbed me with ingratitude
To death—ye wish it—God, ye wish it! Stone—
Gritstone, a-crumble! Clammy squares which sweat
As if the corpse they keep were oozing through—
And no more lapis to delight the world!
Well go! I bless ye. Fewer tapers there,
But in a row: and, going, turn your backs 120 —Ay, like departing akar-ministrants,
And leave me in my church, the church for peace,
That I may watch at leisure if he leers—
Old Gandolf, at me, from his onion-stone,
As still he envied me, so fair she was!
BISHOP BLOUGRAMS APOLOGY.
1855.
No more wine? then we ll push back chairs and talk.
A final glass for me, though: cool, i faith!
We ought to have our Abbey back, you see.
Its different, preaching in basilicas,
And doing duty in some masterpiece
Like this of brother Pugins, bless his heart!
I doubt if theyre half baked, those chalk rosettes,
Ciphers and stucco-twiddlings everywhere;
Its just like breathing in a lime-kiln: eh?
These hot long ceremonies of our church 10
Cost us a little—oh, they pay the price,
You take me—amply pay it! Now, we ll talk.
So, you despise me, Mr. Gigadibs.
No deprecation,—nay, I beg you, sir!
Beside t is our engagement: dont you know,
I promised, if you d watch a dinner out,
We d see truth dawn together?—truth that peeps
Over the glasses edge when dinner s done,
And body gets its sop and holds its noise
And leaves soul free a little. Now s the time: 20
Truths break of day! You do despise me then.
And if I say, "despise me,"—never fear!
I know you do not in a certain sense—
Not in my arm-chair, for example: here,
I well imagine you respect my place

(Status, entourage, worldly circumstance)
Quite to its value–very much indeed:
–Are up to the protesting eyes of you
    M. W.–4 In pride at being seated here for once–
    You ll turn it to such capital account! 30
    When somebody, through years and years to come,
    Hints of the bishop,–names me–thats enough:
    "Blougram? I knew him "–(into it you slide)
    "Dined with him once, a Corpus Christi Day,
    All alone, we two; he s a clever man:
    And after dinner,–why, the wine you know,–
    Oh, there was wine, and good!–what with the wine.
    Faith, we began upon all sorts of talk!
He s no bad fellow, Blougram; he had seen
Something of mine he relished, some review: 40
    Hes quite above their humbug in his heart,
Half-said as much, indeed–the things his trade.
I warrant, Blougram s sceptical at times:
How otherwise? I liked him, I confess! "
Che the, my dear sir, as we say at Rome,
Dont you protest now! Its fair give and take;
You have had your turn and spoken your home-truths:
The hand s mine now, and here you follow suit.
    Thus much conceded, still the first fact stays–You do despise me; your ideal of life
50 Is not the bishops: you would not be I.
You would like better to be Goethe, now,
Or Buonaparte, or, bless me, lower still,
Count DOrsay,–so you did what you preferred,
Spoke as you thought, and, as you cannot help,
Believed or disbelieved, no matter what,
So long as on that point, whateer it was,
You loosed your mind, were whole and sole yourself.
–That, my ideal never can include,
Upon that element of truth and worth 60
    Never be based! for say they make me Pope– (They cant–suppose it for our
argument!)
    Why, there I m at my tethers end, I ve reached
    My height, and not a height which pleases you:
    An unbelieving Pope wont do, you say.
    Its like those eerie stories nurses tell,
    Of how some actor on a stage played Death,
    With pasteboard crown, sham orb and tinselled dart,
    And called himself the monarch of the world;
    Then, going in the tire-room afterward, 70
    Because the play was done, to shift himself,

Got touched upon the sleeve familiarly,
The moment he had shut the closet door,
By Death himself. Thus God might touch a Pope
At unawares, ask what his baubles mean,
And whose part he presumed to play just now.
Best be yourself, imperial, plain and true!
So, drawing comfortable breath again,
You weigh and find, whatever more or less I boast of my ideal realized 80 Is nothing in the balance when opposed
To your ideal, your grand simple life,
Of which you will not realize one jot.
I am much, you are nothing; you would be all, I would be merely much: you beat me there.
No, friend, you do not beat me: hearken why!
The common problem, yours, mine, every ones, Is–not to fancy what were fair in life
Provided it could be,–but, finding first
What may be, then find how to make it fair 90
Up to our means: a very different thing!
No abstract intellectual plan of life
Quite irrespective of lifes plainest laws,
But one, a man, who is man and nothing more,
May lead within a world which (by your leave) Is Rome or London, not Fools-paradise.
Embellish Rome, idealize away,
Make paradise of London if you can,
You re welcome, nay, you re wite.
A simile!
We mortals cross the ocean of this world loo
Each in his average cabin of a life;
The bests not big, the worst yields elbow-room.
Now for our six months voyage–how prepare?
You come on shipboard with a landsmans list
Of things he calls convenient: so they are!
An India screen is pretty furniture,
A piano-forte is a fine resource,
All Balzacs novels occupy one shelf,
The new edition fifty volumes long;
And little Greek books, with the funny type 11 o
They get up well at Leipsic, fill the next:
Go on! slabbed marble, what a bath it makes!
And Parmas pride, the Jerome, let us add!
T were pleasant could Correggios fleeting glow
Hang full in face of one whereer one roams,
Since he more than the others brings with him

Italys self,–the marvellous Modenese!–
Yet was not on your list before, perhaps.
–Alas, friend, here s the agent. is t the name?
The captain, or whoevers master here–120
    You see him screw his face up; whats his cry
Ere you set foot on shipboard? " Six feet square! "
If you wont understand what six feet mean,
Compute and purchaie stores accordingly–
    And if, in pique because he overhauls
    Your Jerome, piano, bath, you come on board
    Bare–why, you cut a figure at the first
    While sympathetic landsmen see you off;
    Not afterward, when long ere half seas over,
    You peep up from your utterly naked boards 130 Into some snug and well-appointed berth,
    Like mine for instance (try the cooler jug–
    Put back the other, but dont jog the ice!)
    And mortified you mutter " Well and good;
    He sits enjoying his sea-furniture;
    Tis stout and proper, and there s store of it:
    Though I Ve the better notion, all agree,
    Of fitting rooms up. Hang the carpenter,
    Neat ship-shape fixings and contrivances–139 I would have brought my Jerome, frame and all!"
    And meantime you bring nothing: never mind–
    Youve proved your artist-nature: what you dont
    You might bring, so despise me, as I say.
    Now come, lets backward to the starting-place. See my way: we re two college friends, suppose. Prepare together for our voyage, then; Each note and check the other in his work,–Here s mine, a bishops outfit; criticise! Whats wrong? why wont you be a bishop too? 149
    Why first, you dont believe, you dont and cant, (Not statedly, that is, and fixedly And absolutely and exclusively) In any revelation called divine. No dogmas nail your faith; and what remains But say so, like the honest man you are? First, therefore, overhaul theology!
    Nay, I too, not a fool, you please to think,
    Must find believing every whit as hard:
    And if I do not frankly say as much,
    The ugly consequence is clear enough. 160
    Now wait, my friend: well, I do not believe–If you ll accept no faith that is not fixed, Absolute and exclusive, as you say. You re wrong–I mean to prove it in due time. Meanwhile, I know where difficulties lie I could not, cannot solve, nor ever shall, So give up hope accordingly to solve–(To you, and over the wine). Our dogmas then With both of us, though in unlike degree, Missing full credence–overboard with

them! 170 I mean to meet you on your own premise: Good, there go mine in company
with yours!

And now what are we? unbelievers both,
Calm and complete, determinately fixed
To-day, to-morrow and forever, pray?
You Ml guarantee me that? Not so, I think!
In no wise! all we ve gained is, that belief,
As unbelief before, shakes us by fits,
Confounds us like its predecessor. Where s
The gain? how can we guard our unbelief, 180
 Make it bear fruit to us?–the problem here.
Just when we are safest, there s a sunset-touch,
A fancy from a flower-bell, some ones death,
A chorus-ending from Euripides,–
And thats enough for fifty hopes and fears
As old and new at once as natures self,
To rap and knock and enter in our soul,
Take hands and dance there, a fantastic ring,
 Round the ancient idol, on his base again,–
The grand Perhaps! We look on helplessly. 190
There the old misgivings, crooked questions are–
This good God,–what he could do, if he would,
Would, if he could–then must have done long since:
If so, when, where and how? seme way must be,–
Once feel about, and soon or late you hit
Some sense, in which it might be, after all.
Why not, "The Way, the Truth, the Life? lv –That way
 Over the mountain, which who stands upon
Is apt to doubt if it be meant for a road;
While, if he views it from the waste itself, 200
 Up goes the line there, plain from base to brow,
Not vague, mistakable! whats a break or two
Seen from the unbroken desert either side?
And then (to bring in fresh philosophy)
What if the breaks themselves should prove at last
The most consummate of contrivances
To train a mans eye, teach him what is faith?
And so we stumble at truths very test!
All we have gained then by our unbelief
Is a life of doubt diversified by faith, 210
 For one of faith diversified by doubt:
We called the chess-board white,–we call it black.

 "Well," you rejoin, " the end s no worse, at least;
We ve reason for both colors on the board:

Why not confess then, where I drop the faith
And you the doubt, that I m as right as you?"
    Because, friend, in the next place, this being so, And both things even,–faith and unbelief
    Left to a mans choice,–we ll proceed a tep, Returning to our image, which I like. 220
    A mans choice, yes–but a cabin-passengers–
The man made for the special life o the world–
Do you forget him? I remember though!
Consult our ships conditions and you find
One and but one choice suitable to all;
The choice, that you unluckily prefer,
Turning things topsy-turvy–they or it
Going to the ground. Belief or unbelief
Bears upon life, determines its whole course,
Begins at its beginning. See the world 230
    Such as it is,–you made it not, nor I;
I mean to take it as it is,–and you,
Not so you ll take it,–though you get naught else.
I know the special kind of life I like,
What suits the most my idiosyncrasy,
Brings out the best of me and bears me fruit
In power, peace, pleasantness and length of days.
I find that positive belief does this
For me, and unbelief, no whit of this.
–For you, it does, however?–that, we ll try! 240
T is clear, I cannot lead my life, at least,
Induce the world to let me peaceably,
Without declaring at the outset, "Friends,
I absolutely and peremptorily
Believe! "–I say, faith is my waking life:
One sleeps, indeed, and dreams at intervals,
We know, but waking s the main point with us,
And my provisions for lifes waking part.
Accordingly, I use heart, head and hand 249
    All day, I build, scheme, study, and make friends;
And when night overtakes me, down I lie,
    Sleep, dream a little, and get done with it,
    The sooner the better, to begin afresh.
    Whats midnight doubt before the daysprings faith?
    You, the philosopher, that disbelieve,
    That recognize the night, give dreams their weight–
    To be consistent you should keep your bed,
    Abstain from healthy acts that prove you man,
    For fear you drowse perhaps at unawares!

And certainly at night you ll sleep and dream, 260
Live through the day and bustle as you please.
And so you live to sleep as I to wake,
To unbelieve as I to still believe?
Well, and the common sense o the world calls you
Bed-ridden,–and its good things come to me.
Its estimation, which is half the fight,
Thats the first-cabin comfort I secure:
The next. but you perceive with half an eye!
Come, come, its best believing, if we may;
You cant but own that!
Next, concede again, 270
If once we choose belief, on all accounts
We cant be too decisive in our faith,
Conclusive and exclusive in its terms,
To suit the world which gives us the good things.
In every mans career are certain points
Whereon he dares not be indifferent;
The world detects him clearly, if he dare,
As baffled at the game, and losing life.
He may care little or he may care much
For riches, honor, pleasure, work, repose, 280
Since various theories of life and lifes
Success are extant which might easily
Comport with either estimate of these;
And whoso chooses wealth or poverty,
Labor or quiet, is not judged a fool
Because his fellow would choose otherwise:
We let him choose upon his own account
So long as he s consistent with his choice.
But certain points, left wholly to himself,
When once a man has arbitrated on, 290
We say he must succeed there or go hang.
Thus, he should wed the woman he loves most
Or needs most, whatsoeer the love or need–
For he cant wed twice. Then, he must avouch,
Or follow, at the least, sufficiently,
The form of faith his conscience holds the best,
Whateer the process of conviction was:
For nothing can compensate his mistake
On such a point, the man himself being judge:
He cannot wed twice, nor twice lose his soul. 300
Well now, theres one great form of Christian faith
I happened to be born in–which to teach
Was given me as I grew up, on all hands,

As best and readiest means of living by;
The same on examination being proved
The most pronounced moreover, fixed, precise
And absolute form of faith in the whole world–
Accordingly, most potent of all forms
For working on the world. Observe, my friend!
Such as you know me, I am free to say, 310 In these hard latter days which hamper one,
Myself–by no immoderate exercise
Of intellect and learning, but the tact
To let external forces work for me,
–Bid the streets stones be bread and they are bread;
Bid Peters creed, or rather, Hildebrands,
     Exalt me oer my fellows in the world
     And make my life an ease and joy and pride; It does so,–which for me s a great point gained,
     Who have a soui and body that exact 320
     A comfortable care in many ways.
     There s power in me and will to dominate
     Which I must exercise, they hurt me else: In many ways I need mankinds respect,
     Obedience, and the love thats born of fear:
     While at the same time, there s a taste I have,
     A toy of soul, a titillating thing,
     Refuses to digest these dainties crude.
     The naked life is gross till clothed upon: I must take what men offer, with a grace 330
     As though I would not, could I help it, take!
     An uniform I wear though over-rich–
     Something imposed on me, no choice of mine;
     No fancy-dress worn for pure fancys sake
     And despicable therefore! now folk kneel
     And kiss my hand–of course the Churchs hand.
     Thus I am made, thus life is best for me,
     And thus that it should be I have procured;
     And thus it could not be another way, I venture to imagine.
     You ll reply, 340
     So far my choice, no doubt, is a success;
But were I made of better elements,
With nobler instincts, purer tastes, like you,
I hardly would account the thing success
Though it did all for me I say.
     But, friend,
     We speak of what is; not of what might be,
And how twere better if twere otherwise.
     I am the man you see here plain enough:

Grant Im a beast, why, beasts must lead beasts lives!
Suppose I own at once to tail and claws; 350
The tailless man exceeds me: but being tailed I ll lash out lion fashion, and leave apes
To dock their stump and dress their haunches up.
My business is not to remake myself,
But make the absolute best of what God made.
Or–our first simile–though you prove me doomed
To a viler berth still, to the steerage-hole,
The sheep-pen or the pig-stye, I should strive
To make what use of each were possible;
And as this cabin gets upholstery, 360
That hutch should rustle with sufficient straw.
But, friend, I dont acknowledge quite so fast
I fail of all your manhoods lofty tastes
Enumerated so complacently,
On the mere ground that you forsooth can find
In this particular life I choose to lead
No fit provision for them. Can you not?
Say you, my fault is I address myself
To grosser estimators than should judge?
And thats no way of holding up the soul, 370
Which, nobler, needs mens praise perhaps, yet knows
One wise mans verdict outweighs all the fools–
Would like the two, but, forced to choose, takes that.
I pine among my million imbeciles
(You think) aware some dozen men of sense
Eye me and know me, whether I believe
In the last winking Virgin, as I vow,
And am a fool, or disbelieve in her
And am a knave,–approve in neither case,
Withhold their voices though I look their way: 3 80
Like Verdi when, at his worst operas end (The thing they gave at Florence,–whats its name?)
While the mad housefuls plaudits near outbang
His orchestra of salt-box, tongs and bones,
He looks through all the roaring and the wreaths
Where sits Rossini patient in his stall.
Nay, friend, I meet you with an answer here–
That even your prime men who appraise their kind
Are men still, catch a wheel within a wheel,
See more in a truth than the truths simple self, 390
Confuse themselves. You see lads walk the street
Sixty the minute; whats to note in that?
You see one lad oerstride a chimney-stack;

Him you must watch—he s sure to fall, yet stands!
Our interests on the dangerous edge of things.
The honest thief, the tender mu-derer,
The superstitious atheist, demirep
That loves and saves her soul in new French books—
We watch while these in equilibrium keep
The giddy line midway: one step aside, 400
    They re classed and done with. I, then, keep the line
    Before your sages,—just the men to shrink
From the gross weights, coarse scales and labels broad
You offer their refinement. Fool or knave?
Why needs a bishop be a fool or knave
When there s a thousand diamond weights between?
So, I enlist them. Your picked twelve, you ll find,
Profess themselves indignant, scandalized
At thus being held unable to explain
How a superior man who disbelieves 410
    May not believe as well: thats Schellings way!
    Its through my coming in the tail of time,
    Nicking the minute with a happy tact.
    Had I been born three hundred years ago
    Theyd say, "Whats strange? Blougram of course believes;"
    And, seventy years since, "disbelieves of course."
But now, "He may believe; and yet, and yet
How can he?" All eyes turn with interest.
Whereas, step off the line on either side—
You, for example, clever to a fault, 420
    The rough and ready man who write apace,
Read somewhat seldomer, think perhaps even less—
You disbelieve! Who wonders and who cares?
Lord So-and-so—his coat bedropped with wax,
All Peters chains about his waist, his back
Brave with the needlework of Noodledom—
Believes! Again, who wonders and who cares?
But I, the man of sei. se and learning too,
The able to think yet act, the this, the that,
I, to believe at this late time of day! 430
    Enough; you see, I need not fear contempt.
    —Except its yours! Admire me as these may, You dont. But whom at least do you admire? Present your own perfection, your ideal, Your pattern man for a minute—oh, make haste, Is it Napoleon you would have us grow? Concede the means; allow his head and hand, (A large concession, clever as you are) Good! In our common primal element Of unbelief (we cant believe, you know—440 We re still at that admission, recollect!) Where do you find—apart from, towering oer The secondary temporary aims

Which satisfy the gross taste you despise–
Where do you find his star?–his crazy trust
God knows through what or in what? its alive
And shines and leads him, and thats all we want.
Have we aught in our sober night shall point
Such ends as his were, and direct the means
Of working out our purpose straight as his, 450
Nor bring a moments trouble on success
With after-care to justify the same?
–Be a Napoleon, and yet disbelieve–
Why, the man s mad, friend, take his light away!
Whats the vague good o the world, for which you dare
With comfort to yourself blow millions up?
We neither of us see it! we do see
The blown-up millions–spatter of their brains
And writhing of their bowels and so forth,
In that bewildering entanglement 460
　　Of horrible eventualities
Past calculation to the end of time!
Can I mistake for some clear word of God
(Which were my ample warrant for it all)
His puff of hazy instinct, idle talk,
"The State, thats I," quack-nonsense about crowns,
And (when one beats the man to his last hold)
A vague idea of setting things to rights,
Policing people efficaciously,
　　More to their profit, most of all to his own; 470
　　The whole to end that dismallest of ends
By an Austrian marriage, cant to us the Church,
And resurrection of the old regime?
Would I, who hope to live a dozen years,
Fight Austerlitz for reasons such and such?
No: for, concede me but the merest chance
　　Doubt may be wrong–there s judgment, life to come!
With just that chance, I dare not. Doubt proves right?
This present life is all?–you offer me
Its dozen noisy years, without a chance 480
　　That wedding an archduchess, wearing lace,
And getting called by divers new-coined names,
Will drive off ugly thoughts and let me dine,
Sleep, read and chat in quiet as I like!
Therefore I will not.
　　Take another case;
Fit up the cabin yet another way.
What say you to the poets? shall we write

Hamlet, Othello–make the world our own,
Without a risk to run of either sort?
I cant!–to put the strongest reason first. 490
    "But try," you urge, "the trying shall suffice;
The aim, if reached or not, makes great the life:
Try to be Shakespeare, leave the rest to fate! "
Spare my self-knowledge–there s no fooling me!
If I prefer remaining my poor self,
I say so not in self-dispraise but praise.
If I m a Shakespeare, let the well alone;
Why should I try to be what now I am?
If I m no Shakespeare, as too probable,–
His power and consciousness and self-delight 500
    And all we want in common, shall I find–
Trying forever? while on points of taste
Wherewith, to speak it humbly, he and I
Are dowered alike–I ll ask you, I or he,
Which in our two lives realizes most?
Much, he imagined–somewhat, I possess.
He had the imagination; stick to that!
Let him say, "In the face of my souls worki
    Your world is worthless and I touch it not 509
    Lest I should wrong them "–I ll withdraw my plea.
    But does he say so? look upon his life!
    Himself, who only can, gives judgment there.
    He leaves his towers and gorgeous palaces
    To build the trimmest house in Stratford town;
    Saves money, spends it, owns the worth of things,
    Giulio Romanos pictures, Dowlands lute;
    Enjoys a show, respects the puppets, too,
    And none more, had he seen its entry once,
    Than " Pandulph, of fair Milan cardinal."
    Why then should I who play that personage, 520
    The very Pandulph Shakespeares fancy made,
    Be told that had the poet chanced to start
    From where I stand now (some degree like mine
    Being just the goal he ran his race to reach)
    He would have run the whole race back, forsooth,
    And left being Pandulph, to begin write plays?
    Ah, the earths best can be but the earths best!
    Did Shakespeare live, he could but sit at home
    And get himself in dreams the Vatican,
    Greek busts, Venetian paintings, Roman walls, 530
    And English books, none equal to his own,
    Which I read, bound in gold (he never did).

–Ternis fall, Naples bay and Gothards top–
Eh, friend? I could not fancy one of these;
But, as I pour this claret, there they are: I ve gained them–crossed St. Gothard last
July
    With ten mules to the carriage and a bed
Slung inside; is my hap the worse for that?
We want the same things, Shakespeare and myself,
And what I want, I have: he, gifted more, 540
Could fancy he too had them when he liked,
But not so thoroughly that, if fate allowed,
M. W.–5
He would not have them also in my sense.
We play one game; I send the ball aloft
No less adroitly that of fifty strokes
Scarce five go oer the wall so wide and high
Which sends them back to me: I wish and get.
He struck balls higher and with better skill,
But at a poor fence level with his head,
And hit–his Stratford house, a coat of arms, 5 50
Successful dealings in his grain and wool,–
While I receive heavens incense in my nose
And style myself the cousin of Queen Bess.
Ask him, if this life s all, who wins the game?
    Believe–and our whole argument breaks up. Enthusiasm s the best thing, I repeat;
Only, we cant command it; fire and life Are all, dead matters nothing, we agree: And
be it a mad dream or Gods very breath, The facts the same,–beliefs fire, once in us,
560 Makes of all else mere stuff to show itself: We penetrate our life with such a glow
As fire lends wood and iron–this turns steel, That burns to ash–all s one, fire proves
its power For good or ill, since men call flare success. But paint a fire, it will not
therefore burn. Light one in me, Ill find it food enough! Why, to be Luther–that s
a life to lead, Incomparably better than my own. He comes, reclaims Gods earth for
God, he says, 570 Sets up Gods rule again by simple means, Re-opens a shut book,
and all is done. He flared out in the flaring of mankind; Such Luthers luck was: how
shall such be mine? If he succeeded, nothings left to do:
    And if he did not altogether–well,
Strauss is the next advance. All Strauss should be I might be also. But to what
result?
    He looks upon no future: Luther did.
What can I gain on the denying side? 580 Ice makes no conflagration. State the
facts,
    Read the text right, emancipate the world–
The emancipated world enjoys itself
With scarce a thank-you: Blougram told it first It could not owe a farthing,–not to
him
More than Saint Paul! twould press its pay, you think?

Then add theres still that plaguy hundredth chance
Strauss may be wrong. And so a risk is run–
For what gain? not for Luthers, who secured
A real heaven in his heart throughout his life, 590
Supposing death a little altered things.

"Ay, but since really you lack faith," you cry, You run the same risk really on all sides, In cool indifference as bold unbelief. As well be Strauss as swing twixt Paul and him. Its not worth having, such imperfect faith, No more available to do faiths work Than unbelief like mine. Whole faith, or none!"

Softly, my friend! I must dispute that point. Once own the use of faith, I Ml find you faith. 600 We re back on Christian ground. You call for faith: I show you doubt, to prove that faith exists. The more of doubt, the stronger faith, I say, If faith oercomes doubt How I know it does? By life and mans free will, God gave for that! To mould life as we choose it, shows our choice:

Thats our one act, the previous work s his own.
You criticise the soul? it reared this tree–
This broad life and whatever fruit it bears!
What matter though I doubt at every pore, 610
    Head-doubts, heart-doubts, doubts at my fingers ends,
Doubts in the trivial work of every day,
Doubts at the very bases of my soul
In the grand moments when she probes herself—
If finally I have a life to show,
The thing I did, brought out in evidence
Against the thing done to me underground
By hell and all its brood, for aught I know?
I say, whence sprang this? shows it faith or doubt?
Alls doubt in me; wheres break of faith in this? 6zo
It is the idea, the feeling and the love,
God means mankind should strive for and show forth
Whatever be the process to that end,–
And not historic knowledge, logic sound,
And metaphysical acumen, sure!
"What think ye of Christ," friend? when alls done and said,
    Like you this Christianity or not?
It may be false, but will you wish it true?
Has it your vote to be so if it can?
Trust you an instinct silenced long ago 630
    That will break silence and enjoin you love
What mortified philosophy is hoarse,
And all in vain, with bidding you despise?
If you desire faith–then you ve faith enough:
What else seeks God–nay, what else seek ourselves i
You form a notion of me, well suppose,
On hearsay; its a favorable one:

"But still" (you add), "there was no such good man,
Because of contradiction in the facts.
    One proves, for instance, he was born in Rome, 640
This Blougram; yet throughout the tales of him
I see he figures as an Englishman."
Well, the two things are reconcilable.
But would I rather you discovered that,
Subjoining–" Still, what matter though they be?
Blougram concerns me naught, born here or there."
    Pure faith indeed–you know not what you ask!
Naked belief in God the Omnipotent,
Omniscient, Omnipresent, sears too much
The sense of conscious creatures to be borne. 650
It were the seeing him, no flesh shall dare.
Some think, Creations meant to show him forth:
I say its meant to hide him all it can,
And thats what all the blessed evils for.
Its use in Time is to environ us,
Our breath, our drop of dew, with shield enough
Against that sight till we can bear its stress.
Under a vertical sun, the exposed brain
And lidless eye and disemprisoned heart
Less certainly would wither up at once 660
    Than mind, confronted with the truth of him.
But time and earth case-harden us to live;
The feeblest sense is trusted most; the child
Feels God a moment, ichors oer the place.
Plays on and grows to be a man like us.
With me, faith means perpetual unbelief
Kept quiet like the snake neath Michaels foot
Who stands calm just because he feels it writhe.
Or, if thats too ambitious,–here s my box–
I need the excitation of a pinch 670
    Threatening the torpor of the inside-nose
Nigh on the imminent sneeze that never comes.
" Leave it in peace" advise the simple folk:
Make it aware of peace by itching-fits,
Say I–let doubt occasion still more faith!
    You ll say, once all believed, man, woman, child,
In that dear middle-age these noodles praise.
How you d exult if I could put you back
Six hundred years, blot out cosmogony,
Geology, ethnology, what not, 680 (Greek endings, each the little passing-bell
That signifies some faith s about to die),
And set you square with Genesis again,–

When such a traveller told you his last news,
He saw the ark a-top of Ararat
But did not climb there since twas getting dusk
And robber-bands infest the mountains foot!
How should you feel, I ask, in such an age,
How act? As other people felt and did;
With soul more blank than this decanters knob, 690
Believe—and yet lie, kill, rob, fornicate
Full in beliefs face, like the beast you d be!
    No, when the fight begins within himself,
A man s worth something. God stoops oer his head,
Satan looks up between his feet—both tug—
Hes left, himself, i the middle: the soul wakes
And grows. Prolong that battle through his life!
Never leave growing till the life to come!
Here, we ve got callous to the Virgins winks
That used to puzzle people wholesomely: 700
    Men have outgrown the shame of being fools.
What are the laws of nature, not to bend
If the Church bid them?—brother Newman asks,
Up with the Immaculate Conception, then—
    On to the rack with faith!—is my advice.
Will not that hurry us upon our knees,
Knocking our breasts, "It cant be—yet it shall!
Who am I, the worm, to argue with my Pope?
Low things confound the high things! " and so forth.
Thats better than acquitting God with grace 710
As some folk do. He s tried—no case is proved.
Philosophy is lenient—he may go!
    Youll say, the old system s not so obsolete
But men believe still: ay, but who and where?
King Bombas lazzaroni foster yet
The sacred flame, so Antonelli writes;
But even of these, what ragamuffin-saint
Believes God watches him continually,
As he believes in fire that it will burn,
Or rain that it will drench him? Break fires law, 720
Sin against rain, although the penalty
Be just a singe or soaking? " No," he smiles;
"Those laws are laws that can enforce themselves."
    The sum of all is—yes, my doubt is great,
My faith s still greater, then my faith s enough.
I have read much, thought much, experienced much,
Yet would die rather than avow my fear
The Naples liquefaction may be false,

When set to happen by the palace-clock
According to the clouds or dinner-time. 730 I hear you recommend, I might at least
Eliminate, decrassify my faith
Since I adopt it; keeping what I must
And leaving what I can—such points as this.
I wont—that is, I cant throw one away.
Supposing there s no truth in what I hold
    About the need of trial to roans faith,
    Still, when you bid me purify the same,
    To such a process I discern no end.
    Clearing off one excrescence to see two, 740
    There s ever a next in size, now grown as big,
    That meets the knife: I cut and cut again!
    First cut the Liquefaction, what comes last
    But Fichtes clever cut at God himself?
    Experimentalize on sacred things!
    I trust nor hand nor eye nor heart nor brain
    To stop betimes: they all get drunk alike.
    The first step, I am master not to take.
    You d find the cutting-process to your taste As much as leaving growths of lies
unpruned, 750 Nor see more danger in it,–you retort. Your taste s worth mine; but my
taste proves more wise
    When we consider that the steadfast hold
On the extreme end of the chain of faith
Gives all the advantage, makes the difference
With the rough purblind mass we seek to rule:
We are their lords, or they are free of us,
Just as we tighten or relax our hold.
So, other matters equal, we ll revert
To the first problem—which, if solved my way 760
And thrown into the balance, turns the scale–
How we may lead a comfortable life,
How suit our luggage to the cabins size.
    Of course you are remarking all this time
How narrowly and grossly I view life,
Respect the creature-comforts, care to rule
The masses, and regard complacently
"The cabin," in our old phrase. Well, I do.
    I act for, talk for, live for this world now,
    As this world prizes action, life and talk: 770
    No prejudice to what next world may prove,
    Whose new laws and requirements, my best pledge
    To observe then, is that I observe these now,
    Shall do hereafter what I do meanwhile.
    Let us concede (gratuitously though)

Next life relieves the soul of body, yields
Pure spiritual enjoyment: well, my friend,
Why lose this life i the meantime, since its use
May be to make the next life more intense?
Do you know, I have often had a dream 780 (Work it up in your next months article)
Of mans poor spirit in its progress, still
Losing true life forever and a day
Through ever trying to be and ever being–
In the evolution of successive spheres–
Before its actual sphere and place of life,
Halfway into the next, which having reached,
It shoots with corresponding foolery
Halfway into the next still, on and off!
As when a traveller, bound from North to South, 790
Scouts fur in Russia: whats its use in France?
In France spurns flannel: where s its need in Spain?
In Spain drops cloth, too cumbrous for Algiers!
Linen goes next, and last the skin itself,
A superfluity at Timbuctoo.
    When, through his journey, was the fool at ease?
Im at ease now, friend; worldly in this world,
I take and like its way of life; I think
My brothers, who administer the means,
Live better for my comfort–that s good too; 800
And God, if he pronounce upon such iife,
    Approves my service, which is better still.
    If he keep silence,–why, for you or me
    Or that brute beast pulled-up in to-days " Times,"
    What odds is t, save to ourselves, what life we lead i
    You meet me at this issue: you declare,–
All special-pleading done with–truth is truth,
And justifies itself by undreamed ways.
You dont fear but its better, if we doubt,
To say so, act up to our truth perceived 810
    However feebly. Do then,–act away!
T is there Im on the watch for you. How one acts
Is, both of us agree, our chief concern:
And how you ll act is what I fain would see
If, like the candid person you appear,
You dare to make the most of your lifes scheme
As I of mine, live up to its full law
Since theres no higher law that counterchecks.
Put natural religion to the test 819
    You ve just demolished the revealed with–quick,
Down to the root of all that checks your will,

All prohibition to lie, kill and thieve,
Or even to be an atheistic priest!
Suppose a pricking to incontinence–
Philosophers deduce you chastity
Or shame, from just the fact that at the first
Whoso embraced a woman in the field,
Threw club down and forewent his brains beside,
So, stood a ready victim in the reach
Of any brother savage, club in hand; 830
    Hence saw the use of going out of sight
In wood or cave to prosecute his loves:
I read this in a French book t other day.
Does law so analyzed coerce you much?
Oh, men spin clouds of fuzz where matters end,
But you who reach where the first thread begins,
Youll soon cut that!–which means you can, but wont,
    Through certain instincts, blind, unreasoned-out,
You dare not set aside, you cant tell why,
But there they are, and so you let them rule. 840
Then, friend, you seem as much a slave as I,
A liar, conscious coward and hypocrite,
Without the good the slave expects to get,
In case he has a master after all!
You own your instincts? why, what else do I,
Who want, am made for, and must have a God
Ere I can be aught, do aught?–no mere name
Want, but the true thing with what proves its truth,
To wit, a relation from that thing to me, 849
    Touching from head to foot–which touch I feel,
And with it take the rest, this life of ours!
I live my life here; yours you dare not live.
    –Not as I state it, who (you please subjoin)
Disfigure such a life and call it names.
While, to your mind, remains another way
For simple men: knowledge and power have rights,
But ignorance and weakness have rights too.
There needs no crucial effort to find truth
If here or there or anywhere about:
We ought to turn each side, try hard and see, 860
And if we cant, be glad we ve earned at least
The right, by one laborious proof the more,
To graze in peace earths pleasant pasturage.
Men are not angels, neither are they brutes:
Something we may see, all we cannot see.
What need of lying? I say, I see all,

And swear to each detail the most minute In what I think a Pans face–you, mere
cloud: I swear I hear him speak and see him wink,
    For fear, if once I drop the emphasis, 870
    Mankind may doubt there s any cloud at all.
    You take the simple life–ready to see,
    Willing to see (for no clouds worth a face)–
    And leaving quiet what no strength can move,
    And which, who bids you move? who has the right?
    I bid you; but you are Gods sheep, not mine:
    "Pastor est tui Dominus." You find In this the pleasant pasture of our life
    Much you may eat without the least offence,
    Much you dont eat because your maw objects, 880
    Much you would eat but that your fellow-flock
    Open great eyes at you and even butt,
    And thereupon you like your mates so well
    You cannot please yourself, offending them;
    Though when they seem exorbitantly sheep,
    You weigh your pleasure with their butts and bleats
    And strike the balance. Sometimes certain fears
    Restrain you, real checks since you find them so;
    Sometimes you please yourself and nothing checks:
    And thus you graze through life with not one lie, 890
    And like it best.
    But do you, in truths name?
If so, you beat–which means you are not I–
Who needs must make earth mine and feed my fill
Not simply unbutted at, unbickered with,
But motioned to the velvet of the sward
By those obsequious wethers very selves.
Look at me. sir; my age is double yours:
At yours, I knew beforehand, so enjoyed,
What now I should be–as, permit the word, I pretty well imagine your whole range
900
    And stretch of tether twenty years to come.
    We both have minds and bodies much alike: In truths name, dont you want my
bishopric,
    My daily bread, my influence and my state?
    You re young. I m old; you must be old one day;
    Will you find then, as I do hour by hour,
    Women their lovers kneel to, who cut curls
    From your tat lap-dogs ear to grace a brooch–
    Dukes, who petition just to kiss your ring–
    With much beside you know or may conceive? 910
    Suppose we die to-night: well, here am I,
    Such were my gains, life bore this fruit to me,

While writing all the same my articles
On music, poetry, the fictile vase
Found at Albano, chess, Anacreons Greek.
But you–the highest honor in your life,
The thing you ll crown yourself with, all your days, Is–dining here and drinking
this last glass I pour you out in sign of amity
Before we part forever. Of your power 920
And social influence, worldly worth in short,
Judge whats my estimation by the fact, I do not condescend to enjoin, beseech,
Hint secrecy on one of all these words!
You re shrewd and know that should you publish one
The world would brand the lie–my enemies first,
Who d sneer–"the bishops an arch-hypocrite
And knave perhaps, but not so frank a fool."
Whereas I should not dare for both my ears
Breathe one such syllable, smile one such smile, 930
Before the chaplain who reflects myself–
My shade s so much more potent than your flesh.
Whats your reward, self-abnegating friend?
Stood you confessed of those exceptional
And privileged great natures that dwarf mine–
A zealot with a mad ideal in reach,
A poet just about to print his ode,
A statesman with a scheme to stop this war,
An artist whose religion is his art– I should have nothing to object: such men 940
Carry the fire, all things grow warm to them,
Their druggets worth my purple, they beat me.
But you,–you re just as little those as I–
You, Gigadibs, who, thirty years of age,
Write stately for Blackwoods Magazine,
Believe you see two points in Hamlets soul
Unseized by the Germans yet–which view you ll print–
Meantime the best you have to show being still
That lively lightsome article we took
Almost for the true Dickens,–whats its name? 950
"The Slum and Cellar, or Whitechapel life
Limned after dark! " it made me laugh, I know,
And pleased a month, and brought you in ten pounds.
–Success I recognize and compliment,
And therefore give you, if you choose, three words
(The card and pencil-scratch is quite enough)
Which whether here, in Dublin or New York,
Will get you, prompt as at my eyebrows wink,
Such terms as never you aspired to get
In all our own reviews and some not ours. 960

Go write your lively sketches! be the first
"Blougram, or The Eccentric Confidence "–
Or better simply say, "The Outward-bound."
Why, men as soon would throw it in my teeth
As copy and quote the infamy chalked broad
About me on the church-door opposite.

Voa will not wait for that experience though, I fancy, howsoever you decide,
To discontinue–not detesting, not
Defaming, but at least–despising me l 970

Over his wine so smiled and talked his hour Sylvester Blougram, styled in partibus Episcopal, nee non –(the deuce knows what It s changed to by our novel hierarchy) With Gigadibs the literary man, Who played with spoons, explored his plates design, And ranged the olive-stones about its edge, While the great bishop rolled him out a mind Long crumpled, till creased consciousness lay smooth.

For Blougram, he believed, say, half he spoke. 980 The other portion, as he shaped it thus For argumentatory purposes, He felt his foe was foolish to dispute. Some arbitrary accidental thoughts That crossed his mind, amusing because new, He chose to represent as fixtures there, Invariable convictions (such they seemed Beside his interlocutors loose cards Flung daily down, and not the same way twice) 989 While certain hell-deep instincts, rrans weak tongue Is never bold to utter in their truth Because styled hell-deep (t is an old mistake To place hell at the bottom of the earth) He ignored these,–not having in readiness Their nomenclature and philosophy: He said true things, but called them by wrong names. "On the whole," he thought, "Ijustify myself On every point where cavillers like this

Oppugn my life: he tries one kind of fence, I close, hes worsted, thats enough for him. 1000

He s on the ground: if ground should break away I take my stand on, there s a firmer yet
Beneath it, both of us may sink and reach.
His ground was over mine and broke the first:
So, let him sit with me this many a year!"
He did not sit five minutes. Just a week
Sufficed his sudden healthy vehemence.
Something had struck him in the "Outward-bound"
Another way than Blougrams purpose was:
And having bought, not cabin-furniture 1010
But settlers-implements (enough for three)
And started for Australia–there, I hope,
By this time he has tested his first plough,
And studied his last chapter of St. John.
CLEON.
"As certain also of your own poets have said—1855.
Cleon the poet (from the sprinkled isles,
Lily on lily, that oerlace the sea,
And laugh their pride when the light wave lisps

"Greece")–
To Protus in his Tyranny: much health!
    They give thy letter to me, even now:
I read and seem as if I heard thee speak.
The master of thy galley still unlades
    Gift after gift; they block my court at last
    And pile themselves along its portico
    Royal with sunset, like a thought of thee: 1 o
    And one white she-slave from the group dispersed
    Of black and white slaves (like the chequer-work
    Pavement, at once my nations work and gift,
    Now covered with this settle-down of doves),
    One lyric woman, in her crocus vest
    Woven of sea-wools, with her two white hands
    Commends to me the strainer and the cup
    Thy lip hath bettered ere it blesses mine.
    Well-counselled, king, in thy munificence!
For so shall men remark, in such an act 20
    Of love for him whose song gives life its joy,
Thy recognition of the use of life;
Nor call thy spirit barely adequate
To help on life in straight ways, broad enough
For vulgar souls, by ruling and the rest.
Thou, in the daily building of thy tower,–
Whether in fierce and sudden spasms of toil,
Or through dim lulls of unapparent growth,
Or when the general work mid good acclaim
Climbed with the eye to cheer the architect,–30
Didst neer engage in work for mere works sake–
Hadst ever in thy heart the luring hope
Of some eventual rest a-top of it,
Whence, all the tumult of the building hushed,
Thou first of men mightst look out to the East:
The vulgar saw thy tower, thou sawest the sun.
For this, I promise on thy festival
To pour libation, looking oer the sea,
M. iking this slave narrate thy fortunes, speak
Thy great words, and describe thy royal face–40
    M. W.–6
    Wishing thee wholly where Zeus lives the most,
Within the eventual element of calm.
    Thy letters first requirement meets me here.
It is as thou hast heard: in one short life
I, Cleon, have effected all those things
Thou wonderingly dost enumerate.

That epos on thy hundred plates of gold
Is mine,–and also mine the little chant,
So sure to rise from every fishing-bark
When, lights at prow, the seamen haul their net. 50
The image of the sun-god on the phare,
Men turn from the suns self to see, is mine;
The Poecile, oer-storied its whole length,
As thou didst hear, with painting, is mine too.
I know the true proportions of a man
And woman also, not observed before;
And I have written three books on the soul,
Proving absurd all written hitherto,
And putting us to ignorance again.
For music,–why, I have combined the moods, 60
Inventing one. In brief, all arts are mine;
Thus much the people know and recognize,
Throughout our seventeen islands. Marvel not.
We of these latter days, with greater mind
Than our forerunners, since more composite,
Look not so great, beside their simple way,
To a judge who only sees one way at once,
One mind-point and no other at a time,–
Compares the small part of a man of us
With some whole man of the heroic age, 70
    Great in his way–not ours, nor meant for ours.
And ours is greater, had we skill to know:
For, what we call this life of men on earth,
    This sequence of the souls achievements here
    Being, as I find much reason to conceive, Intended to be viewed eventually
As a great whole, not analyzed to parts,
But each part having reference to all,–
How shall a certain part, pronounced complete,
Endure effacement by another part? 80
Was the thing done?–then, whats to do again?
See, in the chequered pavement opposite,
Suppose the artist made a perfect rhomb,
And next a lozenge, then a trapezoid–
He did not overlay them, superimpose
The new upon the old and blot it out,
But laid them on a level in his work,
Making at last a picture; there it lies.
So, first the perfect separate forms were made,
The portions of mankind; and after, so, 90
Occurred the combination of the same.
For where had been a progress, otherwise?

Mankind, made up of all the single men,– In such a synthesis the labor ends.
Now mark me! those divine men of old time
Have reached, thou sayest well, each at one point
The outside verge that rounds our faculty;
And where they reached, who can do more than reach It takes but little water just
to touch
At some one point the inside of a sphere, loo
And, as we turn the sphere, touch all the rest In due succession: but the finer air
Which not so palpably nor obviously,
Though no less universally, can touch
The whole circumference of that emptied sphere,
Fills it more fully than the water did;
Holds thrice the weight of water in itself
Resolved into a subtler element.
And yet the vulgar call the sphere first full
Up to the visible height.–and after, void; 110
Not knowing airs more hidden properties.
And thus our soul, misknown, cries out to Zeus
To vindicate his purpose in our life:
Why stay we on the earth unless to grow?
Long since, I imaged, wrote the fiction out,
That he or other god descended here
And, once for all, showed simultaneously
What, in its nature, never can be shown,
Piecemeal or in succession;–showed, I say,
The worth both absolute and relative 1 20
Of all his children from the birth of time,
His instruments for all appointed work.
I now go on to image,–might we hear
The judgment which should give the due to each,
Show where the labor lay and where the ease,
And prove Zeus self, the latent everywhere!
This is a dream:–but no dream, let us hope,
That years and days, the summers and the springs,
Follow each other with unwaning powers.
The grapes which dye thy wine are richer far, 130
Through culture, than the wild wealth of the rock;
The suave plum than the savage-tasted drupe;
The pastured honey-bee drops choicer sweet;
The flowers turn double, and the leaves turn flowers;
That young and tender crescent-moon, thy slave,
Sleeping above her robe as buoyed by clouds,
Refines upon the women of my youth.
What, and the soul alone deteriorates?
I have not chanted verse like Homer, no–139

Nor swept string like Terpander, no–nor carved
And painted men like Phidias and his friend: I am not great as they are, point by point.
But I have entered into sympathy
With these four, running these into one soul,
Who, separate, ignored each others art.
Say, is it nothing that I know them all?
The wild flower was the larger; I have dashed
Rose-blood upon its petals, pricked its cups
Honey with wine, and driven its seed to fruit,
And show a better flower if not so large: 150 I stand myself. Refer this to the gods
Whose gift alone it is! which, shall I dare (All pride apart) upon the absurd pretext
That such a gift by chance lay in my hand,
Discourse of lightly or depreciate?
It might have fallen to anothers hand: what then?
I pass too surely: let at least truth stay!
And next, of what thou followest on to ask.
This being with me as I declare, O king,
My works, in all these varicolored kinds, 160
So done by me, accepted so by men–
Thou askest, if (my soul thus in mens hearts)
I must not be accounted to attain
The very crown and proper end of life?
Inquiring thence how, now life closeth up,
I face death with success in my right hand:
Whether I fear death less than dost thyself
The fortunate of men? "For " (writest thou)
"Thou leavest much behind, while I leave naught.
Thy life stays in the poems men shall sing, 170
The pictures men shall study; while my life,
Complete and whole now in its power and joy,
Dies altogether with my brain and arm,
Is lost indeed; since, what survives myself?
The brazen statue to oerlook my grave,
Set on the promontory which I hamed.
And that–some supple courtier of my heir
Shall use its robed and sceptred arm, perhaps,
To fix the rope to, which best drags it down.
I go then: triumph thou, who dost not go! " 180
Nay, thou art worthy of hearing my whole mind. Is this apparent, when thou turnst to muse Upon the scheme of earth and man in chief, That admiration grows as knowledge grows? That imperfection means perfection hid, Reserved in part, to grace the after-time? If, in the morning of philosophy, Ere aught had been recorded, nay perceived, Thou, with the light now in thee, couldst have looked
On all earths tenantry, from worm to bird, 190

Ere man, her last, appeared upon the stage—
Thou wouldst have seen them perfect, and deduced
The perfectness of others yet unseen.
Conceding which,—had Zeus then questioned thee
"Shall I go on a step, improve on this,
Do more for visible creatures than is done?"
Thou wouldst have answered, "Ay, by making each
Grow conscious in himself—by that alone.
All s perfect else: the shell sucks fast the rock, 199
The fish strikes through the sea, the snake both swims
And slides, forth range the beasts, the birds take flight,
    Till lifes mechanics can no further go—
And all this joy in natural life is put
Like fire from off thy finger into each,
So exquisitely perfect is the same.
    But t is pure fire, and they mere matter are; It has them, not they it: and so I choose
    For man, thy last premeditated work (If I might acid a glory to the scheme)
    That a third thing should stand apart from both, 21O
    A quality arise within his soul,
    Which, intro-active, made to supervise
    And feel the force it has, may view itself,
    And so be happy." Man might live at first
    The animal life: but is there nothing more?
    In due time, let him critically learn
    How he lives; and, the more he gets to know
    Of his own lifes adaptabilities,
    The more joy-giving will his life become.
    Thus man, who hath this quality, is best. 220
    But thou, king, hadst more reasonably said:
"Let progress end at once,—man make no step
Beyond the natural man, the better beastv
Using his senses, not the sense of sense."
In man theres failure, only since he left
The lower and" inconscious forms of life.
We called it an advance, the rendering plain
Mans spirit might grow conscious of mans life,
And, by new lore so added to the old,
Take each step higher over the brutes head. 230
    This grew the only life, the pleasure-house,
Watch-tower and treasure-fortress of the soul,
Which whole surrounding flats of natural life
Seemed only fit to yield subsistence to;
A tower that crowns a country. But alas,
The soul now climbs it just to perish there!

For thence we have discovered (t is no dream—
We know this, which we had not else perceived)
  That theres a world of capability
  For joy, spread round about us, meant for us, 240 Inviting us; and still the soul craves all,
  And still the flesh replies, "Take no jot more
  Than ere thou clombst the tower to look abroad!
  Nay, so much less as that fatigue has brought
  Deduction to it." We struggle, fain to enlarge
  Our bounded physical recipiency, Increase our power, supply fresh oil to life,
  Repair the waste of age and sickness: no, It skills not! life s inadequate to joy,
  As the soul sees joy, tempting life to take 150
  They praise a fountain in my garden here
  Wherein a Naiad sends the water-bow
  Thin from her tube; she smiles to see it rise.
  What if I told her, it is just a thread
  From that great river which the hills shut up,
  And mock her with my leave to take the same I
  The artificer has given her one small tube
  Past power to widen or exchange—what boots
  To know she might spout oceans if she could?
  She cannot lift beyond her first thin thread: 260
  And so a man can use but a mans joy
  While he sees Gods. Is it for Zeus to boast,
  "See, man, how happy I live, and despair—
  That I may be still happier—for thy use!"
  If this were so, we could not thank our Lord,
  As hearts beat on to doing; tis not so—
  Malice it is not. Is it carelessness?
  Still, no. If care—where is the sign? I ask,
  And get no answer, and agree in sum,
  O king, with thy profound discouragement, 270
  Who seest the wider but to sigh the more.
  Most progress is most failure: thou sayest well.
  The last point now:—thou dost except a case—
Holding joy not impossible to one
With artist-gifts—to such a man as I
Who leave behind me living works indeed;
For, such a poem, such a painting lives.
What? dost thou verily trip upon a word,
Confound the accurate view of what joy is
(Caught somewhat clearer by my eyes than thine) 280
With feeling joy? confound the knowing how
And showing how to live (my faculty)
With actually living?—Otherwise

Where is the artists vantage oer the king?
Because in my great epos I display
How divers men young, strong, fair, wise, can act—
Is this as though I acted? if I paint,
Carve the young Phoebus, am I therefore young?
Methinks I m older that I bowed myself
The many years of pain that taught me art! 290 Indeed, to know is something, and to prove
How all this beauty might be enjoyed, is more:
But, knowing naught, to enjoy is something too.
Yon rower, with the moulded muscles there,
Lowering the sail, is nearer it than I.
I can write love-odes: thy fair slaves an ode.
I get to sing of love, when grown too gray
For being beloved: she turns to that young man,
The muscles all a-ripple on his back.
I know the joy of kingship: well, thou art king! 300
     "But," sayest thou—(and I marvel, I repeat,
To find thee trip on such a mere word) " what
Thou writest, paintest, stays; that does not die:
Sappho survives, because we sing her songs,
And Eschylus, because we read his plays! "
     Why, if they live still, let them come and take
     Thy slave in my despite, drink from thy cup,
     Speak in my place. Thou diest while I survive?
     Say rather that my fate is deadlier still, In this, that every day my sense of joy 310
     Grows more acute, my soul (intensified
     By power and insight) more enlarged, more keen;
     While every day my hairs fall more and more,
     My hand shakes, and the heavy years increase—
     The horror quickening still from year to year,
     The consummation coming past escape
     When I shall know most, and yet least enjoy—
     When all my works wherein I prove my worth,
     Being present still to mock me in mens mouths,
     Alive still, in the praise of such as thou, 320 I, I the feeling, thinking, acting man,
     The man who loved his life so over-much,
     Sleep in my urn. It is so horrible, I dare at times imagine to my need
     Some future state revealed to us by Zeus,
     Unlimited in capability
     For joy, as this is in desire for joy, —To seek which, the joy-hunger forces us:
     That, stung by straitness of our life, made strait
     On purpose to make prized the life at large—330
     Freed by the throbbing impulse we call death,
     We burst there as the worm into the fly,

Who, while a worm still, wants his wings. But no!
Zeus has not yet revealed it; and alas,
He must have done so, were it possible!
Live long and happy, and in that thought die: Glad for what was! Farewell. And
for the rest, I cannot tell thy messenger aright
Where to deliver what he bears of thine
To one called Paulus; we have heard his fame 340 Indeed, if Christus be not one
with him— I know not, nor am troubled much to know.
Thou canst not think a mere barbarian Jew,
As Paulus proves to be, one circumcised,
Hath access to a secret shut from us?
Thou wrongest our philosophy, O king, f In stooping to inquire of such an one,
As if his answer could impose at all!
He writeth, doth he? well, and he may write.
Oh, the Jew findeth scholars! certain slaves 3 50
Who touched on this same isle, preached him and
Christ;
And (as I gathered from a bystander)
Their doctrine could be held by no sane man.

RUDEL TO THE LADY OF TRIPOLI. 1842.
I Know a Mount, the gracious Sun perceives
First, when he visits, last, too, when he leaves
The world; and, vainly favored, it repays
The day-long glory of his steadfast gaze
By no change of its large calm front of snow.
And underneath the Mount, a Flower I know,
He cannot have perceived, that changes ever
At his approach; and, in the lost endeavor
To live his life, has parted, one by one,
With all a flowers true graces, for the grace 1O Of being but a foolish mimic sun,
With ray-like florets round a disk-like face.
Men nobly call by many a name the Mount
As over many a land of theirs its large
Calm front of snow like a triumphal targe Is reared, and still with old names, fresh
names vie,
Each to its proper praise and own account:
Men qall the Flower, the Sunflower, sportively.
Oh, Angel of the East, one, one gold look
Across the waters to this twilight nook, 20 –The far sad waters, Angel, to this nook!
in.
Dear Pilgrim, art thou for the East indeed?
Go!–saying ever as thou dost proceed,
That I, French Rudel, choose for my device
A sunflower outspread like a sacrifice
Before its idol. See! These inexpert

And hurried fingers could not fail to hurt
The woven picture; t is a womans skill Indeed; but nothing baffled me, so, ill
Or well, the work is finished. Say, men feed 30
On songs I sing, and therefore bask the bees
On my flowers breast as on a platform broad:
But, as the flowers concern is not for these
But solely for the sun, so men applaud In vain this Rudel, he not looking here
But to the East–the East! Go, say this, Pilgrim dear! ONE WORD MORE.1
To E. B. B.
1855.
There they are, my fifty men and women
Naming me the fifty poems finished!
Take them, Love, the book and me together:
Where the heart lies, let the brain lie also.

Rafael made a century of sonnets,
Made and wrote them in a certain volume
Dinted with the silver-pointed pencil
Else he only used to draw Madonnas:
These, the world might view–but one, the volume.
Who that one, you ask? Your heart instructs you. 10
Did she live and love it all her life-time?
Did she drop, his lady of the sonnets,
Die, and let it drop beside her pillow
Where it lay in place of Rafaels glory,
Rafaels cheek so duteous and so loving–
Cheek, the world was wont to hail a painters,
Rafaels cheek, her love had turned a poets?
ra.
You and I would rather read that volume, (Taken to his beating bosom by it)
Lean and list the bosom-beats of Rafael, 20 1 Originally appended to the collection
of Poems called " Men and Women," the greater portion of which has now been, mor
correctly, distributed under the other titles of this edition.–R. B.

Would we not? than wonder at Madonnas–
Her, San Sisto names, and Her, Foligno,
Her, that visits Florence in a vision,
Her, thats left with lilies in the Louvre–
Seen by us and all the world in circle.
1v.
You and I will never read that volume.
Guido Reni, like his own eyes apple
Guarded long the treasure-book and loved it.
Guido Reni dying, all Bologna 29
Cried, and the world cried too, "Ours, the treasure!"
Suddenly, as rare things will, it vanished.
Dante once prepared to paint an angel:

Whom to please? You whisper "Beatrice."
While he mused and traced it and retraced it, (Peradventure with a pen corroded
Still by drops of that hot ink he dipped for,
When, his left-hand i the hair o the wicked,
Back he held the brow and pricked its stigma,
Bit into the live mans flesh for parchment,
Loosed him, laughed to see the writing rankle, 40
Let the wretch go festering through Florence)–
Dante, who loved well because he hated,
Hated wickedness that hinders loving,
Dante standing, studying his angel,– In there broke the folk of his Inferno.
Says he–" Certain people of importance"
(Such he gave his daily dreadful line to)
"Entered and would seize, forsooth, the poet."
Says the poet–" Then I stopped my painting."
vl.
You and I would rather see that angel, 50
Painted by the tenderness of Dante,
Would we not?–than read a fresh Inferno.
vll.
You and I will never see that picture.
While he mused on love and Beatrice,
While he softened oer his outlined angel,
In they broke, those "people of importance:"
We and Bice bear the loss forever.
vlll.
What of Rafaels sonnets, Dantes picture?
This; no artist lives and loves, that longs not
Once, and only once, and for one only, 60 (Ah, the prize!) to find his love a language
Fit and fair and simple and sufficient–
Using nature thats an art to others, . Not, this one time, art thats turned his nature.
Ay, of all the artists living, loving,
None but would forego his proper dowry,–
Does he paint? he fain would write a poem,–
Does he write? he fain would paint a picture,
Put to proof art alien to the artists,
Once, and only once, and for one only, 70
So to be the man and leave the artist,
Gain the mans joy, miss the artists sorrow.
Wherefore? Hearens gift takes earths abatement! He who smites the rock and spreads the water. Bidding drink and live a crowd beneath him,
Even he, the minute makes immortal,
Proves, perchance, but mortal in the minute,
Desecrates, belike, the deed in doing.

While he smites, how can he but remember,
So he smote before, in such a peril, 80
When they stood and mocked–"Shall smiting help us?"
When they drank and sneered–"A stroke is easy! " When they wiped their mouths
and went their journey, Throwing him for thanks–"But drought was pleasant."
Thus old memories mar the actual triumph;
Thus the doing savors of disrelish;
Thus achievement lacks a gracious somewhal;;
Oer-importuned brows becloud the mandate,
Carelessness or consciousness–the gesture.
For he bears an ancient wrong about him, 90
Sees and knows again those phalanxed faces,
Hears, yet one time more, the customed prelude–
"How shouldst thou, of all men, smite, and save us? "
Guesses what is like to prove the sequel–
"Egypts flesh-pots–nay, the drought was better."
Oh, the crowd must have emphatic warrant!
Theirs, the Sinai-foreheads cloven brilliance,
Right-arms rod-sweep, tongues imperial fiat.
Never dares the man put off the prophet.
    x1.
Did he love one face from out the thousands, 100
(Were she Jethros daughter, white and wifely,
Were she but the Ethiopian bondslave,)
He would envy yon dumb patient camel,
    Keeping a reserve of scanty water
    Meant to save his own life in the desert;
    Ready in the desert to deliver (Kneeling down to let his breast be opened)
    Hoard and life together for his mistress.
    x11.
I shall never, in the years remaining,
Paint you pictures, no, nor carve you statues, j: o
Make you music that should all-express me;
So it seems: I stand on my attainment.
This of verse alone, one life allows me;
Verse and nothing else have I to give you.
Other heights in other lives, God willing:
All the gifts from all the heights, your own, Love!
    x1ll.
Yet a semblance of resource avails us–
Shade so finely touched, loves sense must seize it.
Take these lines, look lovingly and nearly,
Lines I write the first time and the last time. 1 20
He who works in fresco, steals a hair brush,
Curbs the liberal hand, subservient proudly,

Cramps his spirit, crowds its all in little,
Makes a strange art of an art familiar,
Fills his ladys missal-marge with flowerets.
He who blows thro bronze, may breathe thro silver,
Fitly serenade a slumbrous princess.
He who writes, may write for once as I do.
xiv.
Love, you saw me gather men and women,
Live or dead or fashioned by my fancy, 130
Enter each and all, and use their service,
M. w.–7
Speak from every mouth,–the speech, a poem.
Hardly shall I tell my joys and sorrows,
Hopes and fears, belief and disbelieving: I am mine and yours–the rest be all mens,
Karshish, Cleon, Norbert and the fifty.
Let me speak this once in my true person,
Not as Lippo, Roland or Andrea,
Though the fruit of speech be just this sentence:
Pray you, look on these my men and women, 140
Take and keep my fifty poems finished;
Where my heart lies, let my brain lie also!
Poor the speech; be how I speak, for all things.
xv.
Not but that you know me! Lo, the moons self!
Here in London, yonder late in Florence,
Still we find her face, the thrice-transfigured.
Curving on a sky imbrued with color,
Drifted over Fiesole by twilight,
Came she, our new crescent of a hairs-breadth.
Full fhe flared it, lamping Samminiato, I JO
Rounder twixt the cypresses and rounder,
Perfect till the nightingales applauded.
Now, a piece of her old self, impoverished,
Hard to greet, she traverses the houseroofs,
Hurries with unhandsome thrift of silver,
Goes dispiritedly, glad to finish.
xvl.
What, there s nothing in the moon noteworthy?
Nay: for if that moon could love a mortal,
Use, to charm him (so to fit a fancy),
All her magic (t is the old sweet mythos), 160 She would turn a new side to her mortal,
Side unseen of herdsman, huntsman, steersman–
Blank to Zoroaster on his terrace,
Blind to Galileo on his turret,

Dumb to Homer, dumb to Keats–him, even!
Think, the wonder of the moonstruck mortal–
When she turns round, comes again in heaven,
Opens out anew for worse or better!
Proves she like some portent of an iceberg
Swimming full upon the ship it founders, 170
Hungry with huge teeth of splintered crystals?
Proves she as the paved work of a sapphire
Seen by Moses when he climbed the mountain?
Moses, Aaron, Nadab and Abihu
Climbed and saw the very God, the Highest,
Stand upon the paved work of a sapphire.
Like the bodied heaven in his clearness
Shone the stone, the sapphire of that paved work,
When they ate and drank and saw God also! 179 xv11.
What were seen? None knows, none ever shall know.
Only this is sure–the sight were other,
Not the moons same side, born late in Florence,
Dying now impoverished here in London.
God be thanked, the meanest of his creatures
Boasts two soul-sides, one to face the world with,
One to show a woman when he loves her!
xvm.
This I say of me, but think of you, Love!
This to you–yourself my moon of poets! 188
Ah, but thats the worlds side, there s the wonder,
Thus they see you, praise you, think they know you!
There, in turn I stand with them and praise you–
Out of my own self, I dare to phrase it.
But the best is when I glide from out them,
Cross a step or two of dubious twilight,
Come out on the other side, the novel
Silent silver lights and darks undreamed of,
Where I hush and bless myself with silence.
    xlx.
Oh, their Rafael of the dear Madonnas,
Oh, their Dante of the dread Inferno,
Wrote one song–and in my brain I sing it, 200
Drew one angel–borne, see, on my bosom!
R. B IN A BALCONY.
1855.
PERSONS.
NORBERT.
    Constance.
The Queen.

Constance and Norbert.

Norbert, Now!

Constance. Not now!

Norbert. Give me them again, those hands:

Put them upon my forehead, how it throbs!

Press them before my eyes, the fire comes through!

You cruellest, you dearest in the world,

Let me! The Queen must grant whateer I ask—

How can I gain you and not ask the Queen?

There she stays waiting for me, here stand you;

Some time or other this was to be asked;

Now is the one time—what I ask, I gain:

Let me ask now, Love!

   Constance. Do, and ruin us. 10

   Norbert. Let it be now, Love! All my soul breaks forth.

   How I do lov. e you! Give my love its way!

A man can have but one life and one death,

One heaven, one hell. Let me fulfil my fate—

Grant me my heaven now! Let me know you mine,

Prove you mine, write my name upon your brow,

   Hold you and have you, and then die away,

If God please, with completion in my soul!

   Constance. I am not yours then? How content this man!

   I am not his—who change into himself, 20

   Have passed into his heart and beat its beats,

Who give my hands to him, my eyes, my hair,

Give all that was of me away to him—

So well, that now, my spirit turned his own,

Takes part with him against the woman here,

Bids him not stumble at so mere a straw

As caring that the world be cognizant

How he loves her and how she worships him.

You have this woman, not as yet that world.

Go on, I bid, nor stop to care for me 30

   By saving what I cease to care about,

The courtly name and pride of circumstance—

The name you ll pick up and be cumbered with

Just for the poor parades sake, nothing more;

Just that the world may slip from under you—

Just that the world may cry " So much for him—

The man predestined to the heap of crowns:

There goes his chance of winning one, at least! "

   Norbert. The world!

   Constance. You love it. Love me quite as well, And see if I shall pray for this in vain! 40

Why must you ponder what it knows or thinks?
Norbert. You pray for—what, in vain?
Constance. Oh my hearts heart,
How I do love you, Norbert! That is right:
But listen, or I take my hands away!
You say, " let it be now: you would go now
And tell the Queen, perhaps six steps from us.
You love me—so you do, thank God!
Norbert. Thank God!
Constance. Yes, Norbert,—but you fain would tell your love,
And, what succeeds the telling, ask of her
My hand. Now take this rose and look at it, 50
Listening to me. You are the minister,
The Queens first favorite, nor without a cause.
To-night completes your wonderful years-work
(This palace-feast is held to celebrate)
Made memorable by her lifes success,
The junction of two crowns, on her sole head,
Her house had only dreamed of anciently:
That this mere dream is grown a stable truth,
To-nights feast makes authentic. Whose the praise?
Whose genius, patience, energy, achieved 60
What turned the many heads and broke the hearts?
You are the fate, your minutes in the heaven.
Next comes the Queens turn. " Name your own reward!"
With leave to clench the past, chain the to-come,
Put out an arm and touch and take the sun
And fix it ever full-faced on your earth,
Possess yourself supremely of her life,—
You choose the single thing she will not grant;
Nay, very declaration of which choice
Will turn the scale and neutralize your work: 70
At best she will forgive you, if she can.
You think I ll let you choose—her cousins hand?
Norbert. Wait. First, do you retain your old belief The Queen is generous,—nay, is just?
Constance. There, there!
So men make women love them, while they know
No more of womens hearts than., look you here,
You that are just and generous beside,
Make it your own case! For example now, I Ml say—I let you kiss me, hold my hands—79
Why? do you know why? I ll instruct you, then—
The kiss, because you have a name at court;
This hand and this, that you may shut in each

A jewel, if you please to pick up such.
Thats horrible? Apply it to the Queen–
Suppose I am the Queen to whom you speak:
"I was a nameless man; you needed me:
Why did I proffer you my aid? there stood
A certain pretty cousin at your side.
Why did I make such common cause with you?
Access to her had not been easy else. 90
You give my labor here abundant praise?
Faith, labor, which she overlooked, grew play.
How shall your gratitude discharge itself?
Give me her hand!"
Norbert. And still I urge the same.
Js the Queen just? just—generous or no!
Constance. Yes, just. You love a rose; no harm in that:
But was it for the roses sake or mine
You put it in your bosom? mine, you said–
Then, mine you still must say or else be talse.
You told the Queen you served her for herself; 100
If so, to serve her was to serve yourself,
She thinks, for all your unbelieving face!
I know her. In the hall, six steps from us,
One sees the twenty pictures; theres a life
Better than life, and yet no life at all.
Conceive her born in such a magic dome,
Pictures all round her! why, she sees the world,
Can recognize its given things and facts,
The fight of giants or the feast of gods,
    Sages in senate, beauties at the bath, no
    Chases and battles, the whole earths display,
    Landscape and sea-piece, down to flowers and fruit–
    And who shall question that she knows them all, In better semblance than the things
outside?
    Yet bring into the silent gallery
    Some live thing to contrast in breath and blood,
    Some lion, with the painted lion there—
    You think shell understand composedly?
    –Say, " thats his fellow in the hunting-piece
    Yonder, Ive turned to praise a hundred times?" 120
    Not so. Her knowledge of our actual earth, Its hopes and fears, concerns and
sympathies,
    Must be too far, too mediate, too unreal.
    The real exists for us outside, not her:
    How should it, with that life in these four walls–
    That father and that mother, first to last

No father and no mother–friends, a heap,
Lovers, no lack–a husband in due time,
And every one of them alike a lie!
Things painted by a Rubens out of naught 130 Into what kindness, friendship, love should be;
All better, all more grandiose than the life,
Only no life; mere cloth and surface-paint,
You feel, while you admire. How should she feel?
Yet now that she has stood thus fifty years
The sole spectator in that gallery,
You think to bring this warm real struggling Jove In to her of a sudden, and suppose
Shell keep her state untroubled? Heres the truth–
Shell apprehend truths value at a glance, 140
Prefer it to the pictured loyalty?
You only have to say, "so men are made,
For this they act; the thing has many names,
But this the right one: and now, Queen, be just! "
Your life slips back; you lose her at the word:
You do not even for amends gain me.
He will not understand; oh, Norbert, Norbert,
Do you not understand?
    Norbert. The Queen s the Queen: I am myself–no picture, but alive
In every nerve and every muscle, here 1 50
    At the palace-window oer the peoples street,
As she in the gallery where the pictures glow:
The good of life is precious to us both.
She cannot love; what do I want with rule?
When first I saw your face a year ago
I knew my lifes good, my soul heard one voice–
"The woman yonder, there s no use of life
But just to obtain her! heap earths woes in one
And bear them–make a pile of all earths joys
And spurn them, as they help or help not this; 160
Only, obtain her! " How was it to be?
I found you were the cousin of the Queen;
I must then serve the Queen to get to you.
No other way. Suppose there had been one,
And I, by saying prayers to some white star
With promise of my body and my soul,
Might gain you,–should I pray the star or no?
Instead, there was the Queen to serve! I served,
Helped, did what other servants failed to do.
Neither she sought nor I declared my end. 170
    Her good is hers, my recompense be mine,–
I therefore name you as that recompense.

She dreamed that such a thing could never be?
Let her wake now. She thinks there was more cause
In love of power, high fame, pure loyalty?
Perhaps she fancies men wear out their lives
  Chasing such shades. Then, I ve a fancy too;
I worked because I want you with my soul:
I therefore ask your hand. Let it be now! 179
  Constance. Had I not loved you from the very first,
Were I not yours, could we not steal out thus
So wickedly, so wildly, and so well,
You might become impatient. Whats conceived
Of us without here, by the folk within?
Where are you now? immersed in cares of state—
Where am I now? intent on festal robes—
We two, embracing under deaths spread hand!
What was this thought for, what that scruple of yours
Which broke the council up?—to bring about
One minutes meeting in the corridor! 190
  And then the sudden sleights, strange secrecies,
Complots inscrutable, deep telegraphs,
Long-planned chance-meetings, hazards of a look,
"Does she know? does she not know? saved or lost? "
A year of this compressions ecstasy
All goes for nothing! you would give this up
For the old way, the open way, the worlds,
His way who beats, and his who sells his wife!
What tempts you?—their notorious happiness
Makes you ashamed of ours? The best you ll gain 200
Will be—the Queen grants all that you require,
Concedes the cousin, rids herself of you
And me at once, and gives us ample leave
To live like our five hundred happy friends.
The world will show us with officious hand
Our chamber-entry, and stand sentinel
Where we so oft have stolen across its traps!
Get the worlds warrant, ring the falcons feet,
And make it duty to be bold and swift,
Which long ago was nature. Have it so! 21O
We never hawked by rights till flung from fist?
Oh, the mans thought! no woman s such a fool.
Norbert. Yes, the mans thought and my thought, which is more—
  One made to love you, let the world take note!
Have I done worthy work? be loves the praise,
Though hampered by restrictions, barred against
By set forms, blinded by forced secrecies!

Set free my love, and see what love can do
Shown in my life—what work will spring from that!
The world is used to have its business done 220
    On other grounds, find great effects produced
For powers sake, fames sake, motives in mens mouth.
So, good: but let my low ground shame their high!
Truth is the strong thing. Let mans life be true!
And love s the truth of mine. Time prove the rest!
I choose to wear you stamped all over me,
Your name upon my forehead and my breast,
You, from the swords blade to the ribbons edge,
That men may see, all over, you in me—
That pale loves may die out of their pretence 230
In face of mine, shames thrown on love fall off.
Permit this, Constance! Love has been so long
Subdued in me, eating me through and through,
That now tis all of me and must have way.
Think of my work, that chaos of intrigues,
Those hopes and fears, surprises and delays,
That long endeavor, earnest, patient, slow,
Trembling at last to its assured result:
Then think of this revulsion! I resume
Life after death, (it is no less than life, 240
    After such long unlovely laboring days)
And liberate to beauty lifes great need
O the beautiful, which, while it prompted work.
    Suppressed itself erewhile. This eves the time,
    This eve intense with yon first trembling star
    We seem to pant and reach; scarce aught between
    The earth that rises and the heaven that bends;
    All nature self-abandoned, every tree
    Flung as it will, pursuing its own thoughts
    And fixed so, every flower and every weed, 250
    No pride, no shame, no victory, no defeat;
    All under God, each measured by itself.
    These statues round us stand abrupt, distinct,
    The strong in strength, the weak in weakness fixed,
    The Muse forever wedded to her lyre,
    Nymph to her fawn, and Silence to her rose:
    See Gods approval on his universe!
    Let us do so—aspire to live as these In harmony with truth, ourselves being true!
    Take the first way, and let the second come! 260
    My first is to possess myself of you;
    The music sets the march-step—forward, then!
    And theres the Queen, I go to claim you of,

The world to witness, wonder and applaud.
Our flower of life breaks open. No delay!
Constance. And so shall we be ruined, both of us. Norbert, I know her to the skin and bone: You do not know her, were not born to it, To feel what she can see or cannot see. Love, she is generous,–ay, despite your smile, 270 Generous as you are: for, in that thin frame Pain-twisted, punctured through and through with cares, There lived a lavish soul until it starved, Debarred of healthy food. Look to the soul–Pity that, stoop to that, ere you begin (The true mans-way) on justice and your rights, Exactions and acquittance of the past!
Begin so–see what justice she will deal!
We women hate a debt as men a gift.
Suppose her some poor keeper of a school 280
Whose business is to sit thro summer months
And dole out children leave to go and play,
Herself superior to such lightness–she In the arm-chairs state and paedagogic pomp–
To the life, the laughter, sun and youth outside:
We wonder such a face looks black on us?
I do not bid you wake her tenderness, (That were vain truly–none is left to wake)
But let her think her justice is engaged
To take the shape of tenderness, and mark 290 If shell not coldly pay its warmest debt!
Does she love me, I ask you? not a whit:
Yet, thinking that her justice was engaged
To help a kinswoman, she took me up–
Did more on that bare ground than other loves
Would do on greater argument. For me, I have no equivalent of such cold kind
To pay her with, but love alone to give If I give anything. I give her love: I feel I ought to help her, and I will. 300
So, for her sake, as yours, I tell you twice
That women hate a debt as men a gift.
If I were you, I could obtain this grace–
Could lay the whole I did to loves account,
Nor yet be very false as courtiers go–
Declaring my success was recompense; It would be so, in fact: what were it else?
And then, once loose her generosity,–
Oh, how I see it!–then, were I but you,
To turn it, let it seem to move itself, 310
And make it offer what I really take,
Accepting just, in the poor cousins hand,
Her value as the next thing to the Queens–
Since none love Queens directly, none dare that,
And a things shadow or a names mere echo
Suffices those who miss the name and thing!
You pick up just a ribbon she has worn,

To keep in proof how near her breath you came.
Say, I m so near I seem a piece of her–
Ask for me that way–(oh, you understand) 320
You d find the same gift yielded with a grace,
Which, if you make the least show to extort.
–You ll see! and when you have ruined both of us,
Dissertate on the Queens ingratitude!
Norbert. Tnen, if I turn it that way, you consent?
T is not my way; I have more hope in truth:
Still, if you wont have truth–why, this indeed,
Were scarcely false, as I d express the sense.
Will you remain here?
Constance. O best heart of mine,
How I have loved you! then, you take my way? 330
Are mine as you have been her minister,
Work out my thought, give it effect for me,
Paint plain my poor conceit and make it serve?
I owe that withered woman everything–
Life, fortune, you, remember! Take my part–
Help me to pay her! Stand upon your rights?
You, with my rose, my hands, my heart on you?
Your rights are mine–you have no rights but
mine.
Norbert. Remain here. How you know me!
Constance. Ah, but still /fr breaks from her: she remains. Dance-music from
within. Enter the Queen.
Queen. Constance? She is here as he said. Speak quick! 340 Is it so? Is it true or
false? One word!
Constance. True.
Queen. Mercifullest Mother, thanks to thee!
Constance. Madam?
Queen. I love you, Constance, from my soul.
Now say once more, with any words you will,
T is true, all true, as true as that I speak.
Constance. Why should you doubt it?
Queen. Ah, why doubt? why doubt?
Dear, make me see it! Do you see it so?
None see themselves; another sees them best.
You say "why doubt li " –you see him and me.
It is because the Mother has such grace 350
That if we had but faith–wherein we fail–
Whateer we yearn for would be granted us;
Yet still we let our whims prescribe despair,
Our fancies thwart and cramp our will and power,
And while, accepting life, abjure its use.

Constance, I had abjured the hope of love
And being loved, as truly as yon palm
The hope of seeing Egypt from that plot.
    Constance. Heaven!
    Queen. But it was so, Constance, it was so
    Men say—or do men say it? fancies say—360
    "Stop here, your life is set, you are grown old.
Too late—no love for you, too late for love—
Leave love to girls. Be queen: let Constance love."
One takes the hint—half meets it like a child,
Ashamed at any feelings that oppose.
"Oh love, true, never think of love again!
    am a queen: I rule, not love forsooth."
    So it goes on; so a face grows like this,
    Hair like this hair, poor arms as lean as these,
    Till,—nay, it does not end so, I thank God! 370
    Constance. I cannot understand—
    Queen. The happier you!
    Constance, I know not how it is with men:
For women (I am a woman now like you)
There is no good of life but love—but love!
What else looks good, is some shade flung from love;
Love gilds it, gives it worth. Be warned by me,
Never you cheat yourself one instant! Love,
Give love, ask only love, and leave the rest!
    0 Constance, how I love you!
    Constance. I love you. 379
    Queen. I do believe that all is come through you.
    I took you to my heart to keep it warm
    When the last chance of love seemed dead in me;
I thought your fresh youth warmed my withered heart.
    Oh, I am very old now, am I not?
Not so! it is true and it shall be true!
    Constance. Tell it me: let me judge if true or false.
    Queen. Ah, but I fear you! you will look at me And say, " she s old, she s grown
unlovely quite Who neer was beauteous: men want beauty still." Well, so I feared—the
curse! so I felt sure! 390 Constance. Be calm. And now you feel not sure, you say?
Queen. Constance, he came,—the coming was not strange—
    Do not I stand and see men come and go?
I turned a half-look from my pedestal
M. w.—8
    Where I grow marble—" one young man the more I
    He will love some one; that is naught to me:
    What would he with my marble stateliness?"
    Yet this seemed somewhat worse than heretofore;

The man more gracious, youthful, like a god,
And I still older, with less flesh to change—400
We two those dear extremes that long to touch.
Jt seemed still harder when he first began
To labor at those state-affairs, absorbed
The old way for the old end—interest.
Oh, to live with a thousand beating hearts
Around you, swift eyes, serviceable hands,
Professing they ve no care but for your cause,
Thought but to help you, love but for yourself,—
And you the marble statue all the time
They praise and point at as preferred to life, 41 o
Yet leave for the first breathing womans smile,
First dancers, gipsys or street baladines!
Why, how I have ground my teeth to hear mens speech
Stifled for fear it should alarm my ear,
Their gait subdued lest step should startle me,
Their eyes declined, such queendom to respect.
Their hands alert, such treasure to preserve,
While not a man of them broke rank and spoke,
Wrote me a vulgar letter all of love,
Or caught my hand and pressed it like a hand! 420
There have been moments, if the sentinel
Lowering his halbert to salute the queen,
Had flung it brutally and clasped my knees,
I would have stooped and kissed him with my soul.
    Constance. Who could have comprehended?
    Queen. Ay, who—who /
Why, no one, Constance, but this one who did.
Not they, not you, not I. Even now perhaps
It comes too late—would you but tell the truth.
    Constance. I wait to tell it.
    Queen. Well, you see, he came,
Outfaced the others, did a work this year 430
Exceeds in value all was ever done,
You know—it is not I who say it—all
Say it. And so (a second pang and worse)
I grew aware not only of what he did,
But why so wondrously. Oh, never work
Like his was done for works ignoble sake—
Souls need a finer aim to light and lure!
I felt, I saw, he loved—loved somebody.
And Constance, my dear Constance, do you know,
I did believe this while twas you he loved. 440
    Constance. Me, madam?

Queen. It did seem to me, your face
Met him whereer he looked: and whom but you
Was such a man to love? It seemed to me,
You saw he loved you, and approved his love,
And both of you were in intelligence.
You could not loiter in that garden, step
Into this balcony, but I straight was stung
And forced to understand. It seemed so true,
So right, so beautiful, so like you both,
That all this work should have been done by him 450
Not for the vulgar hope of recompense,
But that at last–suppose, some night like this–
Borne on to claim his due reward of me,
He might say " Give her hand and pay me so."
And I (O Constance, you shall love me now!)
I thought, surmounting all the bitterness,
–" And he shall have it. I will make her blest,
My flower of youth, my womans self that was.
　　My happiest womans self that might have been! 459 These two shall have their joy
and leave me here." Yes–yes!
　　Constance. Thanks!
　　Queen. And the word was on my 5p
When he burst in upon me. I looked to hear
A mere calm statement of his just desire
For payment of his labor. When–O heaven,
How can I tell you? lightning on my eyes
And thunder in my ears proved that first word
Which told twas love of me, of me, did all–
He loved me–from the first step to the last,
Loved me!
　　Constance. You hardly saw, scarce heard him speak Of love: what if you should mistake?
　　Queen. No, no–470
No mistake! Ha, there shall be no mistake!
He had not dared to hint the love he felt–
You were my reflex–(how I understood!)
He said you were the ribbon I had worn,
He kissed my hand, he looked into my eyes,
And love, love came at end of every phrase.
Love is begun; this much is come to pass:
The rest is easy. Constance, I am yours!
I will learn, I will place my life on you,
Teach me but how to keep what I have won! 480
Am I so old? This hair was early gray;
But joy ere now has brought hair brown again,

And joy will bring the cheeks red back, I feel.
I could sing once too; that was in my youth.
Still, when men paint me, they declare me. yes,
Beautiful–for the last French painter did!
I know they flatter somewhat; you are frank–
I trust you. How I loved you from the first!
   Some queens would hardly seek a cousin out
And set her by their side to take the eye: 490 I must have felt that good would
come from you.
   I am not generous–like him–like you!
But he is not your lover after all: It was not you he looked at. Saw you him?
You have not been mistaking words or looks?
He said you were the reflex of myself.
And yet he is not such a paragon
To you, to younger women who may choose
Among a thousand Norberts. Speak the truth!
You know you never named his name to me: 500
You know, I cannot give him up–ah God,
Not up now, even to you!
   Constance. Then calm yourself.
   Queen. See, I am old–look here, you happy girl
I will not play the fool, deceive–ah, whom?
Tis all gone: put your cheek beside my cheek
And what a contrast does the moon behold!
But then I set my life upon one chance,
The last chance and the best–am / not left,
My soul, myself? All women love great men
If young or old; it is in all the tales: 510
   Young beauties love old poets who can love–
Why should not he, the poems in my soul,
The passionate faith, the pride of sacrifice,
Life-long, death-long? I throw them at his feet.
Who cares to see the fountains very shape,
Whether it be a Tritons or a Nymphs
That pours the foam, makes rainbows all around?
You could not praise indeed the empty conch;
But I ll pour floods of love and hide myself.
How I will love him! Cannot men love love? 520
Who was a queen and loved a poet once
   Humpbacked, a dwarf? ah, women can do that!
Well, but men too; at least, they tell you so.
They love so many women in their youth,
And even in age they all love whom they please;
And yet the best of them confide to friends
That t is not beauty makes the lasting love–

They spend a day with such and tire the next:
They like soul,—well then, they like phantasy,
Novelty even. Let us confess the truth, 530
    Horrible though it be, that prejudice,
Prescription. curses! they will love a queen.
They will, they do: and will not, does not—he?
    Constance. How can he? You are wedded: t is a name
    We know, but still a bond. Your rank remains,
His rank remains. How can he, nobly souled
As you believe and I incline to think,
Aspire to be your favorite, shame and all?
    Queen. Hear her! There, there now—could she love like me?
    What did I say of smooth-cheeked youth and grace? 540
See all it does or could do! so youth loves!
Oh, tell him, Constance, you could never do
What I will—you, it was not born in! I
Will drive these difficulties far and fast
As yonder mists curdling before the moon.
I ll use my light too, gloriously retrieve
My youth from its enforced calamity,
Dissolve that hateful marriage, and be his,
His own in the eyes alike of God and man.
    Constance. You will do—dare do. pause on what you say! 550
    Queen. Hear her! I thank you, sweet, for that surprise.
    You have the fair face: for the soul, see mine!
    I have the strong soul: let me teach you, here.
    I think I have borne enough and long enough,
    And patiently enough, the world remarks,
    To have my own way now, unblamed by all.
    It does so happen (I rejoice for it)
    This most unhoped-for issue cuts the knot.
    There s not a better way of settling claims
    Than this; God sends the accident express: 560
    And were it for my subjects good, no more,
    Twere best thus ordered. I am thankful now,
    Mute, passive, acquiescent. I receive,
    And bless God simply, or should almost fear
    To walk so smoothly to my ends at last.
    Why, how I baffle obstacles, spurn fate!
    How strong I am! Could Norbert see me now!
    Constance-Let me consider. It is all too strange.
    Queen. You, Constance, learn of me; do you, like me!
    You are young, beautiful: my own, best girl, 570
You will have many lovers, and love one—
Light hair, not hair like Norberts, to suit yours:

Taller than he is, since yourself are tall.
Love him, like me! Give all away to him;
Think never of yourself; throw by your pride,
Hope, fear,–your own good as you saw it once,
And love him simply for his very self.
Remember, I (and what am I to you?)
Would give up all for one, leave throne, lose life,
Do all but just unlove him! He loves me. 5 80
    Constance. He shall.
    Queen. You, step inside my inmost heart!
    Give me your own heart: let us have one heart!
I ll come to you for counsel; " this he says,
    This he does; what should this amount to, pray?
Beseech you, change it into current coin i
. Is that worth kisses? Shall I please him there? "
And then we ll speak in turn of you–what else?
Your love, according to your beautys worth,
For you shall have some noble love, all gold: 589
Whom choose you?-we will get him at your choice.
–Constance, I leave you. Just a minute since,
I felt as I must die or be alone
Breathing my soul into an ear like yours:
Now, I would face the world with my new life,
Wear my new crown. I ll walk around the rooms,
And then come back and tell you how it feels.
How soon a smile of God can change the world!
How we are made for happiness–how work
Grows play, adversity a winning fight!
True, I have lost so many years: what then? 600
Many remain: God has been very good.
You, stay here! Tis as different from dreams,
From the minds cold calm estimate of bliss,
As these stone statues from the flesh and blood.
The comfort thou hast caused mankind, Gods moon!
She goes out, leaving Constance. Dance-
music from to it bin.
    Norbert enters.
    Norbert. Well? we have but one minute and one word!
    Constance. I am yours, Norbert!
Norbert. Yes, mine.
    Constance. Not till now!
    You were mine. Now I give myself to you.
Norbert. Constance?
Constance. Your own! I know the thriftier way
    Of giving–haply, tis the wiser way. 610

Meaning to give a treasure, I might dole
Coin after coin out (each, as that were all,
With a new largess still at each despair)
And lorce you keep in sight the deed, preserve
Exhaustless till the end my part and yours,
My giving and your taking; both our joys
Dying together. Is it the wiser way?
I choose the simpler; I give all at once.
Know what you have to trust to, trade upon!
Use it, abuse it,—anything but think 620
Hereafter, "Had I known she loved me so,
And what my means, I might have thriven with it."
This is your means. I give you all myself.
Norbert. I take you and thank God.
Constance. Look on through years!
We cannot kiss, a second day like this;
Else were this earth no earth.
Norbert, With this days heat
We shall go on through years of cold.
Constance. So, best!
—I try to see those years—I think I see. You walk quick and new warmth comes;
you look back
And lay all to the first glow—not sit down 630
Forever brooding on a day like this
While seeing embers whiten and love die.
Yes, love lives best in its effect; and mine,
Full in its own life, yearns to live in yours.
Norbert. Just so. I take and know you all at once.
Your soul is disengaged so easily,
Your face is there, I know you; give me time,
Let me be proud and think you shall know me.
My soul is slower: in a life I roll
The minute out whereto you condense yours—640
The whole slow circle round you I must move,
To be just you. I look to a long life
To decompose this minute, prove its worth.
Tis the sparks long succession one by one
Shall show you, in the end, what fire was crammed In that mere stone you struck:
how could you know, If it lay ever unproved in your sight,
As now my heart lies? your own warmth would hide Its coldness, were it cold.
Constance. But how prove, how? 649
Norbert. Prove in my life, you ask?
Constance. Quick, Norbert—how?
Norbert. That s easy told. I count life just a stuff

To try the souls strength on, educe the man.
Who keeps one end in view makes all things serve.
As with the body—he who hurls a lance
Or heaps up stone on stone, shows strength alike:
So must I seize and task all means to prove
And show this soul of mine, you crown as yours,
And justify us both.
    Constance. Could you write books,
    Paint pictures! One sits down in poverty
And writes or paints, with pity for the rich. 660
    Norbert. And loves ones painting and ones writ-
ing, then,
    And not ones mistress! All is best, believe,
And we best as no other than we are.
We live, and they experiment on life—
Those poets, painters, all who stand aloof
To overlook the farther. Let us be
The thing they look at! I might take your face
    And write of it and paint it—to what end?
    For whom? what pale dictatress in the air
    Feeds, smiling sadly, her fine ghost-like form 670
    With earths real blood and breath, the beauteous life
    She makes despised forever? You are mine,
    Made for me, not for others in the world,
    Nor yet for that which I should call my art,
    The cold calm power to see how fair you look.
    I come to you; I leave you not, to write
    Or paint. You are, I am: let Rubens there
    Paint us!
    Constance. So, best!
    Norbert. I understand your soul.
    You live, and rightly sympathize with life, 679
    With action, power, success. This way is straight;
And time were short beside, to let me change
The craft my childhood learnt: my craft shall serve.
Men set me here to subjugate, enclose,
Manure their barren lives, and force thence fruit
First for themselves, and afterward for me
In the due tithe; the task of some one soul,
Through ways of work appointed by the world.
I am not bid create—men see no star
Transfiguring my brow to warrant that—
But find and bind and bring to bear their wills. 690
So I began: to-night sees how I end.
What if it see, too, powers first outbreak here

Amid the warmth, surprise and sympathy,
And instincts of the heart that teach the head?
What if the people have discerned at length
The dawn of the next nature, novel brain
Whose will they venture in the place of theirs,
Whose work, they trust, shall find them as novel ways
To untried heights which yet he only sees?
    I felt it when you kissed me. See this Queen, 700
    This people–in our phrase, this mass of men–
    See how the mass lies passive to my hand
    Now that my hand is plastic, with you by
    To make the muscles iron! Oh, an end
    Shall crown this issue as this crowns the first!
    My will be on this people! then, the strain,
    The grappling of the potter with his clay,
    The long uncertain struggle,–the success
    And consummation of the spirit-work,
    Some vase shaped to the curl of the gods lip, 710
    While rounded fair for human sense to see
    The Graces in a dance men recognize
    With turbulent applause and laughs of heart!
    So triumph ever shall renew itself;
    Ever shall end in efforts higher yet,
    Ever begin.
    Constance. I ever helping?
    Norbert. Thus!
As be embraces her, the Queen enters. Constance. Hist, madam! So have I
performed my part.
    You see your gratitudes true decency,
Norbert? A little slow in seeing it!
Begin, to end the sooner! Whats a kiss? 720
    Norbert. Constance?
    Constance. Why, must I teach it you again;
    You want a witness to your dulness, sir?
What was I saying these ten minutes long?
Then I repeat–when some young handsome man
Like you has acted out a part like yours,
Is pleased to fall in love with one beyond,
So very far beyond him, as he says–
So hopelesslv in love that but to speak
    Would prove him mad,–he thinks judiciously,
    And makes some insignificant good soul, 730
    Like me, his friend, adviser, confidant,
    And very stalking-horse to cover him In following after what he dares not face.
    When his ends gained–(sir, do you understand?)

When she, he dares not face, has loved him first, –May I not say so, madam?–tops his hope,

And overpasses so his wildest dream,

With glad consent of all, and most of her

The confidant who brought the same about–

Why, in the moment when such joy explodes, 740 I do hold that the merest gentleman

Will not start rudely from the stalking-horse,

Dismiss it with a " There, enough of you!"

Forget it, show his back unmannerly:

But like a liberal heart will rather turn

And say, "A tingling time of hope was ours;

Betwixt the fears and falterings, we two lived

A chanceful time in waiting for the prize:

The confidant, the Constance, served not ill.

And though I shall forget her in due time, 750

Her use being answered now, as reason bids,

Nay as herself bids from her heart of hearts,–

Still, she has rights, the first thanks-go to her,

The first good praise goes to the prosperous tool,

And the first–which is the last—rewarding kiss."

Norbert. Constance, it is a dream–ah, see, you smile!

Constance. So, now his part being properly performed,

Madam, I turn to you and finish mine

As duly; I do justice in my turn.

Yes, madam, he has loved you–long and well; 760

He could not hope to tell you so–twas I

Who served to prove your soul accessible, I led his thoughts on, drew them to their place

When they had wandered else into despair,

And kept love constant toward its natural aim.

Enough, my part is played; you stoop half-way

And meet us royally and spare our fears:

Tis like yourself. He thanks you, so do I.

Take him–with my full heart! my work is praised

By what comes of it. Be you both happy, both! 770

Yourself–the only one on earth who can–

Do all for him, much more than a mere heart

Which though warm is not useful in its warmth

As the silk vesture of a queen! fold that

Around him gently, tenderly. For him–

For him,–he knows his own part!

Norbert. Have you done?

I take the jest at last. Should I speak now?

Was yours the wager, Constance, foolish child;

Or did you but accept it? Well–at least
You lose by it.

    Constance. Nay, madam, tis your turn! 780
Restrain him still from speech a little more,
And make him happier as more confident!
Pity him, madam, he is timid yet!
Mark, Norbert! Do not shrink now! Here I yield
My whole right in you to the Queen, observe!
With her go put in practice the great schemes
You teem with, follow the career else closed–
Be all you cannot be except by her!
Behold her!–Madam, say for pitys sake
Anything–frankly say you love him! Else 790
He ll not believe it: there s more earnest in
His fear than you conceive: I know the man!

    Norbert. I know the woman somewhat, and confess I thought she had jested better: she begins To overcharge her part. I gravely wait Your pleasure, madam: where is my reward?

    Queen. Norbert, this wild girl (whom I recognize
Scarce more than you do, in her fancy-fit,
Eccentric speech and variable mirth,
Not very wise perhaps and somewhat bold, 800
    Yet suitable, the whole nights work being strange)
.–May still be right: I may do well to speak
And make authentic what appears a dream
To even myself. For, what she says, is true:
Yes, Norbert–what you spoke just now of love,
Devotion, stirred no novel sense in me,
But justified a warmth felt long before.
Yes, from the first–I loved you, I shall say:
Strange! but I do grow stronger, now tis said.
Your courage helps mine: you did well to speak 8ro
To-night, the night that crowns your twelvemonths toil:
    But still I had not waited to discern
Your heart so long, believe me! From the first
The source of so much zeal was almost plain,
In absence even of your own words just now
Which hazarded the truth. Tis very strange,
But takes a happy ending–in your love
Which mine meets: be it so! as you chose me,
So I choose you.

    Norbert. And worthily you choose.
    I will not be unworthy your esteem, 820
    No, madam. I do love you; I will meet
Your nature, now I know it. This was well:

I see,–you dare and you are justified:
But none had ventured such experiment,
    Less versed than you in nobleness of heart,
    Less confident of finding such in me.
    I joy that thus you test me ere you grant
    The dearest richest beauteousest and best
    Of women to my arms: t is like yourself.
    So–back again into my parts set words–830
    Devotion to the uttermost is yours,
    But no, you cannot, madam, even you,
    Create in me the love our Constance does.
    Or–something truer to the tragic phrase–
    Not yon magnolia-bell superb with scent Invites a certain insect–thats myself–
    But the small eye-flower nearer to the ground.
    I take this lady.
    Constance. Stay–not hers, the trap–Stay, Norbert–that mistake were worst of all!
He is too cunning, madam! It was I, 840 I, Norbert, who.
    Norbert. You, was it, Constance? Then,
    But for the grace of this divinest hour
Which gives me you, I might not pardon here!
I am the Queens; she only knows my brain:
She may experiment upon my heart
And I instruct her too by the result.
But you, sweet, you who know me, who so long
Have told my heart-beats over, held my life
In those white hands of yours,–it is not well! 849
    Constance. Tush! I have said it, did I not say it all? The life, for her–the heart-beats,
for her sake!
    Norbert. Enough! my cheek grows red, I think.
    Your test?
    There s not the meanest woman in the world,
Not she I least could love in all the world,
Whom, did she love me, had love proved itself.
    I dare insult as you insult me now.
    Constance, I could say, if it must be said,
    "Take back the soul you offer, I keep mine!"
    But–" Take the soul still quivering on your hand,
    The soul so offered, which I cannot use, 860
    And, please you, give it to some playful friend,
    For–whats the trifle he requites me with?
    I, tempt a woman, to amuse a man,
    That two may mock her heart if it succumb?
    No: fearing God and standing neath his heaven, I would not dare insult a woman
so,
    Were she the meanest woman in the world,

And he, I cared to please, ten emperors!

Constance. Norbert!

Norbert. I love once as I live but once.

What case is this to think or talk about? 870 I love you. Would it mend the case at all

If such a step as this killed love in me?

Your part were done: account to God for it!

But mine—could murdered love get up again,

And kneel to whom you please to designate,

And make you mirth? It is too horrible.

You did not know this, Constance? now you know

That body and soul have each one life, but one:

And here s my love, here, living, at your feet.

Constance. See the Queen! Norbert—this one more last word—880 If thus you have taken jest for earnest—thus

Loved me in earnest.

Norbert. Ah, no jest holds here!

Where is the laughter in which jests break up,

And what this horror that grows palpable?

Madam—why grasp you thus the balcony?

Have I done ill? Have I not spoken truth?

M. W.–9

How could I other? Was it not your test,

To try me, what my love for Constance meant?

Madam, your royal soul itself approves,

The first, that I should choose thus! so one takes 890

A beggar,—asks him, what would buy his child?

And then approves the expected laugh of scorn

Returned as something noble from the rags.

Speak, Constance, I m the beggar! Ha, whats this?

You two glare each at each like panthers now.

Constance, the world fades; only you stand there!

You did not, in to-nights wild whirl of things,

Sell me—your soul of souls for any price)

No—no—t is easy to believe in you!

Was it your loves mad trial to oertop 900

Mine by this vain self-sacrifice? well, still—

Though I might curse, I love you. I am love

And cannot change: loves self is at your feet!

The Queen goes out.

Constance. Feel my heart; let it die against your own!

Norbert. Against my own. Explain not; let this be! This is lifes height.

Constance. Yours, yours, yours!

Norbert. You and I—

Why care by what meanders we are here
I the centre of the labyrinth? Men have died
Trying to find this place, which we have found. 909
    Constance. Found, found!
    Norbert. Sweet, never fear what she can do!
We are past harm now.
    Constance. On the breast of God.
I thought of men–as if you were a man.
Tempting him with a crown!
    Norbert. This must end here: It is too perfect.
    Constance. There s the music stopped. What measured heavy tread? It is one
blaze About me and within me.
    Norbert. Oh, some death
Will run its sudden finger round this spark
And sever us from the rest!
    Constance. And so do well.
Now the doors open.
    Norbert. T is the guard comes.
    Constance. Kiss!
DRAMATIS PERSONS.
1864.
JAMES LEES WIFE.
I.–JAMES LEES WIFE SPEAKS AT THE WINDOW.
Ah, Love, but a day
    And the world has changed!
The sun s away,
    And the bird estranged;
The wind has dropped.
    And the sky s deranged:
Summer has stopped.
    Look in my eyes!
    Wilt thou change too?
Should I fear surprise? 10
    Shall I find aught new
In the old and dear, In the good and true,
With the changing year?
    in.
    Thou art a man,
    But I am thy love.
For the lake, its swan;
    For the dell, its dove;
    And for thee–(oh, haste!)
    Me, to bend above, 20
    Me, to hold embraced.

II.–BY THE FIRESIDE.

1.

It all our fire of shipwreck wood,
    Oak and pine?
Oh, for the ills half-understood,
    The dim dead woe
    Long ago
Befallen this bitter coast of France!
Well, poor sailors took their chance; I take mine.
    n. A ruddy shaft our fire must shoot
    Oer the sea: lo
Do sailors eye the casement–mute,
    Drenched and stark,
    From their bark–
And envy, gnash their teeth for hate
O the warm safe house and happy freight –Thee and me?
    in.
God help you, sailors, at your need!
    Spare the curse!
For some ships, safe in port indeed,
    Rot and rust, 20
    Run to dust,
    All through worms i the wood, which crept,
Gnawed our hearts out while we slept:
    That is worse.
    1v.
Who lived here before us two?
    Old-world pairs.
Did a woman ever–would I knew!–
Watch the man
    With whom began 29
    Loves voyage full-sail,–(now, gnash your teeth!)
When planks start, open hell beneath
Unawares i III.–IN THE DOORWAY.
    The swallow has set her six young on the rail,
    And looks sea-ward:
The water s in stripes like a snake, olive-pale
    To the leeward,–
On the weather-side, black, spotted white with the wind.
    "Good fortune departs, and disasters behind,"–Hark, the wind with its wants and
its infinite wail!
    Our fig-tree, that leaned for the saltness, has furled
    Her five fingers, Each leaf like a hand opened wide to the world 10
    Where there lingers

No glint of the gold, Summer sent for her sake:
How the vines writhe in rows, each impaled on its stake!
My heart shrivels up and my spirit shrinks curled.
    In.
    Yet here are we two; we have love, house enough,
    With the field there,
This house of four rooms, that field red and rough,
    Though it yield there,
    For the rabbit that robs, scarce a blade or a bent;
If a magpie alight now, it seems an event; 20
    And they both will be gone at Novembers rebuff.
    iv.
    But why must cold spread? but wherefore bring change
    To the spirit,
God meant should mate his with an infinite range,
    And inherit
    His power to put life in the darkness and cold?
Oh, live and love worthily, bear and be bold!
Whom Summer made friends of, let Winter estrange I IV.–ALONG THE BEACH.
    I WIll be quiet and talk with you,
And reason why you are wrong.
    You wanted my love–is that much true?
    And so I did love, so I do:
What has come of it all along?
    I took you–how could I otherwise?
    For a world to me, and more;
For all, love greatens and glorifies
Till Gods a-glow, to the loving eyes, In what was mere earth before. 10 ni.
    Yes, earth–yes, mere ignoble earth!
    Now do I mis-state, mistake?
Do I wrong your weakness and call it worth?
Expect all harvest, dread no dearth,
    Seal my sense up for your sake?
    Iv.
    Oh, Love, Love, no, Love! not so, indeed!
    You were just weak earth, I knew:
With much in you waste, with many a weed,
And plenty of passions run to seed,
    But a little good grain too. 2C
    And such as you were, I took you for mine:
    Did not you find me yours,
To watch the olive and wait the vine,
And wonder when rivers of oil and wine
    Would flow, as the Book assures?
    Well, and if none of these good things came,

What did the failure prove? The man was my whole world, all the same, With his
flowers to praise or his weeds to blame,

    And, either or both, to love. jc

TO.

Yet this turns now to a fault–there! there!

That I do love, watch too long,

And wait too well, and weary and wear;

And tis all an old story, and my despair

    Fit subject for some new song:

    "How the light, light love, he has wings to fly

    At suspicion of a bond:

    My wisdom has bidden your pleasure good-bye,

Which will turn up next in a laughing eye,

    And why should you look beyond? " 40

V.–ON THE CLIFF.

I Leaned on the turf, I looked at a rock

Left dry by the surf;

For the turf, to call it grass were to mock:

Dead to the roots, so deep was done

The work of the summer sun.

And the rock lay flat

As an anvils face:

No iron like that!

Baked dry; of a weed, of a shell, no trace: 10

Sunshine outside, but ice at the core,

Deaths altar by the lone shore.

in.

On the turf, sprang gay

With his films of blue,

No cricket, I ll say,

But a warhorse, barded and chanfroned too,

The gift of a quixote-mage to his knight,

Real fairy, with wings all right.

1v.

On the rock, they scorch

Like a drop of fire 20

From a brandished torch,

Fall two red fans of a butterfly:

No turf, no rock: in their ugly stead,

See, wonderful blue and red!

Is it not so

With the minds of men?

The level and low,

The burnt and bare, in themselves; but then

With such a blue and red grace, not theirs,–

Love settling unawares! 30
VI.–READING A BOOK, UNDER
THE CLIFF.

" Stlll ailing, Wind? Wilt be appeased or no?
Which needs the others office, thou or I? Dost want to be disburthened of a woe,
And can, in truth, my voice untie Its links, and let it go?
"Art thou a dumb wronged thing that would be righted,
Entrusting thus thy cause to me? Forbear! No tongue can mend such pleadings;
faith, requited
With falsehood,–love, at last aware Of scorn,–hopes, early blighted,–lO in.
"We have them; but I know not any tone
So fit as thine to falter forth a sorrow:
Dost think men would go mad without a moan,
If they knew any way to borrow
A pathos like thy own?
iv.
"Which sigh wouldst mock, of all the sighs? The one So long escaping from lips
starved and blue,
That lasts while on her pallet-bed the nun
Stretches her length; her foot comes through
The straw she shivers on; 20
"You had not thought she was so tall: and spent,
Her shrunk lids open, her lean fingers shut
Close, close, their sharp and livid nails indent
The clammy palm; then all is mute:
That way, the spirit went.
vl.
"Or wouldst thou rather that I understand
Thy will to help me?–like the dog I found
Once, pacing sad this solitary strand,
Who would not take my food, poor hound,
But whined and licked my hand." 30 vn.
All this, and more, comes from some young mans pride
Of power to see,–in failure and mistake,
Relinquishment, disgrace, on every side,–
Merely examples for his sake,
Helps to his path untried: vln.
Instances he must–simply recognize?
Oh, more than so!–must, with a learners zeal, Make doubly prominent, twice
emphasize,
By added touches that reveal The god in babes disguise. 4.0
Oh, he knows what defeat means, and the rest!
Himself the undefeated that shall be:
Failure, disgrace, he flings them you to test,–

His triumph, in eternity
To plainly manifest!
Whence, judge if he learn forthwith what the wind
Means in its moaning–by the happy prompt Instinctive way of youth, I mean; for kind
Calm years, exacting their accompt
Of pain, mature the mind: 50 x1.
And some midsummer morning, at the lull
Just about daybreak, as he looks across
A sparkling foreign country, wonderful
To the seas edge for gloom and gloss,
Next minute must annul,– xn.
Then, when the wind begins among the vines,
So low, so low, what shall it say but this?
"Here is the change beginning, here the lines
Circumscribe beauty, set to bliss
The limit time assigns." 60 xn1.
Nothing can be as it has been before;
Better, so call it, only not the same.
To draw one beauty into our hearts core,
And keep it changeless! such our claim;
So answered,–Never more!
x l v.
Simple? Why, this is the old woe o the world;
Tune, to whose rise and fall we live and die. Rise with it, then! Rejoice that man is hurled
From change to change unceasingly, His souls wings never furled! 70 xv. Thats a new question; still replies the fact,
Nothing endures: the wind moans, saying so; We moan in acquiescence: there s lifes pact,
Perhaps probation–do / know? God does: endure his act!
Only, for man, how bitter not to grave
On his souls hands palms one fair good wise thing Just as he grasped it! For himself, deaths wave;
While time first washes–ah, the sting!–Oer all he d sink to save. 80
VII.–AMONG THE ROCKS.
Oh, good gigantic smile o the brown old earth,
This autumn morning! How he sets his bones To bask i the sun, and thrusts out knees and feet
For the ripple to run over in its mirth;
Listening the while, where on the heap of stones The white breast of the sea-lark twitters sweet.
That is the doctrine, simple, ancient, true;
Such is lifes trial, as old earth smiles and knows. If you loved only what were worth your love, Love were clear gain, and wholly well for you: 10

Make the low nature better by your throes! Give earth yourself, go up for gain above!

VIII.–BESIDE THE DRAWING BOARD.

i.

"As like as a Hand to another Hand!"
  Whoever said that foolish thing,
Could not have studied to understand
  The counsels of God in fashioning,
Out of the infinite love of his heart,
This Hand, whose beauty I praise, apart
From the world of wonder left to praise,
If I tried to learn the other ways
Of love in its skill, or love in its power.
  "As like as a Hand to another Hand": 10
  Who said that, never took his stand,
Found and followed, like me, an hour,
The beauty in this,–how free, how fine
To fear, almost,–of the limit-line!
As I looked at this, and learned and drew,
  Drew and learned, and looked again,
While fast the happy minutes flew, Its beauty mounted into my brain,
  And a fancy seized me; I was fain
  To efface my work, begin anew, 2o
  Kiss what before I only drew;
  Ay, laying the red chalk twixt my lips,
With soul to help if the mere lips failed,
I kissed all right where the drawing ailed,
  Kissed fast the grace that somehow slips
  Still from ones soulless finger-tips.
  T is a clay cast, the perfect thing,
  From Hand live once, dead long ago: Princess-like it wears the ring
  To fancys eye, by which we know 30
  That here at length a master found
  His match, a proud lone soul its mate,
As soaring genius sank to ground,
  And pencil could not emulate
The beauty in this,–how free, how fine
To fear almost!–of the limit-line.
Long ago the god, like me
The worm, learned, each in our degree:
Looked and loved, learned and drew,
  Drew and learned and loved again, 40
  While fast the happy minutes flew,
  Till beauty mounted into his brain And on the finger which outvied

His art he placed the ring thats there, Still by fancys eye descried, In token of a marriage rare:

For him on earth, his arts despair, For him in heaven, his souls fit bride.

Little girl with the poor coarse hand I turned from to a cold clay cast–. 50 I have my lesson, understand

The worth of flesh and blood at last. Nothing but beauty in a Hand?

Because he could not change the hue,

Mend the lines and make them true To this which met his souls demand,–

Would Da Vinci turn from you?

I hear him laugh my woes to scorn–

"The fool forsooth is all forlorn

Because the beauty, she thinks best, 60

Lived long ago or was never born,–

Because no beauty bears the test

In this rough peasant Hand! Confessed!

Art is null and study void!

So sayest thou? So said not I,

Who threw the faulty pencil by, And years instead of hours employed, Learning the veritable use

Of flesh and bone and nerve beneath

Lines and hue of the outer sheath, 70 If haply I might reproduce

One motive of the powers profuse,

Flesh and bone and nerve that make

The poorest coarsest human hand

An object worthy to be scanned A whole life long for their sole sake. Shall earth and the cramped moment-space Yield the heavenly crowning grace? Now the parts and then the whole! Who art thou, with stinted soul 80

And stunted body, thus to cry

I love,–shall that be lifes strait dole?

I must live beloved or die!

This peasant hand that spins the wool

And bakes the bread, why lives it on,

Poor and coarse with beauty gone,–

What use survives the beauty?" Fool!

Go, little girl with the poor coarse hand!

I have my lesson, shall understand. 89 i IX.–ON DECK.

There is nothing to remember in me,

Nothing I ever said with a grace,

Nothing I did that you care to see,

Nothing I was that deserves a place

In your mind, now I leave you, set you free.

ii.

Conceded! In turn, concede to me,

Such things have been as a mutual flame.

Your souls locked fast; but, love for a key,
You might let it loose, till I grew the same In your eyes, as in mine you stand: strange plea T id

For then, then, what would it matter to me
That I was the harsh ill-favored one?

We both should be like as pea and pea;
It was ever so since the world begun:

So, let me proceed with my reverie.

1v.

How strange it were if you had all me,
As I have all you in my heart and brain,

M. W.–10

You, whose least word brought gloom or glee,
Who never lifted the hand in vain–Will hold mine yet, from over the sea! ao
Strange, if a face, when you thought of me,
Rose like your own face present now, With eyes as dear in their due degree,
Much such a mouth, and as bright a brow, Till you saw yourself, while you cried
"Tis She!"

v1.

Well, you may, you must, set down to me
Love that was life, life that was love; A tenure of breath at your lips decree,
A passion to stand as your thoughts approve, A rapture to fall where your foot might be. 30 vn.

But did one touch of such love for me
Come in a word or a look of yours, Whose words and looks will, circling, flee
Round me and round while life endures,–Could I fancy " As I feel, thus feels he ";
v111.

Why, fade you might to a thing like me,
And your hair grow these coarse hanks of hair,
Your skin, this bark of a gnarled tree,–
You might turn myself!–should I know or care
When I should be dead of joy, James Lee f 40

GOLD HAIR:

A STORY OF PORNIc.

Oh, the beautiful girl, too white,
Who lived at Pornic, down by the sea,
Just where the sea and the Loire unite!

And a boasted name in Brittany
She bore, which I will not write.

ii.

Too white, for the flower of life is red;
Her flesh was the soft seraphic screen Of a soul that is meant (her parents said)
To just see earth, and hardly be seen, And blossom in heaven instead. 1O
Yet earth saw one thing, one how fair!

One grace that grew to its full on earth: Smiles might be sparse on her cheek so spare,

And her waist want half a girdles girth, But she had her great gold hair.

1v.

Hair, such a wonder of flix and floss,

Freshness and fragrance—floods of it, too!

Gold, did I say? Nay, gold s mere dross:

Here, Life smiled, "Think what I meant to do!"

And Love sighed, "Fancy my loss! " 2 v. So, when she died, it was scarce more strange

Than that, when delicate evening dies, And you follow its spent suns pallid range,

There s a shoot of color startles the skies With sudden, violent change,– v1.

That, while the breath was nearly to seek,

As they put the little cross to her lips,

She changed; a spot came out on her cheek,

A spark from her eye in mid-eclipse,

And she broke forth, "I must speak! " 30 vn.

"Not my hair! " made the girl her moan–

"All the rest is gone or to go; But the last, last grace, my all, my own,

Let it stay in the grave, that the ghosts may know! Leave my poor gold hair alone!"

vn1.

The passion thus vented, dead lay she;

Her parents sobbed their worst on that; All friends joined in, nor observed degree:

For indeed the hair was to wonder at, As it spread–not flowing free, 40 1x.

But curled around her brow, like a crown,

And coiled beside her cheeks, like a cap,

And calmed about her neck–ay, down

To her breast, pressed flat, without a gap I the gold, it reached her gown.

All kissed that face, like a silver wedge

Mid the yellow wealth, nor disturbed its hair:

Een the priest allowed deaths privilege,

As he planted the crucifix with care

On her breast, twixt edge and edge. 50 x1.

And thus was she buried, inviolate

Of body and soul, in the very space By the altar; keeping saintly state In Pornic church, for her pride of race, Pure life and piteous fate.

xn.

And in after-time would your fresh tear fall,

Though your mouth might twitch with a dubious smile,

As they told you of gold, both robe and pall,

How she prayed them leave it alone awhile,

So it never was touched at all. 60 xn1.

Years flew; this legend grew at last

The life of the lady; all she had done,

All been, in the memories fading fast
Of lover and friend, was summed in one
Sentence survivors passed: x1v.

To wit, she was meant for heaven, not earth;
Had turned an angel before the time: Yet, since she was mortal, in such dearth
Of frailty, all you could count a crime Was–she knew her gold hairs worth. 70
Xv.

At little pleasant Pornic church, It chanced, the pavement wanted repair,
Was taken to pieces: left in the lurch,
A certain sacred space lay bare,
And the boys began research.
xv1.

T was the space where our sires would lay a saint,
A benefactor,–a bishop, suppose, A baron with armor-adornments quaint,
Dame with chased ring and jewelled rose, Things sanctity saves from taint; 80
xv11.

So we come to find them in after-days
When the corpse is presumed to have done with gauds Of use to the living, in many ways:
For the boys get pelf, and the town applauds, And the church deserves the praise.
xv111.

They grubbed with a will: and at length–O cor
Humanum, pectora cteca, and the rest!–
They found–no gaud they were prying for,
No ring, no rose, but–who would have guessed?–
A double Louis-dor! 90 x1x.

Here was a case for the priest: he heard,
Marked, inwardly digested, laid
Finger on nose, smiled, "There s a bird
Chirps in my ear ": then, "Bring a apade,
Dig deeper! "–he gave the word.
xx.

And lo, when they came to the coffin-lid,
Or rotten planks which composed it once,
Why, there lay the girls skull wedged amid
A mint of money, it served for the nonce
To hold in its hair-heaps hid! 1OO xx1.

Hid there? Why? Could the girl be wont (She the stainless soul) to treasure up
Money, earths trash and heavens affront?
Had a spider found out the communion-cup, Was a toad in the christening-font?
xxn.

Truth is truth: too true it was.
Gold! She hoarded and hugged it first, Longed for it, leaned oer it, loved it–alas–
Till the humor grew to a head and burst, And she cried, at the final pass,–HO xx111.

"Talk not of God, my heart is stone!

Nor lover nor friend–be gold for both! Gold I lack; and, my all, my own, It shall
hide in my hair. I scarce die loth If they let my hair alone!"
    xxlv.
    Louis-dor, some six times five,
    And duly double, every piece.
Now do you see? With the priest to shrive,
    With parents preventing her souls release
By kisses that kept alive,–120 xxv.
    With heavens gold gates about to ope,
    With friends praise, gold-like, lingering still,
    An instinct had bidden the girls hand grope
For gold, the true sort–" Gold in heaven, if you will; But I keep earths too, I hope."
    xxvl.
    Enough! The priest took the graves grim yield:
The parents, they eyed that price of sin
    As if thirty pieces lay revealed
    On the place to bury strangers in,
    The hideous Potters Field. 130 xxvn.
    But the priest bethought him: " Milk thats spilt–You know the adage! Watch and
pray!
    Saints tumble to earth with so slight a tilt!
It would build a new altar; that, we may! "
    And the altar therewith was built.
    xxvln.
    Why I deliver this horrible verse?
    As the text of a sermon, which now I preach: Evil or good may be better or worse
In the human heart, but the mixture of each Is a marvel and a curse. 40 xx1X.
    The candid incline to surmise of late
    That the Christian faith proves false, I find;
    For our Essays-and-Reviews debate
Begins to tell on the public mind,
    And Colensos words have weight: xxx.
    I still, to suppose it true, for my part,
See reasons and reasons; this, to begin:
    T is the faith that launched point-blank her dart
At the head of a lie–taught Original Sin,
    The Corruption of Mans Heart. 150
    THE WORST OF IT.
    Would it were I had been false, not you!
    I that am nothing, not you that are all: I, never the worse for a touch or two
On my speckled hide; not you, the pride Of the day, my swan, that a first flecks fall
On her wonder of white must unswan, undo!
    I had dipped in lifes struggle and, out again,
Bore specks of it here, there, easy to see,

When I found my swan and the cure was plain;
The dull turned bright as I caught your white 1O
    On my bosom: you saved me–saved in vain
If you ruined yourself, and all through me!
    Yes, all through the speckled beast that I am,
    Who taught you to stoop; you gave me yourself,
    And bound your soul by the vows that damn:
Since on better thought you break, as you ought,
    Vows–words, no angel set down, some elf
Mistook,–for an oath, an epigram!
    1v.
    Yes, might I judge you, here were my heart,
    And a hundred its like, to treat as you pleased! 20 I choose to be yours, for my proper part,
Yours, leave or take, or mar me or make; If I acquiesce, why should you be teased
    With the conscience-prick and the memory-smart?
    But what will God say? Oh, my sweet,
Think, and be sorry you did this thing!
    Though earth were unworthy to feel your feet,
There s a heaven above may deserve your love:
    Should you forfeit heaven for a snapt gold ring
    And a promise broke, were it just or meet? 30
    And I to have tempted you! I, who tried
Your soul, no doubt, till it sank! Unwise, I loved and was lowly, loved and aspired,
    Loved, grieving or glad, till I made you mad,
    And you meant to have hated and despised–
Whereas, you deceived me nor inquired!
    vn.
    She, ruined? How? No heaven for her?
    Crowns to give, and none for the brow
That looked like marble and smelt like myrrh?
    Shall the robe be worn, and the palm-branch borne 40
    And she go graceless, she graced now
    Beyond all saints, as themselves aver?
    vn1.
    Hardly! That must be understood!
    The earth is your place of penance, then;
And what will it prove? I desire your good.
    But, plot as I may, I can find no way
How a blow should fall, such as falls on men,
    Nor prove too much for your womanhood.
    1x.
    It will come, I suspect, at the end of life,
    When you walk alone, and review the past; 50

And I, who so long shall have done with strife,
And journeyed my stage and earned my wage
    And retired as was right,–I am called at last
When the devil stabs you, to lend the knife.

    He stabs for the minute of trivial wrong,
        Nor the other hours are able to save,
The happy, that lasted my whole life long:
    For a promise broke, not for first words spoke,
The true, the only, that turn my grave
    To a blaze of joy and a crash of song. 60 xi.

    Witness beforehand! Off I trip
On a safe path gay through the flowers you flung: My very name made great by
your lip,
    And my heart a-glow with the good I know Of a perfect year when we both were
young,
    And I tasted the angels fellowship.
    xn.

And witness, moreover. Ah, but wait!
I spy the loop whence an arrow shoots! It may be for yourself, when you meditate,
69
    That you grieve–for slain ruth, murdered truth. "Though falsehood escape in the
end, what boots?

    How truth would have triumphed! "–you sigh too late.
    Ay, who would have triumphed like you, I say!
Well, it is lost now; well, you must bear, Abide and grow fit for a better day:
    You should hardly grudge, could I be your judge! But hush! For you, can be no
despair:
    There s amends: t is a secret: hope and pray!
    x l v.

For I was true at least–oh, true enough!
    And, Dear, truth is not as good as it seems! 80 Commend me to conscience! Idle
stuff!

    Much help is in mine, as I mope and pine, And skulk through day, and scowl in my
dreams
    At my swans obtaining the crows rebuff.
    xv.

Men tell me of truth now–" False! " I cry:
    Of beauty–" A mask, friend! Look beneath!"
We take our own method, the devil and I,
With pleasant and fair and wise and rare:
    And the best we wish to what lives, is–death;
Which even in wishing, perhaps we lie! qo xv1.

    Far better commit a fault and have done–
        As you, Dear!–forever; and choose the pure,

And look where the healing waters run,
And strive and strain to be good again,
And a place in the other world ensure,
All glass and gold, with God for its sun.
xvn.
Misery! What shall I say or do?
I cannot advise, or, at least, persuade:
Most like, you are glad you deceived me–rue
No whit of the wrong: you endured too long, 100 Have done no evil and want no aid,
Will live the old life out and chance the new.
And your sentence is written all the same,
And I can do nothing,–pray, perhaps:
But somehow the world pursues its game,–
If I pray, if I curse,–for better or worse:
And my faith is torn to a thousand scraps,
And my heart feels ice while my words breathe flame.
x1x.
Dear, I look from my hiding-place.
Are you still so fair? Have you still the eyes? 11 o Be happy! Add but the other grace,
Be good! Why want what the angels vaunt? I knew you once: but in Paradise, If we meet, I will pass nor turn my face.
DIs ALITER VISUM; OR, LE BYRON DE NOS JOURS.
Stop, let me have the truth of that!
Is that all true? I say, the day
Ten years ago when both of us
Met on a morning, friends–as thus
We meet this evening, friends or what?–
Did you–because I took your arm
And sillily smiled, "A mass of brass
That sea looks, blazing underneath! "
While up the cliff-road edged with heath,
We took the turns nor came to harm–10
Did you consider " Now makes twice
That I have seen her, walked and talked
With this poor pretty thoughtful thing,
Whose worth I weigh: she tries to sing;
Draws, hopes in time the eye grows nice; nr.
"Reads verse and thinks she understands;
Loves all, at any rate, thats great,
Good, beautiful; but much as we
Down at the bath-house love the sea,
Who breathe its salt and bruise its sands: 20
"While. do but follow the fishing-gull That flaps and floats from wave to cave!

There s the sea-lover, fair my friend!
What then? Be patient, mark and mend!
Had you the making of your skull?"
v l.
And did you, when we faced the church
With spire and sad slate roof, aloof From human fellowship so far,
Where a few graveyard crosses are, And garlands for the swallows perch,–30 vn.
Did you determine, as we stepped
Oer the lone stone fence, "Let me get
Her for myself, and whats the earth
With all its art, verse, music, worth–
Compared with love, found, gained, and kept?
v l n.
"Schumann s our music-maker now;
Has his march-movement youth and mouth? Ingres s the modern man that paints;
Which will lean on me, of his saints? Heine for songs; for kisses, how? " 40 1x.
And did you, when we entered, reached
The votive frigate, soft aloft Riding on air this hundred years,
Safe-smiling at old hopes and fears,–. Did you draw profit while she preached i x.
Resolving, "Fools we wise men grow!
Yes, I could easily blurt out curt Some question that might find reply
As prompt in her stopped lips, dropped eye, And rush qf red to cheek and brow:
50 x1.
"Thus were a match made, sure and fast,
Mid the blue weed-flowers round the mound
Where, issuing, we shall stand and stay
For one more look at baths and bay,
Sands, sea-gulls, and the old church last–
"A match twixt me, bent, wigged and lamed.
Famous, however, for verse and worse,
Sure of the Fortieth spare Arm-chair
When gout and glory seat me there,
So, one whose love-freaks pass unblamed,–60 x1n.
"And this young beauty, round and sound
As a mountain-apple, youth and truth
With loves and doves, at all events
With money in the Three per Cents;
Whose choice of me would seem profound:– x1v.
"She might take me as I take her.
Perfect the hour would pass, alas!
Climb high, love high, what matter? Still,
Feet, feelings, must descend the hill:
An hours perfection cant recur. 70 xv.
"Then follows Paris and full time
For both to reason: Thus with us!

She ll sigh, Thus girls give body and soul
At first word, think they gain the goal,
When t is the starting-place they climb!
"My friend makes verse and gets renown;
Have they all fifty years, his peers?
He knows the world, firm, quiet and gay;
Boys will become as much one day:
They re fools; he cheats, with beard less brown. So
For boys say, Lave me or I die!
He did not say, The truth is, youth
I want, who am old and know too much; Id catch youth: lend me sight and touch!
Drop hearts blood where lifes wheels grate dry/ xvn1.
While I should make rejoinder "–(then It was, no doubt, you ceased that least
Light pressure of my arm in yours) " I can conceive of cheaper cures For a yawning-
fit oer books and men. 90 x1x.
"What? All I am, was, and might be,
All, books taught, art brought, lifes whole strife,
Painful results since precious, just
Were fitly exchanged, in wise disgust,
For two cheeks freshened by youth and sea?
M. w.–ii xx.
"All for a nosegay!–what came first;
With fields on flower, untried each side; I rally, need my books and men,
And find a nosegay: drop it, then, No match yet made for best or worst! " 100
That ended me. You judged the porch
We left by, Norman; took our look
At sea and sky; wondered so few
Find out the place for air and view;
Remarked the sun began to scorch; xxn.
Descended, soon regained the baths,
And then, good-bye! Years ten since then:
Ten years! We meet: you tell me, now,
By a window-seat for that cliff-brow,
On carpet-stripes for those sand-paths. no xx1n.
Now I may speak: you fool, for all
Your lore! Who made things plain in vain? What was the sea for? What, the gray
Sad church, that solitary day, Crosses and graves and swallows call?
xx1v.
Was there naught better than to enjoy?
No feat which, done, would make time break, And let us pent-up creatures through
Into eternity, our due? No forcing earth teach heavens employ? 120 xxv.
No wise beginning, here and now,
What cannot grow complete (earths feat)
And heaven must finish, there and then?
No tasting earths true food for men, Its sweet in sad, its sad in sweet?

No grasping at love, gaining a share
O the sole spark from Gods life at strife
With death, so, sure of range above
The limits here? For us and love,
   Failure; but, when God fails, despair. 130 xxvn.
   This you call wisdom? Thus you add
   Good unto good again, in vain?
You loved, with body worn and weak; I loved, with faculties to seek:
Were both loves worthless since ill-clad?
   xxvln.
   Let the mere star-fish in his vault
Crawl in a wash of weed, indeed, Rose-jacynth to the finger-tips:
He, whole in body and soul, outstrips Man, found with either in default. 140 xx1x.
   But whats whole, can increase no more,
Is dwarfed and dies, since heres its sphere.
   The devil laughed at you in his sleeve!
You knew not? That I well believe;
   Or you had saved two souls: nay, four.
   xxx.
   For Stephanie sprained last night her wrist,
Ankle or something. " Pooh," cry you?
   At any rate she danced, all say,
Vilely; her vogue has had its day.
   Here comes my husband from his whist. 1 50
TOO LATE.
   Here was I with my arm and heart
   And brain, all yours for a word, a want Put into a look—just a look, your part,—
   While mine, to repay it. vainest vaunt, Were the woman, thats dead, alive to hear,
   Had her lover, thats lost, loves proof to show! But I cannot show it; you cannot speak
   From the churchyard neither, miles removed, Though I feel by a pulse within my cheek,
   Which stabs and stops, that the woman I loved 10 Needs help in her grave and finds none near,
   Wants warmth from the heart which sends it—so!
   Did I speak once angrily, all the drear days
   You lived, you woman I loved so well, Who married the other? Blame or praise,
   Where was the use then? Time would tell, And the end declare what man for you,
   What woman for me, was the choice of God. But, Edith dead! no doubting more!
   I used to sit and look at my life so
   As it rippled and ran till, right before,
A great stone stopped it: oh, the strife
   Of waves at the stone some devil threw
In my lifes midcurrent, thwarting God!
   But either I thought, "They may churn and chide

Awhile, my waves which came for their joy And found this horrible stone full-tide:
Yet I see just a thread escape, deploy Through the evening-country, silent and safe,
And it suffers no more till it finds the sea." 30 Or else I would think, "Perhaps some night
When new things happen, a meteor-ball May slip through the sky in a line of light,
And earth breathe hard, and landmarks fall, And my waves no longer champ nor chafe,
Since a stone will have rolled from its place: let be!"
But, dead! Alls done with: wait who may,
Watch and wear and wonder who will. Oh, my whole life that ends to-day!
Oh, my souls sentence, sounding still, 40
"The woman is dead that was none of his;
And the man that was none of hers may go!" There s only the past left: worry that!
Wreak, like a bull, on the empty coat, Rage, its late wearer is laughing at!
Tear the collar to rags, having missed his throat; Strike stupidly on–" This, this and this,
Where I would that a bosom received the blow.1"
I ought to have done more: once my speech,
And once your answer, and there, the end, 50 And Edith was henceforth out of reach!
Why, men do more to deserve a friend, Be rid of a foe, get rich, grow wise,
Nor, folding their arms, stare fate in the face.
Why, better even have burst like a thief
And borne you away to a rock for us two,
In a moments horror, bright, bloody and brief:
Then changed to myself again–"I slew
Myself in that moment; a ruffian lies
Somewhere: your slave, see, born in his place! " 60
What did the other do? You be judge!
Look at us, Edith! Here are we both! Give him his six whole years: I grudge
None of the life with you, nay, loathe Myself that I grudged his start in advance
Of me who could overtake and pass. But, as if he loved you! No, not he,
Nor any one else in the world, tis plain: Who ever heard that another, free
As I, young, prosperous, sound and sane, 70
Poured life out, proffered it–" Half a glance
Of those eyes of yours and I drop the glass!"
Handsome, were you? T is more than they held, More than they said; I was ware and watched: I was the scapegrace, this rat belled
The cat, this fool got his whiskers scratched:
The others? No head that was turned, no heart
Broken, my lady, assure yourself! Each soon made his mind up; so and so
Married a dancer, such and such 80
Stole his friends wife, stagnated slow,
Or maundered, unable to do as much,
And muttered of peace where he had no part:

While, hid in the closet, laid on the shelf,–
On the whole, you were let alone, I think!
So, you looked to the other, who acquiesced; My rival, the proud man,–prize your pink
Of poets! A poet he was! I ve guessed: He rhymed you his rubbish nobody read,
Loved you and doved you–did not I laugh! 90 There was a prize! But we both were tried.
Oh, heart of mine, marked broad with her mark, Tekel, found wanting, set aside,
Scorned! See, I bleed these tears in the dark Till comfort come and the last be bled:
He? He is tagging your epitaph.
If it would only come over again!
–Time to be patient with me, and probe This heart till you punctured the proper vein,
Just to learn what blood is: twitch the robe 100 From that blank lay-figure your fancy draped,
Prick the leathern heart till the–verses spirt! And late it was easy; late, you walked
Where a friend might meet you; Ediths name Arose to ones lip if one laughed or talked; If I heard good news, you heard the same;
When I woke, I knew that your breath escaped;
I could bide my time, keep alive, alert.
And alive I shall keep and long, you will see!
I knew a man, was kicked like a dog 110
From gutter to cesspool; what cared he
So long as he picked from the filth his prog? He saw youth, beauty and genius die,
And jollily lived to his hundredth year.
But I will live otherwise: none of such life!
At once I begin as I mean to end.
Go on with the world, get gold in its strife,
Give your spouse the slip and betray your friend! There are two who decline, a woman and I,
And enjoy our death in the darkness here. 120 I liked that way you had with your curls
Wound to a ball in a net behind:
Your cheek was chaste as a quaker-girls,
And your mouth–there was never, to my mind, Such a funny mouth, for it would not shut;
And the dented chin too–what a chin! There were certain ways when you spoke, some words
That you know you never could pronounce: You were thin, however; like a birds 129
Your hand seemed–some would say the pounce Of a scaly-footed hawk–all but!
The world was right when it called you thin.
Xil.
But I turn my back on the world: I take
Your hand, and kneel, and lay to my lips.

Bid me live, Edith! Let me slake
Thirst at your presence! Fear no slips:
Tis your slave shall pay, while his soul endures,
Full due, loves whole debt, summum jus.
My queen shall have high observance, planned
Courtship made perfect, no least line 140
Crossed without warrant. There you stand,
Warm too, and white too: would this wine Had washed all over that body of yours,
Ere I drank it, and you down with it, thus!
ABT VOGLER.
(after He Has Been Extemporlzlng Upon The Muslcal Instrument Of Hls Inventlon.)
Would that the structure brave, the manifold music I build, Bidding my organ obey,
calling its keys to their work, Claiming each slave of the sound, at a touch, as when
Solomon willed Armies of angels that soar, legions of demons that lurk,
Man, brute, reptile, fly,–alien of end and of aim, Adverse, each from the other
heaven-high, hell-deep removed,–
Should rush into sight at once as he named the ineffable Name,
And pile him a palace straight, to pleasure the princess he loved!
Would it might tarry like his, the beautiful building of mine,
This which my keys in a crowd pressed and importuned to raise! lo Ah, one and
all, how they helped, would dispart now and now combine, Zealous to hasten the
work, heighten their master his praise! And one would bury his brow with a blind
plunge down to hell, Burrow awhile and build, broad on the roots of things, Then up
again swim into sight, having based me my palace well,
Founded it, fearless of flame, flat on the nether springs.
in.
And another would mount and march, like the excellent minion he was, Ay, another
and yet another, one crowd but with many a crest, Raising my rampired walls of gold
as transparent as glass,
Eager to do and die, yield each his place to the rest: 20
For higher still and higher (as a runner tips with fire,
When a great illumination surprises a festal night–
Outlining round and round Romes dome from space to spire)
Up, the pinnacled glory retched, and the pride of my soul was in sight.
lv.
In sight? Not half! for it seemed, it was certain, to match mans birth,
Nature in turn conceived, obeying an impulse as I; And the emulous heaven yearned
down, made effort to reach the earth, As the earth had done her best, in my passion,
to scale the sky: Novel splendors burst forth, grew familiar and dwelt with mine,
Not a point nor peak but found and fixed its wandering star; 30 Meteor-moons,
balls of blaze: and they did not pale nor pine,
For earth had attained to heaven, there was no more near nor far.
Nay more; for there wanted not who walked in the glare and glow, Presences plain
in the place; or, fresh from the
Protoplast, Furnished for ages to come, when a kindlier wind should blow,

Lured now to begin and live, in a house to their liking at last; Or else the wonderful Dead who have passed through the body and gone, But were back once more to breathe in an old world worth their new: What never had been, was now; what was, as it shall be anon;

And what is,–shall I say, matched both I for I was made perfect too. 40 v1.

All through my keys that gave their sounds to a wish of my soul, All through my soul that praised as its wish flowed visibly forth, All through music and me! For think, had I painted the whole, Why, there it had stood, to see, nor the process so wonder-worth: Had I written the same, made verse–still, effect proceeds from cause, Ye know why the forms are fair, ye hear how the tale is told; It is all triumphant art, but art in obedience to laws, Painter and poet are proud in the artist-list enrolled:– vn.

But here is the finger of God, a flash of the will that can,

Existent behind all laws, that made them and, lo, they are! 50

And I know not if, save in this, such gift be allowed to man, That out of three sounds he frame, not a fourth sound, but a star. Consider it well: each tone of our scale in itself is naught; It is everywhere in the world–loud, soft, and all is said:

Give it to me to use! I mix it with two in my thought: And, there! Ye have heard and seen: consider and bow the head!

vn1.

Well, it is gone at last, the palace of music I reared; Gone! and the good tears start, the praises that come too slow; For one is assured at first, one scarce can say that he feared,

That he even gave it a thought, the gone thing was to go. 60

Never to be again! But many more of the kind

As good, nay, better perchance: is this your com-

fort to me?

To me, who must be saved because I cling with my mind

To the same, same self, same love, same God: ay, what was, shall be.

DC.

Therefore to whom turn I but to thee, the ineffable

Name? Builder and maker, thou, of houses not made with hands! What, have fear of change from thee who art ever the same? Doubt that thy power can fill the heart that thy power expands?

There shall never be one lost good! What was, shall live as before; 69

The evil is null, is naught, is silence implying sound;

What was good shall be good, with, for evil, so much good more;

On the earth the broken arcs; in the heaven, a perfect round.

All we have willed or hoped or dreamed of good shall exist; Not its semblance, but itself; no beauty, nor good, nor power Whose voice has gone forth, but each survives for the melodist

When eternity affirms the conception of an hour. The high that proved too high, the heroic for earth too hard, The passion that left the ground to lose itself in the sky,

Are music sent up to God by the lover and the bard;

Enough that he heard it once: we shall hear it by- and-by. 80 x1.

And what is our failure here but a triumphs evidence For the fulness of the days? Have we withered or agonized? Why else was the pause prolonged but that singing might issue thence? Why rushed the discords in but that harmony should be prized?

Sorrow is hard to bear, and doubt is slow to clear, Each sufferer says his say, his scheme of the weal and woe:

But God has a few of us whom he whispers in the ear; The rest may reason and welcome: tis we musicians know.

xn.

Well, it is earth with me; silence resumes her reign: I will be patient and proud, and soberly acquiesce. 90

Give me the keys. I feel for the common chord again, Sliding by semitones, till I sink to the minor,– yes,

And I blunt it into a ninth, and I stand on alien ground, Surveying awhile the heights I rolled from into the deep;

Which, hark, I have dared and done, for my resting-place is found, The C Major of this life: so, now I will try to sleep.

RABBI BEN EZRA.

Grow old along with me!

The best is yet to be,

The last of life, for which the first was made:

Our times are in His hand

Who saith " A whole I planned, Youth shows but half; trust God: see all nor be afraid!"

Not that, amassing flowers,

Youth sighed " Which rose make ours,

Which lily leave and then as best recall?"

Not that, admiring stars, 10 It yearned " Nor Jove, nor Mars; Mine be some figured flame which blends, transcends them all!"

Not for such hopes and fears

Annulling youths brief years,

Do I remonstrate: folly wide the mark!

Rather I prize the doubt

Low kinds exist without,

Finished and finite clods, untroubled by a spark.

1v.

Poor vaunt of life indeed,

Were man but formed to feed 20

On joy, to solely seek and find and feast:

Such feasting ended, then

As sure an end to men; Irks care the crop-full bird? Frets doubt the maw-crammed beast?

Rejoice we are allied

To That which doth provide And not partake, effect and not receive!

A spark disturbs our clod;

Nearer we hold of God 29

Who gives, than of His tribes that take, I must believe.

v1.

Then, welcome each rebuff

That turns earths smoothness rough, Each sting that bids nor sit nor stand but go!

Be our joys three-parts pain!

Strive, and hold cheap the strain; Learn, nor account the pang; dare, never grudge the throe!

For thence,—a paradox

Which comforts while it mocks,—

Shall life succeed in that it seems to fail:

What I aspired to be, 40

And was not, comforts me:

A brute I might have been, but would not sink i the scale.

What is he but a brute

Whose flesh has soul to suit,

Whose spirit works lest arms and legs want play?

To man, propose this test—

Thy body at its best, How far can that project thy soul on its lone way?

Yet gifts should prove their use:

I own the Past profuse 50

Of power each side, perfection every turn:

Eyes, ears took in their dole,

Brain treasured up the whole;

Should not the heart beat once " How good to live and learn"?

Not once beat " Praise be Thine!

I see the whole design,

I, who saw power, see now love perfect too:

Perfect I call Thy plan:

Thanks that I was a man!

Maker, remake, complete,—I trust what Thou shah do!" 60 x1.

For pleasant is this flesh;

Our soul, in its rose-mesh

Pulled ever to the earth, still yearns for rest;

M. W.—12

Would we some prize might hold To match those manifold Possessions of the brute,—gain most, as we did best!

x11.

Let us not always say

"Spite of this flesh to-day I strove, made head, gained ground upon the whole!"

As the bird wings and sings, 70

Let us cry " All good things

Are ours, nor soul helps flesh more, now, than flesh helps soul!"

xin.

Therefore I summon age

To grant youths heritage,
Lifes struggle having so far reached its term:
    Thence shall I pass, approved
    A man, for aye removed From the developed brute; a god though in the germ.
    xlv.
    And I shall thereupon
    Take rest, ere I be gone 80
    Once more on my adventure brave and new:
    Fearless and unperplexed,
    When I wage battle next,
What weapons to select, what armor to indue.
    xv.
    Youth ended, I shall try
    My gain or loss thereby;
Leave the fire ashes, what survives is gold:
    And I shall weigh the same,
    Give life its praise or blame: Young, all lay in dispute; I shall know, being old. 90
xvl.
    For note, when evening shuts,
    A certain moment cuts
The deed off, calls the glory from the gray:
    A whisper from the west
    Shoots–" Add this to the rest, Take it and try its worth: here dies another day."
    So, still within this life,
    Though lifted oer its strife,
Let me discern, compare, pronounce at last,
    "This rage was right i the main, 1 oo
    That acquiescence vain: The Future I may face now I have proved the Past."
    xvl11.
    For more is not reserved
    To man, with soul just nerved
To act to-morrow what he learns to-day:
    Here, work enough to watch
    The Master work, and catch Hints of the proper craft, tricks of the tools true play.
    xlx.
    As it was better, youth
    Should strive, through acts uncouth, 11O
    Toward making, than repose on aught found made:
    So, better, age, exempt
    From strife, should know, than tempt Further. Thou waitedest age: wait death nor
be afraid!
    xx.
    Enough now, if the Right
    And Good and Infinite Be named here, as thou callest thy hand thine own,
    With knowledge absolute,

Subject to no dispute 119
From fools that crowded youth, nor let thee feel alone.
xx1.
Be there, for once and all,
Severed great minds from small, Announced to each his station in the Past!
Was I, the world arraigned,
Were they, my soul disdained,
Right? Let age speak the truth and give us peace at last!
Now, who shall arbitrate?
Ten men love what I hate,
Shun what I follow, slight what I receive;
Ten, who in ears and eyes 130
Match me: we all surmise,
They this thing, and I that: whom shall my soul believe?
xxm.
Not on the vulgar mass
Called " work," must sentence pass, Things done, that took the eye and had the price;
Oer which, from level stand,
The low world laid its hand, Found straightway to its mind, could value in a trice:
Xx1v.
But all, the worlds coarse thumb
And finger failed to plumb, 140
So passed in making up the main account;
All instincts immature,
All purposes unsure,
That weighed not as his work, yet swelled the mans amount: xxv.
Thoughts hardly to be packed
Into a narrow act,
Fancies that broke through language and escaped;
All I could never be,
-All, men ignored in me,
This, I was worth to God, whose wheel the pitcher shaped. 150 xxv1.
Ay, note that Potters wheel,
That metaphor! and feel
Why time spins fast, why passive lies our clay,–
Thou, to whom fools propound,
When the wine makes its round, "Since life fleets, all is change; the Past gone, seize to-day!"
xxvn.
Fool! All that is, at all,
Lasts ever, past recall;
Earth changes, but thy soul and God stand sure:
What entered into thee, 160

That was, is, and shall be: Times wheel runs back or stops: Potter and clay endure.
He fixed thee mid this dance
    Of plastic circumstance,
This Present, thou, forsooth, wouldst fain arrest:
    Machinery just meant
    To give thy soul its bent, Try thee and turn thee forth, sufficiently impressed.
    What though the earlier grooves
    Which ran the laughing loves 170
    Around thy base, no longer pause and press?
    What though, about thy rim,
    Skull-things in order grim Grow out, in graver mood, obey the sterner stress?
    xxx.
    Look not thou down but up!
    To uses of a cup,
The festal board, lamps flash and trumpets peal,
    The new wines foaming flow,
    The Masters lips a-glow!
    Thou, heavens consummate cup, what needst thou with earths wheel? 180 xxxl.
    But I need, now as then,
    Thee, God, who mouldest men;
And since, not even while the whirl was worst,
    Did I,–to the wheel of life
    With shapes and colors rife, Bound dizzily,–mistake my end, to slake Thy thirst:
So, take and use Thy work:
    Amend what flaws may lurk, What strain o the stuff, what warpings past the aim!
    My times be in Thy hand! 190
    Perfect the cup as planned! Let age approve of youth, and death complete the same
I
    A DEATH IN THE DESERT.
    supposed of Pamphylax the Antiochene:
It is a parchment, of my rolls the fifth,
Hath three skins glued together, is all Greek
And goeth from Epsilon down to Mu:
Lies second in the surnamed Chosen Chest,
Stained and conserved with juice of terebinth,
Covered with cloth of hair, and lettered Xi,
From Xanthus, my wifes uncle, now at peace:
Mu and Epsilon stand for my own name., I may not write it, but I make a cross lo
    To show I wait His coming, with the rest,
And leave off here: beginneth Pamphylax.
    I said, "If one should wet his lips with wine,
    And slip the broadest plantain-leaf we find,
    Or else the lappet of a linen robe, Into the water-vessel, lay it right,
    And cool his forehead just above the eyes,
    The while a brother, kneeling either side,

Should chafe each hand and try to make it warm,–
He is not so far gone but he might speak." 20
This did not happen in the outer cave,
Nor in the secret chamber of the rock
Where, sixty days since the decree was out,
We had him, bedded on a camel-skin,
And waited for his dying all the while;
But in the midmost grotto: since noons light
Reached there a little, and we would not lose
The last of what might happen on his face.
I at the head, and Xanthus at the feet,
With Valens and the Boy, had lifted him, 30
And brought him from the chamber in the depths,
And laid him in the light where we might see:
For certain smiles began about his mouth,
And his lids moved, presageful of the end.
Beyond, and halfway up the mouth o the cave,
The Bactrian convert, having his desire,
Kept watch, and made pretence to graze a goat
That gave us milk, on rags of various herb,
Plantain and quitch, the rocks shade keeps alive:
So that if any thief or soldier passed, 4.0 (Because the persecution was aware)
Yielding the goat up promptly with his life,
Such man might pass on, joyful at a prize,
Nor care to pry into the cool o the cave.
Outside was all noon and the burning blue.
"Here is wine," answered Xanthus,–dropped a drop; I stooped and placed the lap
of cloth aright,
Then chafed his right hand, and the Boy his left:
But Valens had bethought him, and produced
And broke a ball of nard, and made perfume. 50
Only, he did–not so much wake, as–turn
And smile a little, as a sleeper does If any dear one call him, touch his face–
And smiles and loves, but will not be disturbed.
Then Xanthus said a prayer, but still he slept: It is the Xanthus that escaped to
Rome,
Was burned, and could not write the chronicle.
Then the Boy sprang up from his knees, and ran,; Stung by the splendor of a sudden
thought,
And fetched the seventh plate of graven lead 60
Out of the secret chamber, found a place,
Pressing with, finger on the deeper dints,
And spoke, as twere his mouth proclaiming first,
"I am the Resurrection and the Life."
Whereat he opened his eyes wide at once,

And sat up of himself, and looked at us;
And thenceforth nobody pronounced a word:
Only, outside, the Bactrian cried his cry
Like the lone desert-bird that wears the ruff,
As signal we were safe, from time to time. 70
First he said, "If a friend declared to me,
This my son Valens, this my other son,
Were James and Peter,—nay, declared as well
This lad was very John,—I could believe!
—Could, for a moment, doubtlessly believe:
So is myself withdrawn into my depths,
The soul retreated from the perished brain
Whence it was wont to feel and use the world
Through these dull members, done with long ago.
Yet I myself remain; I feel myself: 80
    And there is nothing lost. Let be, awhile!"
This is the doctrine he was wont to teach,
How divers persons witness in each man,
Three souls which make up one soul: first, to wit,
A soul of each and all the bodily parts,
    Seated therein, which works, and is what Does,
    And has the use of earth, and ends the man
    Downward: but, tending upward for advice,
    Grows into, and again is grown into
    By the next soul, which, seated in the brain, 90
    Useth the first with its collected use,
    And feeleth, thinketh, willeth,—is what Knows:
    Which, duly tending upward in its turn,
    Grows into, and again is grown into
    By the last soul, that uses both the first,
    Subsisting whether they assist or no,
    And, constituting mans self, is what Is—
    And leans upon the former, makes it play,
    As that played off the first: and, tending up,
    Holds, is upheld by, God, and ends the man loo
    Upward in that dread point of intercourse,
    Nor needs a place, for it returns to Him.
What Does, what Knows, what Is; three souls, one man. I give the glossa of
Theotypas.
    And then, "A stick, once fire from end to end;
    Now, ashes save the tip that holds a spark!
    Yet, blow the spark, it runs back, spreads itself
    A little where the fire was: thus I urge
    The soul that served me, till it task once more
    What ashes of my brain have kept their shape, HO

And these make effort on the last o the flesh,
Trying to taste again the truth of things–"
(He smiled)–" their very superficial truth;
As that ye are my sons, that it is long
Since James and Peter had release by death,
And I am only he, your brother John,
Who saw and heard, and could remember all.
Remember all! It is not much to say.
What if the truth broke on me from above
As once and oft-times? Such might hap again: 120
Doubtlessly He might stand in presence here,
With head wool-white, eyes flame, and feet like brass,
The sword and the seven stars, as I have seen– I who now shudder only and surmise
How did your brother bear that sight and live?
  "If I live yet, it is for good, more love
Through me to men: be naught but ashes here
That keep awhile my semblance, who was John,–
Still, when they scatter, there is left on earth
No one alive who knew (consider this!) 130 –Saw with his eyes and handled with his hands
That which was from the first, the Word of Life.
How will it be when none more saith I saw?
  "Such ever was loves way: to rise, it stoops.
  Since I, whom Christs mouth tauglu, was bidden teach, I went, for many years,
about the world,
Saying It was so; so I heard and saw,
Speaking as the case asked: and men believed.
Afterward came the message to myself
In Patmos isle; I was not bidden teach, 140
  But simply listen, take a book and write,
Nor set down other than the given word,
With nothing left to my arbitrament
To choose or change: I wrote, and men believed.
Then, for my time grew brief, no message more,
No call to write again, I found a way,
And, reasoning from my knowledge, merely taught
Men should, for loves sake, in loves strength believe;
  Or I would pen a letter to a friend
  And urge the same as friend, nor less nor more: 150
Friends said I reasoned rightly, and believed.
But at the last, why, I seemed left alive
Like a sea-jelly weak on Patmos strand,
To tell dry sea-beach gazers how I fared
When there was mid-sea, and the mighty things;
Left to repeat, I saw, I heard, I knew,

And go all over the old ground again,
With Antichrist already in the world,
And many Antichrists, who answered prompt
Am I not Jasper as thyself art John? 160
Nay, young, whereas through age thou mayest forget:
Wherefore, explain, or how shall we believe?
I never thought to call down fire on such,
Or, as in wonderful and early days,
Pick up the scorpion, tread the serpent dumb;
But patient stated much of the Lords life
Forgotten or misdelivered, and let it work:
Since much that at the first, in deed and word,
Lay simply and sufficiently exposed,
Had grown (or else my soul was grown to match, 170
Fed through such years, familiar with such light,
Guarded and guided still to see and speak)
Of new significance and fresh result;
What first were guessed as points, I now knew stars,
And named them in the Gospel I have writ.
For men said, It is getting long ago:
Where is the promise of His coming?–asked
These young ones in their strength, as loth to wait,
Of me who, when their sires were born, was old.
I, for I loved them, answered, joyfully, 180
Since I was there, and helpful in my age;
And, in the main, I think such men believed-
Finally, thus endeavoring, I fell sick,
Ye brought me here, and I supposed the end,
And went to sleep with one thought that, at least,
Though the whole earth should lie in wickedness,
/ We had the truth, might leave the rest to God.
Yet now I wake in such decrepitude
As I had slidden down and fallen afar,
Past even the presence of my former self, 190
    Grasping the while for stay at facts which snap,
Till I am found away from my own world,
Feeling for foot-hold through a blank profound,
Along with unborn people in strange lands,
Who say–I hear said or conceive they say–
Was John at all, and did he say he saw?
Assure us, ere we ask what he might see!
    "And how shall I assure them? Can they share –They, who have flesh, a veil of
youth and strength About each spirit, that needs must bide its time, zoo Living and
learning still as years assist
    Which wear the thickness thin, and let man see–

With me who hardly am withheld at all,
But shudderingly, scarce a shred between,
Lie bare to the universal prick of light?
Is it for nothing we grow old and weak,
We whom God loves? When pain ends, gain ends too.
To me, that story–ay, that Life and Death
Of which I wrote it was–to me, it is; –Is, here and now: I apprehend naught else. 21
o Is not God now i the world His power first made? Is not His love at issue still with
sin,
Visibly when a wrong is done on earth?
Love, wrong, and pain, what see I else around?
Yea, and the Resurrection and Uprise
To the right hand of the throne–what is it beside,
When such truth, breaking bounds, oerfloods my soul,
And, as i saw the sin and death, even so
See I the need yet transiency of both,
The good and glory consummated thence? 220 I saw the power; I see the Love, once
weak,
Resume the Power: and in this word I see,
Lo, there is recognized the Spirit of both
(That moving oer the spirit of man, unblinds
His eye and bids him look. These are, I see;
But ye, the children, His beloved ones too,
Ye need,–as I should use an optic glass
I wondered at erewhile, somewhere i the world,
It had been given a crafty smith to make;
A tube, he turned on objects brought too close, 230
Lying confusedly insubordinate
For the unassisted eye to master once:
Look through his tube, at distance now they lay,
Become succinct, distinct, so small, so clear!
Just thus, ye needs must apprehend what truth
I see, reduced to plain historic fact,
Diminished into clearness, proved a point
And far away: ye would withdraw your sense
From out eternity, strain it upon time,
Then stand before that fact, that Life and Death, 240
Stay there at gaze, till it dispart, dispread,
As though a star should open out, all sides,
Grow the world on you, as it is my world.
"For life, with all it yields of joy and woe,
And hope and fear,–believe the aged friend,–
Is just our chance o the prize of learning love,
How love might be, hath been indeed, and is;
And that we hold thenceforth to the uttermost

Such prize despite the envy of the world,
And, having gained truth, keep truth: that is all. 250
But see the double way wherein we are led,
How the soul learns diversely from the flesh!
With flesh, that hath so little time to stay,
And yields mere basement for the souls emprise,
Expect prompt teaching. Helpful was the light,
And warmth was cherishing and food was choice
To every mans flesh, thousand years ago,
As now to yours and mine; the body sprang
At once to the height, and stayed: but the soul,–no!
Since sages who, this noontide, meditate 260 In Rome or Athens, may descry some point
Of the eternal power, hid yestereve;
And, as thereby the powers whole mass extends,
So much extends the sther floating oer,
The love that tops the might, the Christ in God.
Then, as new lessons shall be learned in these
Till earths work stop and useless time run out,
So duly, daily, needs provision be
For keeping the souls prowess possible,
Building new barriers as the old decay, 270
Saving us from evasion of lifes proof,
Putting the question ever, Does God love,
And will ye hold that truth against the world?
Ye know there needs no second proof with good
Gained for our flesh from any earthly source:
We might go freezing, ages,–give us fire,
Thereafter we judge fire at its full worth,
And guard it safe through every chance, ye know!
That fable of Prometheus and his theft, 279
How mortals gained Joves fiery flower, grows old (I have been used to hear the pagans own)
And out of mind; but fire, howeer its birth,
Here is it, precious to the sophist now
Who laughs the myth of Eschylus to scorn,
As precious to those satyrs of his play,
Who touched it in gay wonder at the thing.
While were it so with the soul,–this gift of truth
Once grasped, were this our souls gain safe, and sure
To prosper as the bodys gain is wont,–
Why, mans probation would conclude, his earth 290
Crumble; for he both reasons and decides,
Weighs first, then chooses: will he give up fire
For gold or purple once he knows its worth?

Could he give Christ up were His worth as plain?
Therefore, I say, to test man, the proofs shift,
Nor may he grasp that fact like other fact,
And straightway in his life acknowledge it,
As, say, the indubitable bliss of fire.
Sigh ye, It had been easier once than now?
To give you answer I am left alive; 300
Look at me who was present from the first!
Ye know what things I saw; then came a test,
My first, befitting me who so had seen:
Forsake the Christ thou sawest transfigured, Him
Who trod the sea and brought the dead to life?
What should wring this from thee!–ye laugh and ask.
What wrung it? Even a torchlight and a noise,
The sudden Roman faces, violent hands,
And fear of what the Jews might do! Just that,
And it is written, I forsook and fled: 310
There was my trial, and it ended thus.
Ay, but my soul had gained its truth, could grow:
Another year or two,–what little child,
What tender woman that had seen no least
Of all my sights, but barely heard them told,
Who did not clasp the cross with a light laugh,
Or wrap the burning robe round, thanking God?
Well, was truth safe forever, then? Not so.
Already had begun the silent work
Whereby truth, deadened of its absolute blaze, 320
Might need loves eye to pierce the oerstretched doubt.
Teachers were busy, whispering All is true
As the aged ones report; but youth can reach
Where age gropes dimly, weak with stir and strain,
And the full doctrine slumbers till to-day.
Thus, what the Romans lowered spear was found,
A bar to me who touched and handled truth,
Now proved the glozing of some new shrewd tongue,
This Ebion, this Cerinthus or their mates,
Till imminent was the outcry Save our Christ! 330
Whereon I stated much of the Lords life
Forgotten or misdelivered, and let it work.
Such work done, as it will be, what comes next?
What do I hear say, or conceive men say,
Was John at all, and did he say he saw?
Assure us, ere we ask what he might see!
Is this indeed a burthen for late days,
And may I help to bear it with you all,

Using my weakness which becomes your strength?
For if a babe were born inside this grot, 340
Grew to a boy here, heard us praise the sun,
Yet had but yon sole glimmer in lights place,–
One loving him and wishful he should learn,
Would much rejoice himself was blinded first
Month by month here, so made to understand
How eyes, born darkling, apprehend amiss:- I think I could explain to such a child
There was more glow outside than gleams he caught,
M. W.–13
Ay, nor need urge I saw it, so believe!
It is a heavy burthen you shall bear 3 50 In latter days, new lands, or old grown strange,
    Left without me, which must be very soon.
What is the doubt, my brothers? Quick with it!
I see you stand conversing, each new face,
Either in fields, of yellow summer eves,
On islets yet unnamed amid the sea;
Or pace for shelter neath a portico
Out of the crowd in some enormous town
Where now the larks sing in a solitude;
Or muse upon blank heaps of stone and sand 360 Idly conjectured to be Ephesus:
And no one asks his fellow any more
Where is the promise of His coming? but
Was he revealed in any of His lives,
As Power, as Love, as Influencing Soul?
"Quick, for time presses, tell the whole mind out,
And let us ask and answer and be saved!
My book speaks on, because it cannot pass;
One listens quietly, nor scoffs but pleads
Here is a tale of things done ages since; 370
    What truth was ever told the second day?
Wonders, that would prove doctrine, go for naught.
Remains the doctrine, love; well, we must love,
And what we love most, power and love in one,
Let us acknowledge on the record here,
Accepting these in Christ: must Christ then be?
Has He been? Did not we ourselves make Him?
Our mind receives but what it holds, no more.
First of the love, then; we acknowledge Christ–
A proof we comprehend His love, a proof 380
    We had such love already in ourselves,
    Knew first what else we should not recognize.
    T is mere projection from mans inmost mind,
    And, what he loves, thus falls reflected back,,

Becomes accounted somewhat out of him;
He throws it up in air, it drops down earths,
With shape, name, story added, mans old way.
How prove you Christ came otherwise at least?
Next try the power: He made and rules the world:
Certes there is a world once made, now ruled, 390
Unless things have been ever as we see.
Our sires declared a charioteers yoked steeds
Brought the sun up the east and down the west,
Which only of itself now rises, sets,
As if a hand impelled it and a will,–
Thus they long thought, they who had will and hands:
But the new questions whisper is distinct,
Wherefore must all force needs be like ourselves?
We have the hands, the will; what made and drives
The sun is force, is law, is named, not known, 400
While will and love we do know; marks of these,
Eye-witnesses attest, so books declare–
As that, to punish or reward our race,
The sun at undue times arose or set
Or else stood still: what do not men affirm?
But earth requires as urgently reward
Or punishment to-day as years ago,
And none expects the sun will interpose:
Therefore it was mere passion and mistake,
Or erring zeal for right, which changed the truth. 410
Go back, far, farther, to the birth of things;
Ever the will, the intelligence, the love,
Mans!–which he gives, supposing he but finds,
As late he gave head, body, hands and feet,
To help these in what forms he called his gods.
First, Joves brow, Junos eyes were swept away,
But Joves wrath, Junos pride continued long;
As last, will, power, and love discarded these,
So law in turn discards power, love, and will.
What proveth God is otherwise at least? 420
All else, projection from the mind of man!
    "Nay, do not give me wine, for I am strong, But place my gospel where I put my hands.
    "I say that man was made to grow, not stop;
That help, he needed once, and needs no more,
Having grown but an inch by, is withdrawn:
For he hath new needs, and new helps to these.
This imports solely, man should mount on each
New height in view; the help whereby he mounts,

The ladder-rung his foot has left, may fall, 430
Since all things suffer change save God the Truth.
Man apprehends Him newly at each stage
Whereat earths ladder drops, its service done;
And nothing shall prove twice what once was proved.
You stick a garden-plot with ordered twigs
To show inside lie germs of herbs unborn,
And check the careless step would spoil their birth;
But when herbs wave, the guardian twigs may go,
Since should ye doubt of virtues, question kinds, It is no longer for old twigs ye look, 440
Which proved once underneath lay store of seed,
But to the herbs self, by what light ye boast,
For what fruits signs are. This books fruit is plain,
Nor miracles need prove it any more.
Doth the fruit show? Then miracles bade ware
At first of root and stem, saved both till now
From trampling ox, rough boar and wanton goat.
What? Was man made a wheelwork to wind up,
And be discharged, and straight wound up anew?
No!–grown, his growth lasts; taught, he neer
forgets: 450
May learn a thousand things, not twice the same.
"This might be pagan teaching: now hear mine.
"I say, that as the babe, you feed awhile,
Becomes a boy and fit to feed himself,
So, minds at first must be spoon-fed with truth:
When they can eat, babes-nurture is withdrawn.
I fed the babe whether it would or no: I bid the boy or feed himself or starve.
I cried once, That ye may believe in Christ,
Behold this blind man shall receive his sight! 460 I cry now, Urgest ihou, for I am shrewd
And smile at stories bow Johns word could cure –
Repeat that miracle and take my faith?
I say, that miracle was duly wrought
When, save for it, no faith was possible.
Whether a change were wrought i the shows o the world,
Whether the change came from our minds which see
Of shows o the world so much as and no more
Than God wills for His purpose,–(what do I
See now, suppose you, there where you see rock 470
Round us?)–I know not; such was the effect,
So faith grew, making void more miracles
Because too much: they would compel, not help.
I say, the acknowledgment of God in Christ

Accepted by thy reason, solves for thee
All questions in the earth and out of it,
And has so far advanced thee to be wise.
    Wouldst thou unprove this to re-prove the proved?
In lifes mere minute, with power to use that proof,
Leave knowledge and revert to how it sprung? 480
Thou hast it; use it and forthwith, or die!
    "For I say, this is death and the sole death,
When a mans loss comes to him from his gain,
Darkness from light, from knowledge ignorance,
And lack of love from love made manifest;
A lamps death when, replete with oil, it chokes;
A stomachs when, surcharged with food, it starves.
With ignorance was surety of a cure.
When man, appalled at nature, questioned first
What if there lurk a might behind this might? 490
He needed satisfaction God could give,
And did give, as ye have the written word:
But when he finds might still redouble might,
Yet asks, Since all is might, what use of will?
–Will, the one source of might,–he being man
With a mans will and a mans might, to teach In little how the two combine in large,–
    That man has turned round on himself and stands,
Which in the course of nature is, to die. 499
    "And when man questioned, What if there be love
Behind the will and might, as real as they?–
He needed satisfaction God could give,
And did give, as ye have the written word:
But when, beholding that love everywhere,
He reasons, Since such love is everywhere,
And since ourselves can love and would be loved,
We ourselves make the love, and Christ was not,–
How shall ye help this man who knows himself,
That he must love and would be loved again,
    Yet, owning his own lovethat proveth Christ, Jio
Rejecteth Christ through very need of Him?
The lamp oerswims with oil, the stomach flags
Loaded with nurture, and that mans soul dies.
    "If he rejoin, But this was all the while
A trick; the fault was, first of all, in thee,
Thy story of the places, names and dates,
Where, when and how the ultimate truth had rise, –Thy prior truth, at last discovered none,
Whence now the second suffers detriment.

What good of giving knowledge if, because 520
O the manner of the gift, its profit fail?
And why refuse what modicum of help
Had stopped the after-doubt, impossible I the face of truth–truth absolute, uniform?
Why must I hit of this and miss of that,
Distinguish just as I be weak or strong,
And not ask of thee and have answer prompt,
Was this once, was it not once?–then and now
And evermore, plain truth from man to man.
Is Johns procedure just the heathen bards? 530
Put question of his famous play again
How for the ephemerals sake Joves fire was filched,
And carried in a cane and brought to earth:
The fact is in the fable, cry the wise,
Mortals obtained the boon, so much is fact,
Though fire be spirit and produced on earth.
As with the Titans, so now with thy tale:
Why breed in us perplexity, mistake,
Nor tell the whole truth in the proper words?
"I answer, Have ye yet to argue out 540
The very primal thesis, plainest law, –Man is not God but hath Gods end to serve,
A master to obey, a course to take,
Somewhat to cast off, somewhat to become?
Grant this, then man must pass from old to new,
From vain to real, from mistake to fact,
From what once seemed good, to what now proves best.
How could man have progression otherwise?
Before the point was mooted What is God?
No savage man inquired What am myself? 550
Much less replied, First, last, and best of things.
Man takes that title now if he believes
Might can exist with neither will nor love, In Gods case–what he names now
Natures Law–
While in himself he recognizes love
No less than might and will: and rightly takes.
Since if man prove the sole existent thing
Where these combine, whatever their degree,
However weak the might or will or love,
So they be found there, put in evidence,–560
He is as surely higher in the scale
Than any might with neither love nor will,
As life, apparent in the poorest midge, (When the faint dust-speck flits, ye guess
its wing) Is marvellous beyond dead Atlas self–
Given to the nobler midge for resting-place!
Thus, man proves best and highest–God, in fine,

And thus the victory leads but to defeat,
The gain to loss, best rise to the worst fall,
His life becomes impossible, which is death. 570
"But if, appealing thence, he cower, avouch
He is mere man, and in humility
Neither may know God nor mistake himself; I point to the immediate consequence
And say, by such confession straight he falls Into mans place, a thing nor God nor beast, /
Made to know that he can know and not more:
Lower than God who knows all and can all,
Higher than beasts which know and can so far
As each beasts limit, perfect to an end, 580
Nor conscious that they know, nor craving more;
While man knows partly but conceives beside,
Creeps ever on from fancies to the fact,
And in this striving, this converting air Into a solid he may grasp and use,
Finds progress, mans distinctive mark alone,
Not Gods, and not the beasts: God is, they are,
Man partly is and wholly hopes to be.
Such progress could no more attend his soul
Were all it struggles after found at first 590
And guesses changed to knowledge absolute,
Than motion wait his body, were all else
Than it the solid earth on every side,
Where now through space he moves from rest to rest.
Man, therefore, thus conditioned, must expect
He could not, what he knows now, know at first;
What he considers that he knows to-day,
Come but to-morrow, he will find misknown;
Getting increase of knowledge, since he learns
Because he lives, which is to be a man, 600
Set to instruct himself by his past self:
First, like the brute, obliged by facts to learn,
Next, as man may, obliged by his own mind,
Bent, habit, nature, knowledge turned to law.
Gods gift was that man should conceive of truth
And yearn to gain it, catching at mistake,
As midway help till he reach fact indeed.
The statuary ere he mould a shape
Boasts a like gift, the shapes idea, and next
The aspiration to produce the same; 6lo
So, taking clay, he calls his shape thereout,
Cries ever Now I have the thing I see:
Yet all the while goes changing what was wrought,
I From falsehood like the truth, to truth itself.

How were it had he cried I see no face,
No breast, no feet i the ineffectual clay?
Rather commend him that he clapped his hands,
And laughed It is my shape and lives again!
Enjoyed the falsehood, touched it on to truth,
Until yourselves applaud the flesh indeed 620 In what is still flesh-imitating clay.
Right in you, right in him, such way be mans!
God only makes the live shape at a jet.
Will ye renounce this pact of creatureship?
The pattern on the Mount subsists no more,
Seemed awhile, then returned to nothingness;
But copies, Moses strove to make thereby,
Serve still and are replaced as time requires:
By these, make newest vessels, reach the type!
If ye demur, this judgment on your head, 630
  Never to reach the ultimate, angels law,
Indulging every instinct of the soul
There where law, life, joy, impulse are one thing!
  "Such is the burthen of the latest time.
  I have survived to hear it with my ears,
  Answer it with my lips: does this suffice?
  For if there be a further woe than such,
  Wherein my brothers struggling need a hand,
  So long as any pulse is left in mine,
  May I be absent even longer yet, 640
  Plucking the blind ones back from the abyss,
  Though I should tarry a new hundred years!"
  But he was dead; t was about noon, the day
Somewhat declining: we five buried him
That eve, and then, dividing, went five ways,
And I, disguised, returned to Ephesus.
  By this, the caves mouth must be filled with sand.
  Valens is lost, I know not of his trace;
  The Bactrian was but a wild childish man,
  And could not write nor speak, but only loved: 650
  So, lest the memory of this go quite,
  Seeing that I to-morrow fight the beasts, I tell the same to Phoebas, whom believe!
  For many look again to find that face,
  Beloved Johns to whom I ministered,
  Somewhere in life about the world; they err:
  Either mistaking what was darkly spoke
  At ending of his book, as he relates,
  Or misconceiving somewhat of this speech
  Scattered from mouth to mouth, as I suppose. 6flo
  Believe ye will not see him any more

About the world with his divine regard!
For all was as I say, and now the man
Lies as he lay once, breast to breast with God.
Cerinthus read and mused; one added this:
"If Christ, as thou afermest, be of men
Mere man, the first and best but nothing more,–
Account Him, for reward of what He was,
Now and forever, wretchedest of all.
For see; Himself conceived of life as love, 670
Conceived of love as what must enter in,
Fill up, make one with His each soul He loved:
Thus much for mans joy, all mens joy for Him.
Well, He is gone, thou sayest, to fit reward.
But by this time are many souls set free,
And very many still retained alive:
Nay, should His coming be delayed awhile,
Say, ten years longer (twelve years, some compute)
See if, for every finger of thy hands,
There be not found, that day the world shall end, 680
Hundreds of souls, each holding by Christs word
That He will grow incorporate with all,
With me as Pamphylax, with him as John,
Groom for each bride! Can a mere man do this?
Yet Christ saith, this He lived and died to do.
Call Christ, then, the illimitable God,
Or lost!"
But t was Cerinthus that is lost.

CALIBAN UPON SETEBOS; OR, NATURAL THEOLOGY IN THE ISLAND.

"Thou thoughtest that I was altogether such a one as thyself."

wlll sprawl, now that the heat of day is best,
Flat on his belly in the pits much mire,
With elbows wide, fists clenched to prop his chin.
And, while he kicks both feet in the cool slush,
And feels about his spine small eft-things course,
Run in and out each arm, and make him laugh:
And while above his head a pompion-plant,
Coating the cave-top as a brow its eye,
Creeps down to touch and tickle hair and beard,
And now a flower drops with a bee inside, 1O
And now a fruit to snap at, catch and crunch,–
He looks out oer yon sea which sunbeams cross
And recross till they weave a spider-web
(Meshes of fire, some great fish breaks at times)
And talks to his own self, howeer he please,
Touching that other, whom his dam called God.

Because to talk about Him, vexes–ha,
Could He but know! and time to vex is now,
When talk is safer than in winter-time.
Moreover Prosper and Miranda sleep 20 In confidence he drudges at their task,
And it is good to cheat the pair, and gibe,
Letting the rank tongue blossom into speech.
    Setebos, Setebos, and Setebos!
    Thinketh, He dwelleth i the cold o the moon.
    Thinketh He made it, with the sun to match,
    But not the stars; the stars came otherwise;
    Only made clouds, winds, meteors, such as that:
    Also this isle, what lives and grows thereon,
    And snaky sea which rounds and ends the same. 30
    Thinketh, it came of being ill at ease:
    He hated that He cannot change His cold,
    Nor cure its ache. Hath spied an icy fish
    That longed to scape the rock-stream where she lived,
    And thaw herself within the lukewarm brine
    O the lazy sea her stream thrusts far amid,
    A crystal spike twixt two warm walls of wave;
    Only, she ever sickened, found repulse
    At the other kind of water, not her life, (Green-dense and dim-delicious, bred o the
sun) 40
    Flounced back from bliss she was not born to breathe,
    And in her old bounds buried her despair,
    Hating and loving warmth alike: so He.
    Thinketh, He made thereat the sun, this isle,
    Trees and the fowls here, beast and creeping thing.
    Yon otter, sleek-wet, black, lithe as a leech;
    Yon auk, one fire-eye in a ball of foam,
    That floats and feeds; a certain badger brown
    He hath watched hunt with that slant white-wedge eye
    By moonlight; and the pie with the long tongue 50
    That pricks deep into oakwarts for a worm,
    And says a plain word when she finds her prize,
    But will not eat the ants; the ants themselves
    That build a wall of seeds and settled stalks
    About their hole–He made all these and more,
    Made all we see, and us, in spjte: how else?
    He could not, Himself, make a second self
    To be His mate; as well have made Himself:
    He would not make what he mislikes or slights,
    An eyesore to Him, or not worth His pains: 60
    But did, in envy, listlessness or sport,
    Make what Himself would fain, in a manner, be–

Weaker in most points, stronger in a few,
Worthy, and yet mere playthings all the while,
Things He admires and mocks too,–that is it.
Because, so brave, so better though they be, It nothing skills if He begin to plague.
Look now, I melt a gourd-fruit into mash,
Add honeycomb and pods, I have perceived,
Which bite like finches when they bill and kiss,–70
Then, when froth rises bladdery, drink up all,
Quick, quick, till maggots scamper through my brain;
Last, throw me on my back i the seeded thyme,
And wanton, wishing I were born a bird.
Put case, unable to be what I wish, I yet could make a live bird out of clay:
Would not I take clay, pinch my Caliban
Able to fly?–for, there, see, he hath wings,
And great comb like the hoopoes to admire,
And there, a sting to do his foes offence, 80
There, and I will that he begin to live,
Fly to yon rock-top, nip me off the horns
Of grigs high up that make the merry din,
Saucy through their veined wings, and mind me not.
In which feat, if his leg snapped, brittle clay,
And he lay stupid-like,–why, I should laugh;
And if he, spying me, should fall to weep,
Beseech me to be good, repair his wrong,
Bid his poor leg smart less or grow again,–
Well, as the chance were, this might take or else 90
Not take my fancy: I might hear his cry,
And give the mankin three sound legs for one,
Or pluck the other off, leave him like an egg,
And lessoned he was mine and merely clay.
Were this no pleasure, lying in the thyme,
Drinking the mash, with brain become alive,
Making and marring clay at will? So He.
    Thinketh, such shows nor right nor wrong in Him,
Nor kind, nor cruel: He is strong and Lord.
Am strong myself compared to yonder crabs loo
    That march now from the mountain to the sea;
Let twenty pass, and stone the twenty-first,
Loving not, hating not, just choosing so.
Say, the first straggler that boasts purple spots
Shall join the file, one pincer twisted off;
Say, this bruised fellow shall receive a worm,
And two worms he whose nippers end in red;
As it likes me each time, I do: so He.

Well then, supposeth He is good i the main,
Placable if His mind and ways were guessed, no
But rougher than His handiwork, be sure!
Oh, He hath made things worthier than Himself,
And envieth that, so helped, such things do more
Than He who made them! What consoles but this?
That they, unless through Him, do naught at all,
And must submit: what other use in things?
Hath cut a pipe of pithless elder-joint
That, blown through, gives exact the scream o the jay
When from her wing you twitch the feathers blue:
Sound this, and little birds that hate the jay 1 20
Flock within stones throw, glad their foe is hurt:
Put case such pipe could prattle and boast forsooth
"I catch the birds, I am the crafty thing,
I make the cry my maker cannot make
With his great round mouth; he must blow through mine! "
Would not I smash it with my foot? So He.
But wherefore rough, why cold and ill at ease?
Aha, that is a question! Ask, for that,
What knows,–the something over Setebos 1 29
That made Him, or He, may be, found and fought,
Worsted, drove off and did to nothing, perchance.
There may be something quiet oer His head,
Out of His reach, that feels nor joy nor grief,
Since both derive from weakness in some way.
I joy because the quails come; would not joy
Could I bring quails here when I have a mind:
This Quiet, all it hath a mind to, doth.
Esteemeth stars the outposts of its couch,
But never spends much thought nor care that way.
It may look up, work up,–the worse for those 140 It works on! Careth but for
Setebos
The many-handed as a cuttle-fish,
Who, making Himself feared through what He does,
Looks up, first, and perceives he cannot soar
To what is quiet and hath happy life;
Next looks down here, and out of very spite
Makes this a bauble-world to ape yon real,
These good things to match those as hips do grapes.
T is solace making baubles, ay, and sport.
Himself peeped late, eyed Prosper at his books 150
Careless and lofty, lord now of the isle:
Vexed, stitched a book of broad leaves, arrow-shaped,
Wrote thereon, he knows what, prodigious words;

Has peeled a wand and called itby a name;
Weareth at whiles for an enchanters robe
The eyed skin of a supple oncelot;
And hath an ounce sleeker than youngling mole,
A four-legged serpent he makes cower and couch,
Now snarl, now hold its breath and mind his eye,
And saith she is Miranda and my wife: 160
Keeps for his Ariel a tall pouch-bill crane
He bids go wade for fish and straight disgorge;
Also a sea-beast, lumpish, which he snared,
Blinded the eyes of, and brought somewhat tame,
And split its toe-webs, and now pens the drudge In a hole o the rock and calls him
Caliban;
A bitter heart that bides its time and bites.
Plays thus at being Prosper in a way,
Taketh his mirth with make-believes: so He.
His dam held that the Quiet made all things 170
Which Setebos vexed only: holds not so.
Who made them weak, meant weakness He might vex.
Had He meant other, while His hand was in,
Why not make horny eyes no thorn could prick,
M. W.–14
Or plate my scalp with bone against the snow,
Or overscale my flesh neath joint and joint,
Like an ores armor? Ay,–so spoil His sport!
He is the One now: only He doth all.
Saith, He may like, perchance, what profits Him.
Ay, himself loves what does him good; but why? 180
Gets good no otherwise. This blinded beast
Loves whoso places flesh-meat on his nose,
But, had he eyes, would want no help, but hate
Or love, just as it liked him: He hath eyes.
Also it pleaseth Setebos to work,
Use all His hands, and exercise much craft,
By no means for the love of what is worked.
Tasteth, himself, no finer good i the world
When all goes right, in this safe summer-time,
And he wants little, hungers, aches not much, 190
Than trying what to do with wit and strength.
Falls to make something: piled yon pile of turfs,
And squared and stuck there squares of soft white chalk,
And, with a fish-tooth, scratched a moon on each,
And set up endwise certain spikes of tree,
And crowned the whole with a sloths skull a-top,
Found dead i the woods, too hard for one to kill.

No use at all i the work, for works sole sake;
Shall some day knock it down again: so He.
Saith He is terrible: watch His feats in proof! 200
One hurricane will spoil six good months hope.
He hath a spite against me, that I know,
Just as He favors Prosper, who knows why?
So it is, all the same, as well I find.
Wove wattles half the winter, fenced them firm
With stone and stake to stop she-tortoises
Crawling to lay their eggs here: well, one wave,
  Feeling the foot of Him upon its neck,
  Gaped as a snake does, lolled out its large tongue,
  And licked the whole labor flat; so much for spite. 210
  Saw a ball flame down late (yonder it lies)
  Where, half an hour before, I slept i the shade:
  Often they scatter sparkles: there is force!
  Dug up a newt He may have envie. i once
  And turned to stone, shut up inside a stone.
  Please Him and hinder this?–What Prosper does?
  Aha, if He would tell me how! Not He!
  There is the sport: discover how or die!
  All need not die, for of the things o the isle
  Some flee afar, some dive, some run up trees; 220
  Those at His mercy,–why, they please Him most
  When. when. well, never try the same way twice!
  Repeat what act has pleased, He may grow wroth.
  You must not know His ways, and play Him off,
  Sure of the issue. Doth the like himself:
  Spareth a squirrel that it nothing fears
  But steals the nut from underneath my thumb,
  And when I threat, bites stoutly in defence:
  Spareth an urchin that contrariwise,
  Curls up into a ball, pretending death 230
  For fright at my approach: the two ways please.
  But what would move my choler more than this,
  That either creature counted on its life
  To-morrow and next day and all days to come,
  Saying, forsooth, in the inmost of its heart,
  "Because he did so yesterday with me,
  And otherwise with such another brute,
  So must he do henceforth and always."–Ay?
  Would teach the reasoning couple what "must"
means! Doth as he likes, or wherefore Lord? So He. 24.0 Conceiveth all things
will continue thus,
  And we shall have to live in fear of Him

So long as He lives, keeps His strength: no change, If He have done His best, make
no new world

To please Him more, so leave off watching this,– If He surprise not even the Quiets
self

Some strange day,–or, suppose, grow into it

As grubs grow butterflies: else, here are we,

And there is He, and nowhere help at all.

Believeth with the life, the pain shall stop. 250

His dam held different, that after death

He both plagued enemies and feasted friends: Idly! He doth His worst in this our
life,

Giving just respite lest we die through pain,

Saving last pain for worst,–with which, an end.

Meanwhile, the best way to escape His ire Is, not to seem too happy. Sees, himself,

Yonder two flies, with purple films and pink,

Bask on the pompion-bell above: kills both.

Sees two black painful beetles roll their ball 260

On head and tail as if to save their lives:

Moves them the stick away they strive to clear.

Even so, would have Him misconceive, suppose

This Caliban strives hard and ails no less,

And always, above all else, envies Him;

Wherefore he mainly dances on dark nights,

Moans in the sun, gets under holes to laugh,

And never speaks his mind save housed as now:

Outside, groans, curses. If He caught me here,

Oerheard this speech, and asked "What chucklest
at?" 270

Would, to appease Him, cut a finger off,

Or of my three kid yearlings burn the best,

Or let the toothsome apples rot on tree,

Or push my tame beast for the ore to taste:

While myself lit a fire, and made a song

And sung it, " What I hate, be consecrate

To celebrate Thee and Thy state, no mate

For Thee; what see for envy in poor me? "

Hoping the while, since evils sometimes mend,

Warts rub away and sores are cured with slime, 280

That some strange day, will either the Quiet catch

And conquer Setebos, or likelier He

Decrepit may doze, doze, as good as die.

What, what? A curtain oer the world at once!

Crickets stop hissing; not a bird–or, yes,

There scuds His raven that has told Him all!

It was fools play, this prattling! Ha! The wind

Shoulders the pillared dust, deaths house o the move,
And fast invading fires begin! White blaze–
A trees head snaps–and there, there, there, there,
there,, 290
    His thunder follows! Fool to gibe at Him!
Lo! Lieth flat and loveth Setebos!
Maketh his teeth meet through his upper lip,
Will let those quails fly, will not eat this month
One little mess of whelks, so he may scape! J
    CONFESSIONS.
    What is he buzzing in my ears?
    "Now that I come to die,
Do I view the world as a vale of tears? "
    Ah, reverend sir, not I!
    What I viewed there once, what I view again
    Where the physic bottles stand
On the tables edge,–is a suburb lane,
    With a wall to my bedside hand.
    ra.
    That lane sloped, much as the bottles do,
    From a house you could descry 10
    Oer the garden-wall: is the curtain blue
Or green to a healthy eye?
    nf,
    To mine, it serves for the old June weather
    Blue above lane and wall;
And that farthest bottle labelled "Ether"
    Is the house oertopping all.
    At a terrace, somewhere near the stopper,
    There watched for me, one June, A girl: I know, sir, its improper.
    My poor mind s out of tune. 20 v1.
    Only, there was a way. you crept
    Close by the side to dodge
Eyes in the house, two eyes except:
    They styled their house "The Lodge."
    vn.
    What right had a lounger up their lane?
    But, by creeping very close, With the good walls help,–their eyes might strain
    And stretch themselves to Oes, v111.
    Yet never catch her and me together,
    As she left the attic, there, 30
    By the rim of the bottle labelled " Ether,"
And stole from stair to stair,
    And stood by the rose-wreathed gate. Alas,
    We loved, sir–used fo meet: How sad and bad and mad it was–

But then, how it was sweet!
MAY AND DEATH.
I W1sh that when you died last May,
Charles, there had died along with you
    Three parts of springs delightful things;
Ay, and, for me, the fourth part too.
    A foolish thought, and worse, perhaps!
    There must be many a pair of friends Who, arm in arm, deserve the warm
    Moon-births and the long evening-ends.
    So, for their sake, be May still May!
    Let their new time, as mine of old, 10
    Do all it did for me: I bid
    Sweet sights and sounds throng manifold.
    1v.
    Only, one little sight, one plant,
    Woods have in May, that starts up green
Save a sole streak which, so to speak, Is springs blood, spilt its leaves between,–
    That, they might spare; a certain wood
    Might miss the plant; their loss were small:
But I,–wheneer the leaf grows there, Its drop comes from my heart, thats all. 20
DEAF AND DUMB.
A GROUP BY WOOLNER.
    Only the prisms obstruction shows aright
The secret of a sunbeam, breaks its light
Into the jewelled bow from blankest white;
    So may a glory from defect arise:
Only by Deafness may the vexed Love wreak
Its insuppressive sense on brow and cheek,
Only by Dumbness adequately speak
    As favored mouth could never, through the eyes, PROSPICE.
    Fear death?–to feel the fog in my throat,
    The mist in my face,
When the snows begin, and the blasts denote I am nearing the place,
The power of the night, the press of the storm.
    The post of the foe;
Where he stands, the Arch Fear in a visible form, j
    Yet the strong man must go:
For the journey is done and the summit attained,
    And the barriers fall, 10
    Though a battles to fight ere the guerdon be gained,
    The reward of it all.
I was ever a fighter, so–one fight more,
    The best and the last!
I would hate that death bandaged my eyes, and forbore,

And bade me creep past.
No! let me taste the whole of it, fare like my peers
    The heroes of old,
Bear the brunt, in a minute pay glad lifes arrears
    Of pain, darkness and cold. 20
    For sudden the worst turns the best to the brave,
    The black minute s at end,
And the elements rage, the fiend-voices that rave,
    Shall dwindle, shall blend,
Shall change, shall become first a peace out of pain,
    Then a light, then thy breast,
O thou soul of my soul! I shall clasp thee again,
    Aad with God be the rest!

EURYDICE TO ORPHEUS.

A PICTURE BY LEIGHTON.

But give them me, the mouth, the eyes, the brow!
    Let them once more absorb me! One look now
Will lap me round forever, not to pass
Out of its light, though darkness lie beyond:
Hold me but safe again within the bond
    Of one immortal look! All woe that was,
Forgotten, and all terror that may be,
Defied,—no past is mine, no future: look at me I

YOUTH AND ART.

It once might have been, once only:
    We lodged in a street together,
You, a sparrow on the housetop lonely, I, a lone she-bird of his feather.

    Your trade was with sticks and clay,
    You thumbed, thrust, patted and polished,
    Then laughed "They will see some day
Smith made, and Gibson demolished."

    My business was song, song, song; I chirped, cheeped, trilled and twittered, IO "
Kate Brown s on the boards ere long,
    And Grisis existence embittered J"
    1v.

I earned no more by a warble
Than you by a sketch in plaster; You wanted a piece of marble, I needed a music-
master.

    We studied hard in our styles,
    Chipped each at a crust like Hindoos,
    For air looked out on the tiles,
    For fun watched each others windows. 20 v1.

    You lounged, like a boy of the South,
    Cap and blouse—nay, a bit of beard too;

Or you got it, rubbing your mouth
With fingers the clay adhered to.
    v11.
And I–soon managed to find
Weak points in the flower-fence facing,
    Was forced to put up a blind
And be safe in my corset-lacing.
    v111.
No harm! It was not my fault If you never turned your eyes tail up, 30 As I shook
upon E in alt,
    Or ran the chromatic scale up: 1x.
For spring bade the sparrows pair,
And the boys and girls gave guesses,
    And stalls in our street looked rare
With bulrush and watercresses.
    Why did not you pinch a flower In a pellet of clay and fling it? Why did not I put
a power
    Of thanks in a look, or sing it? 40 x1.
I did look, sharp as a lynx, (And yet the memory rankles) When models arrived,
some minx
    Tripped up-stairs, she and her ankles.
    xn.
But I think I gave you as good!
"That foreign fellow,–who can know How she pays, in a playful mood,
    For his tuning her that piano?"
    x1n.
Could you say so, and never say
"Suppose we join hands and fortunes, 50
And I fetch her from over the way,
    Her, piano, and long tunes and short tunes"?
    X1v.
No, no: you would not be rash,
Nor I rasher and something over: Youve to settle yet Gibsons hash,
    And Grisi yet lives in clover.
    xv.
But you meet the Prince at the Board, Im queen myself at bah-pare, I ve married a
rich old lord,
    And you re dubbed knight and an R. A. 60 xv1.
Each life unfulfilled, you see; It hangs still, patchy and scrappy:
    We have not sighed deep, laughed free,
    Starved, feasted, despaired,–been happy.
    xvn.
And nobody calls you a dunce,
    And people suppose me clever:
This could but have happened once,

And we missed it, lost it forever.

A FACE.

If one could have that little head of hers

Painted upon a background of pale gold, Such as the Tuscans early art prefers!

No shade encroaching on the matchless mould Of those two lips, which should be opening soft In the pure profile; not as when she laughs, For that spoils all: but rather as if aloft

Yon hyacinth, she loves so, leaned its staffs

Burthen of honey-colored buds to kiss

And capture twixt the lips apart for this. 10

Then her lithe neck, three fingers might surround,

How it should waver on the pale gold ground

Up to the fruit-shaped, perfect chin it lifts!

I know, Correggio loves to mass, in rifts

Of heaven, his angel faces, orb on orb

Breaking its outline, burning shades absorb:

But these are only massed there, I should think,

Waiting to see some wonder momently

Grow out, stand full, fade slow against the sky (Thats the pale ground you d see this sweet face by), 20

All heaven, meanwhile, condensed into one eye Which fears to lose the wonder, should it wink.

A LIKENESS.

Some people hang portraits up In a room where they dine or sup:

And the wife clinks tea-things under, And her cousin, he stirs his cup,

Asks, "Who was the lady, I wonder? " "Tis a daub John bought at a sale,"

Quoth the wife,–looks black as thunder:

"What a shade beneath her nose!

Snuff-taking, I suppose,–"

Adds the cousin, while Johns corns ail. 10

Or else, there s no wife in the case,

But the portraits queen of the place,

Alone mid the other spoils

Of youth,–masks, gloves and foils,

And pipe-sticks, rose, cherry-tree, jasmine,

And the long whip, the tandem-lasher,

And the cast from a fist ("not, alas! mine,

But my masters, the Tipton Slasher"), And the cards where pistol-balls mark ace,

And a satin shoe used for cigar-case, 20

And the chamois-horns (" shot in the Chablais")

And prints–Rarey drumming on Cruiser,

And Sayers, our champion, the bruiser, And the little edition of Rabelais:

Where a friend, with both hands in his pockets,

May saunter up close to examine it,

And remark a good deal of Jane Lamb in it,

"But the eyes are half out of their sockets;
That hairs not so bad, where the gloss is,
But they ve made the girls nose a proboscis: 30
Jane Lamb, that we danced with at Vichy!
What, is not she Jane? Then, who is she? "
    All that I own is a print,
An etching, a mezzotint;
Tis a study, a fancy, a fiction,
Yet a fact (take my conviction)
Because it has more than a hint
    Of a certain face, I never
Saw elsewhere touch or trace of
In women I ve seen the face of: 40
    Just an etching, and, so far, clever.
    I keep my prints, an imbroglio,
Fifty in one portfolio.
When somebody tries my claret,
We turn round chairs to the fire,
Chirp over days in a garret,
    Chuckle oer increase of salary,
Taste the good fruits of our leisure,
Talk about pencil and lyre,
    And the National Portrait Gallery: 50
    Then I exhibit my treasure.
After we ve turned over twenty,
    And the debt of wonder my crony owes Is paid to my Marc Antonios,
He stops me–" Festina lente!
Whats that sweet thing there, the etching? "
How my waistcoat-strings want stretching,
    How my cheeks grow red as tomatos, How my heart leaps! But hearts, after leaps,
ache.
    "By the by, you must take, for a keepsake, 60
    That other, you praised, of Volpatos." The fool! would he try a flight further and
say–He never saw, never before to-day, What was able to take his breath away, A face
to lose youth for, to occupy age With the dream of, meet death with,–why, I ll not
engage
    But that, half in a rapture and half in a rage,
I should toss him the things self–" Tis only a duplicate,
A thing of no value! Take it, I supplicate! "
    MR. SLUDGE, "THE MEDIUM."
    Now, dont, sir! Dont expose me! Just this once!
    This was the first and only time, I ll swear,–
    Look at me,–see, I kneel,–the only time, I swear, I ever cheated,–yes, by the soul
Of rler who hears–(your sainted mother, sir!)
    All, except this last accident, was truth–

This little kind of slip!–and even this, It was your own wine, sir, the good champagne, (I took it for Catawba, you re so kind)

Which put the folly in my head!

"Get up?" 10

You still inflict on me that terrible face?

You show no mercy?–Not for Her dear sake,

The sainted spirits, whose soft breath even now

Blows on my cheek–(dont you feel something, sir?) You ll tell?

Go tell, then! Who the devil cares What such a rowdy chooses to.

Aie–aie–aie!

Please, sir! your thumbs are through my windpipe, sir! Ch–ch!

Well, sir, I hope you ve done it now! Oh Lord! I little thought, sir, yesterday, When your departed mother spoke those words 20 Of peace through me, and moved you, sir, so much, You gave me–(very kind it was of you) These shirt-studs–(better take them back again, Please, sir)–yes, little did I think so soon A trifle of trick, all through a glass too much Of his own champagne, would change my best of friends Into an angry gentleman!

Though, twas wrong.

I dont contest the point; your anger s just:

Whatever put such folly in my head,

I know twas wicked of me. Theres a thick 30

Dusk undeveloped spirit (I ve observed)

Owes me a grudge–a negros, I should say,

Or else an Irish emigrants; yourself

Explained the case so well last Sunday, sir,

When we had summoned Franklin to clear up

A point about those shares i the telegraph:

Ay, and he swore. or might it be Tom Paine?.

Thumping the table close by where I crouched,

He d do me soon a mischief: thats come true!

Why, now your face clears! I was sure it would! 40

Then, this one time. dont take your hand away,

M. W.–15

Through yours I surely kiss your mothers hand.

You ll promise to forgive me?–or, at least,

Tell nobody of this? Consider, sir!

What harm can mercy do? Would but the shade

Of the venerable dead-one just vouchsafe

A rap or tip! What bit of paper s here?

Suppose we take a pencil, let her write,

Make the least sign, she urges on her child 49

Forgiveness? There now! Eh? Oh! T was your foot,

And not a natural creak, sir?

Answer, then! Once, twice, thrice. see, I m waiting to say

"thrice!"

All to no use! No sort of hope for me?
Its all to post to Greeleys newspaper?
    What? If I told you all about the tricks?
    Upon my soul!–the whole truth, and naught else,
    And how theres been some falsehood–for your part,
    Will you engage to pay my passage out,
    And hold your tongue until I m safe on board?
    England s the place, not Boston–no offence! 60 I see what makes you hesitate:
dont fear!
    I mean to change my trade and cheat no more,
    Yes, this time really its upon my soul!
    Be my salvation!–under Heaven, of course.
    I ll tell some queer things. Sixty Vs must do.
    A trifle, though, to start with! We ll refer
    The question to this table?
    How you re changed!
    Then split the difference; thirty more, well say.
Ay, but you leave my presents! Else I ll swear
T was all through those: you wanted yours again, 70
    So, picked a quarrel with me, to get them back!
    Tread on a worm, it turns, sir! If I turn,
    Your fault! T is you Ml have forced me! Who a obliged
    To give up life yet try no self-defence?
At all events, I Ml run the risk. Eh?
    Done!
    May I sit, sir? This dear old table, now!
    Please, sir, a parting egg-nogg and cigar!
    I ve been so happy with you! Nice stuffed chairs,
    And sympathetic sideboards; what an end
    To all the instructive evenings! (Its alight.) 80
    Well, nothing lasts, as Bacon came and said.
    Here goes,–but keep your temper, or I Ml scream!
    Fol-lol-the-rido-liddle-iddle-ol!
    You see, sir, its your own fault more than mine; It s all your fault, you curious
gentlefolk!
    You re prigs,–excuse me,–like to look so spry,
    So clever, while you cling by half a claw
    To the perch whereon you puff yourselves at roost,
    Such piece of self-conceit as serves for perch
    Because you chose it, so it must be safe. 90
    Oh, otherwise you re sharp enough! You spy
    Who slips, who slides, who holds by help of wing,
    Wanting real foothold,–who cant keep upright
    On the other perch, your neighbor chose, not you:
    Theres no outwitting you respecting him!

For instance, men love money—that, you know
And what men do to gain it: well, suppose
A poor lad, say a helps son in your house,
Listening at keyholes, hears the company
Talk grand of dollars, V-notes, and so forth, 1OC
How hard they are to get, how good to hold,
How much they buy,—if, suddenly, in pops he—
"Ive got a V-note! "—what do you say to him?
Whats your first word which follows your last kick?
"Where did you steal it, rascal? " Thats because
He finds you, fain would fool you, off your perch,
Not on the special piece of nonsense, sir,
Elected your parade-ground: let him try
Lies to the end of the list,—"He picked it up,
His cousin died and left it him by will, 11 o
The President flung it to him, riding by,
An actress trucked it for a curl of his hair,
He dreamed of luck and found his shoe enriched,
He dug up clay, and out of clay made gold"–
How would you treat such possibilities?
Would not you, prompt, investigate the case
With cow-hide? "Lies, lies, lies," youd shout: and why?
Which of the stories might not prove mere truth?
This last, perhaps, that clay was turned to coin!
Lets see, now, give him me to speak for him! i 20
How many of your rare philosophers,
In plaguy books I ve had to dip into,
Believed gold could be made thus, saw it made
And made it? Oh, with such philosophers
You re on your best behavior! While the lad–
With him, in a trice, you settle likelihoods,
Nor doubt a moment how he got his prize:
In his case, you hear, judge and execute,
All in a breath: so would most men of sense.
　　But let the same lad hear you talk as grand 130
　　At the same keyhole, you and company,
Of signs and wonders, the invisible world;
How wisdom scouts our vulgar unbelief
　　More than our vulgarest credulity;
　　How good men have desired to see a ghost,
　　What Johnson used to say, what Wesley did,
　　Mother Goose thought, and fiddle-diddle-dee:– If he break in with, "Sir, / saw a ghost!"
　　Ah, the ways change! He finds you perched and prim; Its a conceit of yours that ghosts may be: 140

There s no talk now of cow-hide. "Tell it out!
Dont fear us! Take your time and recollect!
Sit down first: try a glass of wine, my boy!
And, David, (is not that your Christian name?)
Of all things, should this happen twice–it may–
Be sure, while fresh in mind, you let us know!"
Does the boy blunder, blurt out this, blab that,
Break down in the other, as beginners will?
Alls candor, alls considerateness–" No haste!
Pause and collect yourself! We understand! 1 50
Thats the bad memory, or the natural shock,
Or the unexplained phenomena!"
Egad,
The boy takes heart of grace; finds, never fear,
The readiest way Co ope your own heart wide,
Show–what I call your peacock-perch, pet post
To strut, and spread the tail, and squawk upon!
"Just as you thought, much as you might expect!
There be more things in heaven and earth, Hora-
tio,".
And so on. Shall not David take the hint,
Grow bolder, stroke you down at quickened rate? 160
If he ruffle a feather, its " Gently, patiently!
Manifestations are so weak at first!
Doubting, moreover, kills them, cuts all short,
Cures with a vengeance! "
There, sir, thats your style! You and your boy–such pains bestowed on him, Or any headpiece of theaverage worth, To teach, say, Greek, would perfect him apace, Make him a Person (" Person? " thank you, sir!) Much more, proficient in the art of lies. You never leave the lesson! Fire alight, 170
Catch you permitting it to die! You ve friends; Theres no withholding knowledge,– least from those
Apt to look elsewhere for their souls supply:
Why should not you parade your lawful prize?
Who finds a picture, digs a medal up,
Hits on a first edition,–he henceforth
Gives it his name, grows notable: how much more,
Who ferrets out a "medium"? "Davids yours,
You highly-favored man? Then, pity souls
Less privileged! Allow us share your luck!" 180
So, David holds the circle, rules the roast,
Narrates the vision, peeps in the glass ball,
Sets-to the spirit-writing, hears the raps,
As the case may be.
Now mark! To be precise–

Though I say, "lies" all these, at this first stage,
T is just for science sake: I call such grubs
By the name of what theyll turn to, dragonflies.
Strictly, its what good people style untruth;
But yet, so far, not quite the full-grown thing:
Its fancying, fable-making, nonsense-work–190
What never meant to be so very bad–.
The knack of story-telling, brightening up
Each dull old bit of fact that drops its shine.
One does see somewhat when one shuts ones eyes, If only spots and streaks; tables
do tip In the oddest way of themselves: and pens, good Lord,
 Who knows if you drive them or they drive you?
 T is but a foot in the water and out again;
 Not that duck-under which decides your dive.
 Note this, for its important: listen why. 200 Ill prove, you push on David till he
dives
 And ends the shivering. Heres your circle, now:
 Two-thirds of them, with heads like you their host,
 Turn up their eyes, and cry, as you expect,
 "Lord, whod have thought it!" But theres always one
 Looks wise, compassionately smiles, submits
Of your veracity no kind of doubt,
But–do you feel so certain of that boys?
Really, I wonder! I confess myself
More chary of my faith!" Thats galling, sir! 210
What, he the investigator, he the sage,
When all s done? Then, you just have shut your eyes,
Opened your mouth, and gulped down David whole,
You! Terrible were such catastrophe!
So, evidence is redoubled, doubled again,
And doubled besides; once more, "He heard, we heard,
 You and they heard, your mother and your wife,
Your children and the stranger in your gates:
Did they or did they not? " So much for him,
The black sheep, guest without the wedding-garb, 220
The doubting Thomas! Now s your turn to crow:
"He s kind to think you such a fool: Sludge cheats?
Leave you alone to take precautions! "
 Straight
The rest join chorus. Thomas stands abashed,
 Sips silent some such beverage as this,
 Considers if it be harder, shutting eyes
 And gulping David in good fellowship,
 Than going elsewhere, getting, in exchange,
 With no egg-nogg to lubricate the food,

Some just as tough a morsel. Over the way, 230
Holds Captain Sparks his court: is it better there?
Have not you hunting-stories, scalping-scenes,
And Mexican War exploits to swallow plump If youd be free o the stove-side, rocking-chair,
And trio of affable daughters?
Doubt succumbs!
Victory! All your circle s yours again!
Out of the clubbing of submissive wits,
Davids performance rounds, each chink gets patched,
Every protrusion of a points filed fine,
All s fit to set a-rolling round the world, 240
And then return to David finally,
Lies seven-feet thick about his first half-inch.
Heres a choice birth o the supernatural,
Poor David s pledged to! You ve employed no tool
That laws exclaim at, save the devils own,
Yet screwed him into henceforth gulling you
To the top o your bent,—all out of one half-lie!
You hold, if theres one half or a hundredth part
Of a lie, thats his fault,—his be the penalty!
I dare say! You d prove firmer in his place? 250
You d find the courage,—that first flurry over,
That mild bit of romancing-work at end,—
To interpose with " It gets serious, this;
Must stop here. Sir, I saw no ghost at all.
Inform your friends I made. well, fools of them,
And found you ready-made. I ve lived in clover
These three weeks: take it out in kicks of me! "
I doubt it. Ask your conscience! Let me know,
Twelve months hence, with how few embellishments
Youve told almighty Boston of this passage 260
Of arms between us, your first taste o the foil
From Sludge, who could not fence, sir! Sludge, your boy!
I lied, sir,—there! I got up from my gorge
On offal in the gutter, and preferred
Your canvas-backs: I took their carvers size,
Measured his modicum ofintelliger. ee,
Tickled him on the cockles of his heart
With a raven feather, and next week found myselt
Sweet and clean, dining daintily, dizened smart,
Set on a stool buttressed by ladies knees, 270
Every soft smiler calling me her pet,
Encouraging my story to uncoil
And creep out from its hole, inch after inch,

"How last night, I no sooner snug in bed,
Tucked up, just as they left me,–than came raps!
While a light whisked". "Shaped somewhat like a star? " " Well, like some sort of
stars, maam."–" So we thought!
   And any voice? Not yet? Try hard, next time,
If you cant hear a voice; we think you may:
At least, the Pennsylvanian mediums did." 280
Oh, next time comes the voice! "Just as we hoped!"
Are not the hopers proud now, pleased, profuse
O the natural acknowledgment?
   Of course!
   So, off we push, illy-oh-yo, trim the boat,
On we sweep with a cataract ahead,
   We re midway to the Horseshoe: stop, who can,
   The dance of bubbles gay about our prow!
   Experiences become worth waiting for.
   Spirits now speak up, tell their inmost mind,
   And compliment the " medium " properly, 290
   Concern themselves about his Sunday coat,
   See rings on his hand with pleasure. Ask yourself
   How you d receive a course of treats like these!
   Why, take the quietest hack and stall him up,
   Cram him with corn a month, then out with him
   Among his mates on a bright April morn,
   With the turf to tread; see if you find or no
   A caper in him, if he bucks or bolts!
   Much more a youth whose fancies sprout as rank
   As toadstool-clump from melon-bed. T is soon, 300
   "Sirrah, you spirit, come, go, fetch and carry,
   Read, write, rap, rub-a-dub, and hang yourself!"
I m spared all further trouble; all s arranged;
Your circle does my business; I may rave
Like an epileptic dervish in the books,
Foam, fling myself flat, rend my clothes to shreds;
No matter: lovers, friends and countrymen
Will lay down spiritual laws, read wrong things right
By the rule o reverse. If Francis Verulam
Styles himself Bacon, spells the name beside 3 1 o
With a y and a k, says he drew breath in York,
   Gave up the ghost in Wales when Cromwell reigned, (As, sir, we somewhat fear
he was apt to say,
   Before I found the useful book that knows)
   Why, what harm s done? The circle smiles apace,
   "It was not Bacon, after all, you see!
   We understand; the tricks but natural:

Such spirits individuality Is hard to put in evidence: they incline
To gibe and jeer, these undeveloped sorts. 3 20
You see, their world s much like a jail broke loose,
While this of ours remains shut, bolted, barred,
With a single window to it. Sludge, our friend,
Serves as this window, whether thin or thick,
Or stained or stainless; he s the medium-pane
Through which, to see us and be seen, they peep:
They crowd each other, hustle for a chance,
Tread on their neighbors kibes, play tricks enough!
Does Bacon, tired of waiting, swerve aside?
Up in his place jumps Barnum–Im your man, 330
1 ll answer you for Bacon! Try once more! "
　　Or else it s–" Whats a medium? He s a means.
　　Good, bad, indifferent, still the only means
　　Spirits can speak by; he may misconceive,
　　Stutter and stammer,–he s their Sludge and drudge.
　　Take him or leave him; they must hold their peace,
　　Or else, put up with having knowledge strained
　　To half-expression through his ignorance.
　　Suppose, the spirit Beethoven wants to shed
　　New music hes brimful of; why, he turns 340
　　The handle of this organ, grinds with Sludge,
　　And what he poured in at the mouth o the mill
　　As a Thirty-third Sonata, (fancy now!)
　　Comes from the hopper as bran-new Sludge, naught else,
　　The Shakers Hymn in G, with a natural F,
Or the Stars and Stripes set to consecutive fourths."
　　Sir, where s the scrape you did not help me through,
You that are wise? And for the fools, the folk
Who came to see,–the guests, (observe that word!)
Pray do you find guests criticize your wine, 350
Your furniture, your grammar, or your nose?
Then, why your " medium "? Whats the difference?
Prove your madeira red-ink and gamboge,–
Your Sludge, a cheat–then, somebody s a goose
For vaunting both as genuine. " Guests! " Dont fear!
　　Theyll make a wry face, nor too much of that,
And leave you in your glory.
　　　　"No, sometimes
　　They doubt and say as much! " Ay, doubt they do! And what s the consequence?
" Of course they doubt"– (You triumph) "that explains the hitch at once! 360
Doubt posed our medium, puddled his pure mind;
He gave them back their rubbish: pitch chaff in,
Could flour come out o the honest mill?" So, prompt

Applaud the faithful: cases flock in point,
"How, when a mocker willed a medium once
Should name a spirit James whose name was George,
James cried the medium,—twas the test of truth!"
    In short, a hit proves much, a miss proves morel
Does this convince? The better: does it fail?
Time for the double-shotted broadside, then—370
The grand means, last resource. Look black and big!
"You style us idiots, therefore—why stop short?
Accomplices in rascality: this we hear
In our own house, from our invited guest
Found brave enough to outrage a poor boy
Exposed by our good faith! Have you been heard?
Now, then, hear us; one man s not quite worth twelve.
You see a cheat? Here s some twelve see an ass:
    Excuse me if I calculate: good day!"
    Out slinks the sceptic, all the laughs explode. 380
    Sludge waves his hat in triumph!
    Or—he dont.
    Theres something in real truth (explain who can!)
One casts a wistful eye at, like the horse
Who mopes beneath stuffed hay-racks and wont munch
Because he spies a corn-bag: hang that truth,
It spoils all dainties proffered in its place!
I ve felt at times when, cockered, cosseted
And coddled by the aforesaid company,
Bidden enjoy their bullying,—never fear,
But oer their shoulders spit at the flying man,—390
I ve felt a child; only, a fractious child
That, dandled soft by nurse, aunt, grandmother,
Who keep him from the kennel, sun and wind,
Good fun and wholesome mud,—enjoined be sweet,
And comely and superior,—eyes askance
The ragged sons o the gutter at their game,
Fain would be down with them i the thick o the filth,
Making dirt-pies, laughing free, speaking plain,
And calling granny the gray old cat she is.
I ve felt a spite, I say, at you, at them, 400
    Huggings and humbug—gnashed my teeth to mark
A decent dog pass! Its too bad, I say,
Ruining a soul so!
    But whats "so," whats fixed, Where may one stop? Nowhere! The cheating s
nursed

Out of the lying, softly and surely spun
To just your length, sir! I d stop soon enough:
But you re for progress. " All old, nothing new?
    Only the usual talking through the mouth,
    Or writing by the hand? I own, I thought
    This would develop, grow demonstrable, 410
    Make doubt absurd, give figures we might see,
    Flowers we might touch. There s no one doubts you, Sludge!
    You dream the dreams, you see the spiritual sights,
The speeches come in your head, beyond dispute.
Still, for the sceptics sake, to stop all mouths,
We want come outward manifestation!–well,
The Pennsylvanians gained such; why not Sludge?
He may improve with time! "
    Ay, that he may!
    He sees his lot: there s no avoiding fate. 419
    T is a trifle at first. " Eh, David? Did you hear? You jogged the table, your foot
caused the squeak, This time you re. joking, are you not, my boy?" " N-n-no! "–and
I m done for, bought and sold henceforth.
    The old good easy jog-trot way, the. eh?
The. not so very false, as falsehood goes,
The spinning out and drawing fine, you know,–
Really mere novel-writing of a sort,
Acting, or improvising, make-believe,
Surely not downright cheatery,–any how, 429
    Tis done with and my lot cast; Cheats mywiame:
The fatal dash of brandy in your tea
Has settled what you II have the souchongs smack:
The caddy gives way to the dram-bottle.
    Then, its so cruel easy! Oh, those tricks
    That cant be tricks, those feats by sleight of hand,
    Clearly no common conjurors!–no indeed!
    A conjuror? Choose me any craft i the world
A man puts hand to; and with six months pains
I ll play you twenty tricks miraculous
To people untaught the trade: have you seen glass
blown, 440
    Pipes pierced? Why, just this biscuit that I chip,
Did you ever watch a baker toss one flat
To the oven? Try and do it! Take my word,
Practise but half as much, while limbs are lithe,
To turn, shove, tilt a table, crack your joints,
Manage your feet, dispose your hands aright,
Work wires that twitch the curtains, play the glove
At end o your slipper,–then put out the lights

And. there, there, all you want you ll get, I hope!
I found it slip, easy as an old shoe. 450
 Now, lights on table again! I ve done my part,
 You take my place while I give thanks and rest.
 "Well, Judge Humgruffin, whats your verdict, sir?
 You, hardest head in the United States,–
 Did you detect a cheat here? Wait! Lets see!
 Just an experiment first, for candors sake!
 I ll try and cheat you, Judge! The table tilts: Is it I that move it? Write! I ll press
your hand:
 Cry when I push, or guide your pencil, Judge!"
 Sludge still triumphant! " That a rap, indeed? 460
 That, the real writing? Very like a whale!
 Then, if, sir, you–a most distinguished man,
 And, were the Judge not here, I d say,. no matter!
 Well, sir, if you fail, you cant take us in,–
There s little fear that Sludge will! "
 Wont he, maam r But what if our distinguished host, like Sludge,
 Bade God bear witness that he played no trick,
 While you believed that what produced the raps
 Was just a certain child who died, you know, 469
 And whose last breath you thought your lips had felt?
 Eh? Thats a capital point, maam: Sludge begins
 At your entreaty with your dearest dead,
 The little voice set lisping once again,
 The tiny hand made feel for yours once more,
 The poor lost image brought back, plain as dreams,
 Which image, if a word had chanced recall,
 The customary cloud would cross your eyes,
 Your heart return the old tick, pay its pang!
 A right mood for investigation, this!
 One s at ones ease with Saul and Jonathan, 480
 Pompey and Caesar: but ones own lost child.
 I wonder, when you heard the first clod drop
 From the spadeful at the grave-side, felt you free
 To investigate who twitched your funeral scarf
 Or brushed your flounces? Then, it came of course
 You should be stunned and stupid; then, (how else?)
 Your breath stopped with your blood, your brain struck work.
 But now, such causes fail of such effects,
Alls changed,–the little voice begins afresh,
Yet you, calm, consequent, can test and try 490
 And touch the truth. "Tests? Didnt the creature tell Its nurses name, and say it
lived six years,

And rode a rocking-horse? Enough of tests!
Sludge never could learn that! "
    He could not, eh?
    You compliment him. "Could not?" Speak for yourself!
    I d like to know the man I ever saw
    Once,–never mind where, how, why, when,– once saw,
    Of whom I do not keep some matter in mind
He d swear I " could not " know, sagacious soul! 499
What? Do you live in this worlds blow of"blacks,
Palaver, gossipry, a single hour
Nor find one smut has settled on your nose,
Of a smuts worth, no more, no less?–one fact
Out of the drift of facts, whereby you learn
What someone was, somewhere, somewhen, somewhy?
You dont tell folk–" See what has stuck to me!
Judge Humgruffin, our most distinguished man,
Your uncle was a tailor, and your wife
Thought to have married Miggs, missed him, hit you!"–
    Do you, sir, though you see him twice a-week? 510
"No," you reply, " what use retailing it?
Why should I?" But, you see, one day you should,
Because one day there s much use,–when this fact
Brings you the Judge upon both gouty knees
Before the supernatural; proves that Sludge
Knows, as you say, a thing he " could not " know:
Will not Sludge thenceforth keep an outstretched face
The way the wind drives?
    "Could not! " Look you now, Ill tell you a story! Theres a whiskered chap, A
foreigner, that teaches music here 520
    And gets his bread,–knowing no better way:
He says, the fellow who informed of him
And made him fly his country and fall West
Was a hunchback cobbler, sat, stitched soles and sang,
In some outlandish place, the city Rome,
M. w.–16
    In a cellar by their Broadway, all day long;
Never asked questions, stopped to listen or look,
Nor lifted nose from lapstone; let the world
Roll round his three-legged stool, and news run in
The ears he hardly seemed to keep pricked up. 530
Well, that man went on Sundays, touched his pay,
And took his praise from government, you see;
For something like two dollars every week,
He d engage tell you some one little thing
Of some one man, which led to many more,

(Because one truth leads right to the worlds end)
And make you that mans master–when he dined
And on what dish, where walked to keep his health
And to what street. His trade was, throwing thus
His sense out, like an ant-eaters long tongue, 540
Soft, innocent, warm, moist, impassible,
And when twas crusted oer with creatures–slick,
Their juice enriched his palate. " Could not Sludge! "
    I ll go yet a step further, and maintain,
    Once the imposture plunged its proper depth I the rotten of your natures, all of
you,– (If ones not mad nor drunk, and hardly then) Its impossible to cheat–thats, be
found out!
    Go tell your brotherhood this first slip of mine,
    All to-days tale, how you detected Sludge, 550
    Behaved unpleasantly, till he was fain confess,
    And so has come to grief! You ll find, I think,
    Why Sludge still snaps his fingers in your face.
    There now, you ve told them! Whats their prompt reply?
    "Sir, did that youth confess he had cheated me,
I d disbelieve him. He may cheat at times;
Thats in the medium-nature, thus they re made,
    Vain and vindictive, cowards, prone to scratch.
    And so all cats are; still, a cats the beast
    You coax the strange electric sparks from out, 560
    By rubbing back its fur; not so a dog,
    Nor lion, nor lamb: tis the cats nature, sir!
    Why not the dogs? Ask God, who made them beasts!
    D ye think the sound, the nicely-balanced man (Like me "–aside)–" like you
yourself,"– (aloud)
    "–He s stuff to make a medium? Bless your soul,
Tis these hysteric, hybrid half-and-halfs,
Equivocal, worthless vermin yield the fire!
We take such as we find them, ware their tricks,
Wanting their service. Sir, Sludge took in you–570
How, I cant say, not being there to watch:
He was tried, was tempted by your easiness,–
He did not take in me! "
    Thank you for Sludge!
I m to be grateful to such patrons, eh,
When what you hears my best word? Tis a challenge
    "Snap at all strangers, half-tamed prairie-dog,
So you cower duly at your keepers beck!
Cat, show what claws were made for, muffling them
Only to me! Cheat others if you can,
Me, if you dare! " And, my wise sir, I dared–580

Did cheat you first, made you cheat others next,
And had the help o your vaunted manliness
To bully the incredulous. You used me?
Have not I used you, taken full revenge,
Persuaded folk they knew not their own name,
And straight they d own the error! Who was the fool
When, to an awe-struck wide-eyed open-mouthed
 Circle of sages, Sludge would introduce
 Milton composing baby-rhymes, and Locke
 Reasoning in gibberish, Homer writing Greek 590 In naughts and crosses, Asaph
setting psalms
 To crotchet and quaver? I ve made a spirit squeak In sham voice for a minute, then
outbroke
 Bold in my own, defying the imbeciles–
 Have copied some ghosts pothooks, half a page,
 Then ended with my own scrawl undisguised.
 "All right! The ghost was merely using Sludge,
 Suiting itself from his imperfect stock!"
 Dont talk of gratitude to me! For what?
 For being treated as a showmans ape, 600
 Encouraged to be wicked and make sport,
 Fret or sulk, grin or whimper, any mood
 So long as the ape be in it and no man–
 Because a nut pays every mood alike.
 Curse your superior, superintending sort,
 Who, since you hate smoke, send up boys that climb
 To cure your chimney, bid a " medium " lie
 To sweep you truth down! Curse your women too,
 Your insolent wives and daughters, that fire up
 Or faint away if a male hand squeeze theirs, 610
 Yet, to encourage Sludge, may play with Sludge
 As only a " medium," only the kind of thing
 They must humor, fondle. oh, to misconceive
 Were too preposterous! But I ve paid them out!
 They ve had their wish–called for the naked truth,
 And in she tripped, sat down and bade them stare:
 They had to blush a little and forgive!
 "The fact is, children talk so; in next world
 All our conventions are reversed,–perhaps
 Made light of: something like old prints, my dear! 620
 The Judge has one, he brought from Italy,
 A metropolis in the background,–oer a bridge,
A team of trotting roadsters,–cheerful groups
Of wayside travellers, peasants at their work,
And, full in front, quite unconcerned, why not?

Three nymphs conversing with a cavalier,
And never a rag among them: fine, folk cry—
And heavenly manners seem not much unlike!
Let Sludge go on; we ll fancy its in print! "
If such as came for wool, sir, went home shorn, 630
Where is the wrong I did them? T was their choice;
They tried the adventure, ran the risk, tossed up
And lost, as some one s sure to do in games;
They fancied I was made to lose,—smoked glass
Useful to spy the sun through, spare their eyes:
And had I proved a red-hot iron plate
They thought to pierce, and, for their pains, grew blind,
    Whose were the fault but theirs? While, as things go,
Their loss amounts to gain, the mores the shame!
They ve had their peep into the spirit-world, 640
And all this world may know it! They ve fed fat
Their self-conceit which else had starved: what chance
Save this, of cackling oer a golden egg
And compassing distinction from the flock,
Friends of a feather? Well, they paid for it,
And not prodigiously; the price o the play,
Not counting certain pleasant interludes,
Was scarce a vulgar plays worth. When you buy
The actors talent, do you dare propose
For his soul beside? Whereas my soul you buy! 650
Sludge acts Macbeth, obliged to be Macbeth,
Or you ll not hear his first word! Just go through
That slight formality, swear himselfs the Thane,
And thenceforth he may strut and fret his hour,
    Spout, spawl, or spin his target, no one cares!
    Why had nt I leave to play tricks, Sludge as Sludge?
    Enough of it all! I ve wiped out scores with you—
Vented your fustian, let myself be streaked
Like tom-fool with your ochre and carmine,
Worn patchwork your respectable fingers sewed 660
To metamorphose somebody,—yes, Ive earned
My wages, swallowed down my bread of shame,
And shake the crumbs off—where but in your face?
As for religion—why, I served it, sir!
I ll stick to that! With my phenomena I laid the atheist sprawling on his back,
Propped up Saint Paul, or, at least, Swedenborg!
In fact, its just the proper way to balk
These troublesome fellows—liars, one and all,
Are not these sceptics? Well, to baffle them, 670
No use in being squeamish: lie yourself!

Erect your buttress just as wide o the line,
Your side, as they build up the wall on theirs;
Where both meet, midway in a point, is truth
High overhead: so, take your room, pile bricks,
Lie! Oh, there s titillation in all shame!
What snow may lose in white, snow gains in rose!
Miss Stokes turns–Rahab,–nor a bad exchange!
Glory be on her, for the good she wrought,
Breeding belief anew neath ribs of death, 680
Browbeating now the unabashed before,
Ridding us of their whole lifes gathered straws
By live coal from the altar! Why, of old,
Great men spent years and years in writing books
To prove we ve souls, and hardly proved it then:
Miss Stokes with her live coal, for you and me!
Surely, to this good issue, all was fair–
Not only fondling Sludge, but, even suppose
He let escape some spice of knavery,–well, In wisely being blind to it! Dont you
praise 690
Nelson for setting spy-glass to blind eye
And saying. what was it–that he could not see
The signal he was bothered with? Ay, indeed!
I ll go beyond: there s a real love of a lie,
Liars find ready-made for lies they make,
As hand for glove, or tongue for sugar-plum.
At best, t is never pure and full belief;
Those furthest in the quagmire,–dont suppose
They strayed there with no warning, got no chance
Of a filth-speck in their face, which they clenched teeth, 700
Bent brow against! Be sure they had their doubts,
And fears, and fairest challenges to try
The floor o the seeming solid sand! But no!
Their faith was pledged, acquaintance too apprised,
AH but the last step ventured, kerchiefs waved,
And Sludge called "pet": twas easier marching on
To the promised land; join those who, Thursday next,
Meant to meet Shakespeare; better follow Sludge–
Prudent, oh sure!–on the alert, how else?–
But making for the mid-bog, all the same! 710
To hear your outcries, one would think I caught
Miss Stokes by the scruff o the neck, and pitched her flat,
Foolish-face-foremost! Hear these simpletons,
Thats all I beg, before my work s begun,
Before I ve touched them with my finger-tip!
Thus they await me (do but listen, now!

Its reasoning, this is,–I cant imitate
The baby voice, though) "In so many tales
   Must be some truth, truth though a pin-point big,
   Yet, some: a single mans deceived, perhaps–720
   Hardly, a thousand: to suppose one cheat
   Can gull all these, were more miraculous far
   Than aught we should confess a miracle "—
And so on. Then the Judge sums up–(it s rare)
Bids you respect the authorities that leap
To the judgment-seat at once,–why dont you note
The limpid nature, the unblemished life,
The spotless honor, indisputable sense
Of the first upstart with his story? What–
Outrage a boy on whom you neer till now 730
Set eyes, because he finds raps trouble him?
   Fools, these are: ay, and how of their opposites
Who never did, at bottom of their hearts,
Believe for a moment?–Men emasculate,
Blank of belief, who played, as eunuchs use,
With superstition safely,–cold of blood,
Who saw what made for them i the mystery,
Took their occasion, and supported Sludge –As proselytes? No, thank you, far too shrewd!
   –But promisers of fair play, encouragers 740
O the claimant; who in candor needs must hoist
Sludge up on Mars Hill, get speech out of Sludge
To carry off, criticise, and cant about!
   Did nt Athens treat Saint Paul so?–at any rate,
Its " a new thing " philosophy fumbles at.
Then there s the other picker-out of pearl
From dung-heaps,–ay, your literary man,
Who draws on his kid gloves to deal with Sludge
Daintily and discreetly,–shakes a dust 749
   O the doctrine, flavors thence, he well knows how,
The narrative or the novel,–half-believes,
   All for the books sake, and the publics stare,
   And the cash thats Gods sole solid in this world!
   Look at him! Try to be too bold, too gross
   For the master! Not you! He s the man for muck;
   Shovel it forth, full-splash, hell smooth your brown Into artistic richness, never fear!
   Find him the crude stuff; when you recognize
   Your lie again, you ll doff your hat to it,
   Dressed out for company! " For company," 760 I say, since there s the relish of success:

Let all pay due respect, call the lie truth,
Save the soft silent smirking gentleman
Who ushered in the stranger: you must sigh
"How melancholy, he, the only one
Fails to perceive the bearing of the truth
Himself gave birth to!"—Theres the triumphs smack!
That man would choose to see the whole world roll
I the slime o the slough, so he might touch the tip
Of his brush with what I call the best of browns—770
Tint ghost-tales, spirit-stories, past the power
Of the outworn umber and bistre!
   Yet I think
There s a more hateful form of foolery—
The social sages, Solomon of saloons
And philosophic diner-out, the fribble
Who wants a doctrine for a chopping-block
To try the edge of his faculty upon,
Prove how much common sense he ll hack and hew
I the critical minute twixt the soup and fish! 779
These were my patrons: "these, and the like of them
Who, rising in my soul now, sicken it,—
These I have injured! Gratitude to these?
   The gratitude, forsooth, of a prostitute
   To the greenhorn and the bully—friends of hers,
   From the wag that wants the queer jokes for his club,
   To the snuff-box-decorator, honest man,
Who just was at his wits end where to find
So genial a Pasiphae! All and each
Pay, compliment, protect from the police:
And how she hates them for their pains, like me! 790
So much for my remorse at thanklessness
Toward a deserving public!
   But, for God?
   Ay, thats a question! Well, sir, since you press—
(How you do tease the whole thing out of me!
I dont mean you, you know, when I say "them":
Hate you, indeed! But that Miss Stokes, that Judge!
Enough, enough—with sugar: thank you, sir!)
Now for it, then! Will you believe me, though?
You ve heard what I confess; I dont unsay
A single word: I cheated when I could, 800
   Rapped with my toe-joints, set sham hands at work,
Wrote down names weak in sympathetic ink,
Rubbed odic lights with ends of phosphor-match,
And all the rest; believe that: believe this,

By the same token, though it seem to set
The crooked straight again, unsay the said,
Stick up what Ive knocked down; I cant help that
Its truth! I somehow vomit truth to-day.
This trade of mine—I dont know, cant be sure
But there was something in it, tricks and all! 810
Really, I want to light up my own mind.
They were tricks,—true, but what I mean to add
Is also true. First,—dont it strike you, sir?
    Go back to the beginning,—the first fact
    We re taught is, theres a world beside this world,
    With spirits, not mankind, for tenantry;
    That much within that world once sojourned here,
    That all upon this world will visit there,
    And therefore that we, bodily here below,
    Must have exactly such an interest 820 In learning what may be the ways o the world
    Above us, as the disembodied folk
    Have (by all analogic likelihood) In watching how things go in the old home
    With us, their sons, successors, and what not.
    Oh yes, with added powers probably,
    Fit for the novel state,—old loves grown pure,
    Old interests understood aright,—they watch!
    Eyes to see, ears to hear, and hands to help,
    Proportionate to advancement: they re ahead, 830
    Thats all—do what we do, but noblier done—
    Use plate, whereas we eat our meals off delf, (To use a figure).
    Concede that, and I ask Next what may be the mode of intercourse Between us men here, and those once-men there? First comes the Bibles speech; then, history With the supernatural element,—you know—. All that we sucked in with our mothers milk, Grew up with, got inside of us at last, Till its found bone of bone and flesh of flesh. 84.0 See now, we start with the miraculous, And know it used to be, at all events: Whats the first step we take, and cant but take, In arguing from the known to the obscure? Why this: "What was before, may be to-day.
    Since Samuels ghost appeared to Saul, of course
    My brothers spirit may appear to me."
    Go tell your teacher that! Whats his reply?
    What brings a shade of doubt for the first time
    Oer his brow late so luminous with faith? 850
    "Such things have been," says he, "and theres no doubt
    Such things may be: but I advise mistrust
Of eyes, ears, stomach, and, more than all, your brain,
    Unless it be of your great-grandmother,
Whenever they propose a ghost to you! "
The end is, there s a composition struck;

T is settled, weve some way of intercourse
Just as in Sauls time; only, different:
How, when and where, precisely,–find it out!
I want to know, then, whats so natural 860
    As that a person born into this world
And seized on by such teaching, should begin
With firm expectancy and a frank look-out
For his own allotment, his especial share
I the secret,–his particular ghost, in fine?
I mean, a person born to look that way,
Since natures differ: take the painter-sort.
One man lives fifty years in ignorance
Whether grass be green or red,–" No kind of eye
For color," say you; while another picks 870
    And puts away even pebbles, when a child,
Because of bluish spots and pinky veins–
"Give him forthwith a paint-box! " Just the same
Was I born." medium," you wont let me say,–
Well, seer of the supernatural
Every when, everyhow and everywhere,–
Will that do?
    I and all such boys of course Started with the same stock of Bible-truth; Only,–what
in the rest you style their sense, Instinct, blind, reasoning but imperative, 880
    This, betimes, taught them the old world had one law And ours another: "New
world, new laws," cried they:
    "None but old laws, seen everywhere at work,"
Cried I, and by their help explained my life
The Jews way, still a working way to me.
Ghosts made the noises, fairies waved the lights,
Or Santa Claus slid down on New Years Eve
And stuffed with cakes the stocking at my bed,
Changed the worn shoes, rubbed clean the fingered slate O the sum that came to grief
the day before. 890
    This could not last long: soon enough I found
Who had worked wonders thus, and to what end:
But did I find all easy, like my mates?
Henceforth no supernatural any more?
Not a whit: what projects the billiard-balls?
"A cue," you answer: "Yes, a cue," said I;
"But what hand, off the cushion, moved the cue?
What unseen agency, outside the world,
Prompted its puppets to do this and that,
Put cakes and shoes and slates into their mind, 900
These mothers and aunts, nay even schoolmasters?"
Thus high I sprang, and there have settled since.

Just so I reason, in sober earnest still,
About the greater godsends, what you call
The serious gains and losses of my life.
What do I know or care about your world
Which either is or seems to be? This snap
O my fingers, sir! My care is for myself;
Myself am whole and sole reality Inside a raree-show and a market-mob 910
Gathered about it: thats the use of things.
T is easy saying they serve vast purposes,
Advantage their grand selves: be it true or false,
Each thing may have two uses. Whats a star?
A world, or a worlds sun: does nt it serve
As taper also, time-piece, weather-glass,
And almanac? Are stars not set for signs
When we should shear our sheep, sow corn, prune trees? The Bible says so.
Well, I add one use
To all the acknowledged uses, and declare 920 If I spy Charless Wain at twelve to-night,
It warns me, "Go, nor lose another day,
And have your hair cut, Sludge! " You laugh: and why?

    Were such a sign too hard for God to give?
No: but Sludge seems too little for such grace:
Thank you, sir! So you think, so does not Sludge!
When you and good men gape at Providence,
Go into history and bid us mark
Not merely powder-plots prevented, crowns
Kept on kings heads by miracle enough, 930

    But private mercies—oh, you ve told me, sir,
Of such interpositions! How yourself
Once, missing on a memorable day
Your handkerchief—just setting out, you know,–
You must return to fetch it, lost the train,
And saved your precious self from what befell
The thirty-three whom Providence forgot.

    You tell, and ask me what I think of this?
    Well, sir, I think then, since you needs must know,
What matter had you and Boston city to boot 940
Sailed skyward, like barnt onion-peelings? Much
To you, no doubt: for me—undoubtedly
The cutting of my hair concerns me more,
Because, however sad the truth may seem,
Sludge is of all-importance to himself.
You set apart that day in every year
For special thanksgiving, were a heathen else:
Well, I who cannot boast the like escape,

Suppose I said "I dont thank Providence
For my part, owing it no gratitude"? 950
"Nay, but you owe as much "–you d tutor me,
"You, every man alive, for blessings gained In every hour o the day, could you but know!
 I saw my crowning mercy: all have such,
 Could they but see!" Well, sir, why dont they see?
 "Because they wont look,–or perhaps, they cant."
Then, sir, suppose I can, and will, and do
Look, microscopically as is right,
Into each hour with its infinitude
Of influences at work to profit Sludge? 960
 For thats the case: I ve sharpened up my sight
To spy a providence in the fires going out,
The kettles boiling, the dimes sticking fast
Despite the hole i the pocket. Call such facts
Fancies, too petty a work for Providence,
And those same thanks which you exact from me
Prove too prodigious payment: thanks for what,
If nothing guards and guides us little men?
No, no, sir! You must put away your pride,
Resolve to let Sludge into partnership! 970 I live by signs and omens: looked at the roof
 Where the pigeons settle–"If the further bird,
 The white, takes wing first, I ll confess when thrashed;
 Not, if the blue does "–so I said to myself
Last week, lest you should take me by surprise:
Off flapped the white,–and I m confessing, sir!
Perhaps t is Providences whim and way
With only me, i the world: how can you tell?
"Because unlikely! " Was it likelier, now,
That this our one out of all worlds beside, 980
The what-dyou-call-em millions, should be just
Precisely chosen to make Adam for,
 And the rest o the tale? Yet the tales true, you know:
 Such undeserving clod was graced so once;
Why not graced likewise undeserving Sludge?
Are we merit-mongers, flaunt we filthy rags?
All you can bring against my privilege
Is, that another way was taken with you,–
Which I dont question. It s pure grace, my luck:
I m broken to the way of nods and winks, 990
 And need no formal summoning. You ve a help;
Holloa his name or whistle, clap your hands,
Stamp with your foot or pull the bell: alls one,

He understands you want him, here he comes.
Just so, I come at the knocking: you, sir, wait
The tongue o the bell, nor stir before you catch
Reasons clear tingle, natures clapper brisk,
Or that traditional peal was wont to cheer
Your mothers face turned heavenward: short of these
There s no authentic intimation, eh? 1000
    Well, when you hear, you ll answer them, start up
And stride into the presence, top of toe,
And there find Sludge beforehand, Sludge that sprang
At noise o the knuckle on the partition-wall!
I think myself the more religious man.
Religions all or nothing; its no mere smile
O contentment, sigh of aspiration, sir–
No quality o the finelier-tempered clay
Like its whiteness or its lightness; rather, stuff
O the very stuff, life of life, and self of self. 1o1q
I tell you, men wont notice; when they do,
They ll understand. I notice nothing else:
I m eyes, ears, mouth of me, one gaze and gape,
Nothing eludes me, everything s a hint,
Handle and help. Its all absurd, and yet
There s something in it all, I know: how much?
No answer! What does that prove? Man s still man,
Still meant for a poor blundering piece of work
When alls done; but, if somewhats done, like this,
Or not done, is the case the same? Suppose 1020
I blunder in my guess at the true sense
O the knuckle-summons, nine times out of ten,–
What if the tenth guess happen to be right?
If the tenth shovel-load of powdered quartz
Yield me the nugget? I gather, crush, sift all,
Pass oer the failure, pounce on the success.
To give you a notion, now–(let who wins, laugh!)
When first I see a man, what do I first?
Why, count the letters which make up his name,
And as their number chances, even or odd, 1030
    Arrive at my conclusion, trim my course:
Hiram H. Horsefall is your honored name,
And have nt I found a patron, sir, in you?
"Shall I cheat this stranger? ". I take apple-pips,
Stick one in either canthus of my eye,
And if the left drops first–(your left, sir, stuck)
Im warned, I let the trick alone this time.
11. w.–17

You, sir, who smile, superior to such trash,
You judge of character by other rules: 1040
    Dont your rules sometimes fail you? Pray, what rule
Have you judged Sludge by hitherto?
    Oh, be sure,
    You, everybody blunders, just as I,
In simpler things than these by far! For see:
I knew two farmers,–one, a wiseacre
Who studied seasons, rummaged almanacs,
Quoted the dew-point, registered the frost,
And then declared, for outcome of his pains,
Next summer must be dampish: twas a drought.
His neighbor prophesied such drought would fall,
Saved hay and corn, made cent, per cent, thereby, 1050
And proved a sage indeed: how came his lore?
Because one brindled heifer, late in March,
Stiffened her tail of evenings, and somehow
He got into his head that drought was meant!
I dont expect all men can do as much:
Such kissing goes by favor. You must take
A certain turn of mind for this,–a twist
I the flesh, as well. Be lazily alive,
Open-mouthed, like my friend the ant-eater,
Letting all natures loosely-guarded motes 1060
    Settle and, slick, be swallowed! Think yourself
The one i the world, the one for whom the world
Was made, expect it tickling at your mouth!
Then will the swarm of busy buzzing flies,
Clouds of coincidence, break egg-shell, thrive,
Breed, multiply, and brjng you food enough.
    I cant pretend to mind your smiling, sir!
    Oh, what you mean is this! Such intimate way,
    Close converse, frank exchange of offices,
    Strict sympathy of the immeasurably great 1070
    With the infinitely small, betokened here
    By a course of signs and omens, raps and sparks,–
    How does it suit the dread traditional text
    O the "Great and Terrible Name"? Shall the
    Heaven of Heavens Stoop to such childs play?
    Please, sir, go with me A moment, and I Ml try to answer you. The " Magnum et
terribile " (is that right?) Well, folk began with this in the early day; And all the acts
they recognized in proof Were thunders, lightnings, earthquakes, whirlwinds, dealt
1080 Indisputably on men whose death they caused.
    There, and there only, folk saw Providence
    At work,–and seeing it, t was right enough

All heads should tremble, hands wring hands amain,
And knees knock hard together at the breath
O the Names first letter; why, the Jews, I m told,
Wont write it down, no, to this very hour,
Nor speak aloud: you know best if t be so.
Each ague-fit of fear at end, they crept (Because somehow people once born must live) 1090
Out of the sound, sight, swing and sway o the Name, Into a corner, the dark rest of the world,
And safe space where as yet no fear had reached;
T was there they looked about them, breathed again,
And felt indeed at home, as we might say.
The current o common things, the daily life,
This had their due contempt; no Name pursued
Man from the mountain-top where fires abide,
To his particular mouse-hole at its foot
Where he ate, drank, digested, lived in short: 1100
Such was mans vulgar business, far too small
To be worth thunder: "small," folk kept on, "small,"
With much complacency in those great days!
A mote of sand, you know, a blade of grass–
What was so despicable as mere grass,
Except perhaps the life o the worm or fly
Which fed there? These were "small " and men were great.
Well, sir, the old way s altered somewhat since,
And the world wears another aspect now:
Somebody turns our spyglass round, or else i 110
Puts a new lens in it: grass, worm, fly grow big:
We find great things are made of little things,
And little things go lessening till at last
Comes God behind them. Talk of mountains now?
We talk of mould that heaps the mountain, mites
That throng the mould, and God that makes the mites.
The Name comes close behind a stomach-cyst,
The simplest of creations, just a sac
Thats mouth, heart, legs and belly at once, yet lives
And feels, and could do neither, we conclude, 11 20
If simplified still further one degree:
The small becomes the dreadful and immense!
Lightning, forsooth? No word more upon that!
A tin-foil bottle, a strip of greasy silk,
With a bit of wire and knob of brass, and there s
Your dollars-worth of lightning! But the cyst–
The life of the least of the little things?
No, no!

Preachers and teachers try another tack,
Come near the truth this time: they put aside 11 30
Thunder and lightning: "Thats mistake," they cry,
"Thunderbolts fall for neither fright nor sport,
But do appreciable good, like tides,
Changes o the wind, and other natural facts–
Good meaning good to man, his body or soul.
Mediate, immediate, all things minister
To man,–thats settled: be our future text
We are His children! " So, they now harangue
About the intention, the contrivance, all
That keeps up an incessant play of love,–
See the Bridgewater book.
Amen to it! 1140
Well, sir, I put this question: I m a child?
I lose no time, but take you at your word:
How shall I act a childs part properly?
Your sainted mother, sir,–used you to live
With such a thought as this a-worrying you?
"She has it in her power to throttle me,
Or stab or poison: she may turn me out,
Or lock me in,–nor stop at this to-day,
But cut me off to-morrow from the estate
I look for "–(long may you enjoy it, sir!) 1150
"In brief, she may unchild the child I am."
You never had such crotchets? Nor have I!
Who, frank confessing childship from the first,
Cannot both fear and take my ease at once,
So, dont fear,–know what might be, well enough,
But know too, child-like, that it will not be,
At least in my case, mine, the son and heir
O the kingdom, as yourself proclaim my style.
But do you fancy I stop short at this?
Wonder if suit and service, son and heir 1160
Needs must expect, I dare pretend to find?
If, looking for signs proper to such an one, I straight perceive them irresistible?
Concede that homage is a sons plain right,
And, never mind the nods and raps and winks,
T is the pure obvious supernatural
Steps forward, does its duty: why, of course!
I have presentiments; my dreams come true: I fancy a friend stands whistling all in white
Blithe as a boblink, and he s dead I learn. 1170
J take dislike to a dog my favorite long,
And sell him; he goes mad next week and snaps.

I guess that stranger will turn up to-day I have not seen these three years; theres his knock.

I wager " sixty peaches on that tree! "–
That I pick up a dollar in my walk,
Thatyourwifesbrotherscousins name was George–
And win on all points. Oh, you wince at this?
You d fain distinguish between gift and gift,
Washingtons oracle and Sludges itch 1! 80
O the elbow when at whist he ought to trump?
With Sludge its too absurd? Fine, draw the line
Somewhere, but, sir, your somewhere is not mine!
Bless us, Im turning poet! Its time to end.
How you have drawn me out, sir! All I ask Is–am I heir or not heir? If I m he,
Then, sir, remember, that same personage (To judge by what we read i the news-paper)

Requires, beside one nobleman in gold
To carry up and down his coronet, 1190 I
Another servant, probably a duke,
To hold egg-nogg in readiness: why want
Attendance, sir, when helps in his fathers house
Abound, I d like to know?
Enough of talk!
My fault is that I tell too plain a truth.
Why, which of those who say they disbelieve,
Your clever people, but has dreamed his dream,
Caught his coincidence, stumbled on his fact
He cant explain, (hell tell you smilingly)
Which he s too much of a philosopher 1200

To count as supernatural, indeed,
So calls a puzzle and problem, proud of it:
Bidding you still be on your guard, you know,
Because one fact dont make a system stand,
Nor prove this an occasional escape
Of spirit beneath the matter: thats the way!
Just so wild Indians picked up, piece by piece,
The fact in California, the fine gold
That underlay the gravel–hoarded these,
But never made a system stand, nor dug! 1210

So wise men hold out in each hollowed palm
A handful of experience, sparkling fact
They cant explain; and since their rest of life
Is all explainable, what proof in this?
Whereas I take the fact, the grain of gold,
And fling away the dirty rest of life,
And add this grain to the grain each fool has found

O the million other such philosophers,–
Till I see gold, all gold and only gold,
Truth questionless though unexplainable, 1220
    And the miraculous proved the commonplace!
The other fools believed in mud, no doubt–
Failed to know gold they saw: was that so strange?
Are all men born to play Bachs fiddle-fugues,
"Time " with the foil in carte, jump their own height,
Cut the mutton with the broadsword, skate a five,
Make the red hazard with the cur, clip nails
    While swimming, in five minutes row a mile,
    Pull themselves three feet up with the left arm,
    Do sums of fifty figures in their head, 1230
    And so on, by the scores of instances?
    The Sludge with luck, who sees the spiritual facts
    His fellows strive and fail to see, may rank
    With these, and share the advantage.
    Ay, but share
    The drawback! Think it over by yourself;
I have not heart, sir, and the fire s gone gray.
Defect somewhere compensates for success,
Every one knows that. Oh, we re equals, sir!
The big-legged fellow has a little arm
And a less brain, though big legs win the race: 1240
Do you suppose I scape the common lot?
Say, I was born with flesh so sensitive,
Soul so alert, that, practice helping both,
I guess what s going on outside the veil,
Just as a prisoned crane feels pairing-time
In the islands where his kind are, so must fall
To capering by himself some shiny night,
As if your back-yard were a plot of spice–
Thus am I ware o the spirit-world: while you,
Blind as a beetle that way,–for amends, 1 250
    Why, you can double fist and floor me, sir!
Ride that hot hardmouthed horrid horse of yours,
Laugh while it lightens, play with the great dog,
Speak your mind though it vex some friend to hear,
Never brag, never bluster, never blush,–
In short, you ve pluck, when I m a coward–there!
I know it, I cant help it,–folly or no,
I m paralyzed, my hand s no more a hand,
Nor my head a head, in danger: you can smile
    And change the pipe in your cheek. Your gift s not mine. 1260
    Would you swap for mine? No! but you d add my gift

To yours: I dare say! I too sigh at times,
Wish I were stouter, could tell truth nor flinch,
Keep cool when threatened, did not mind so much
Being dressed gayly, making strangers stare,
Eating nice things; when I d amuse myself,
I shut my eyes and fancy in my brain
I m—now the President, now Jenny Lind,
Now Emerson, now the Benicia Boy—
With all the civilized world a-wondering 1270
  And worshipping. I know its folly and worse;
I feel such tricks sap, honeycomb the soul,
But I cant cure myself: despond, despair,
And then, hey, presto, theres a turn o the wheel,
Under comes uppermost, fate makes full amends;
Sludge knows and sees and hears a hundred things
You all are blind to,—Ive my taste of truth,
Likewise my touch of falsehood,—vice no doubt,
But you ve your vices also: I m content.
What, sir? You wont shake hands? "Because I cheat! " 1280
  "You ve found me out in cheating! " That s enough
  To make an apostle swear! Why, when I cheat,
Mean to cheat, do cheat, and am caught in the act,
Are you, or, rather, am I sure o the fact?
(There s verse again, but I m inspired somehow.)
Well then I m not sure! I may be, perhaps,
Free as a babe from cheating: how it began,
My gift,—no matter; what t is got to be
In the end now, thats the question; answer that
  Had I seen, perhaps, what hand was holding mine,
  Leading me whither, I had died of fright: 1291
  So, I was made believe I led myself.
  If I should lay a six-inch plank from roof
  To roof, you would not cross the street, one step,
  Even at your mothers summons: but, being shrewd, If I paste paper on each side the plank
  And swear tis solid pavement, why, you ll cross
  Humming a tune the while, in ignorance
  Beacon Street stretches a hundred feet below: I walked thus, took the paper-cheat for stone. 1300
  Some impulse made me set a thing o the move
  Which, started once, ran really by itself;
  Beer flows thus, suck the siphon; toss the kite, It takes the wind and floats of its own force.
  Dont let truths lump rot stagnant for the lack
  Of a timely helpful lie to leaven it!

Put a chalk-egg beneath the clucking hen,
Shell lay a real one, laudably deceived,
Daily for weeks to come. Ive told my lie,
And seen truth follow, marvels none of mine; 1310
All was not cheating, sir, I m positive!
I dont know if I move your hand sometimes
When the spontaneous writing spreads so far, If my knee lifts the table all that
height,
Why the inkstand dont fall off the desk a-tilt,
Why the accordion plays a prettier waltz
Than I can pick out on the piano-forte,
Why I speak so much more than I intend,
Describe so many things I never saw.
I tell you, sir, in one sense, I believe I 3 zo
Nothing at all,–that everybody can,
Will, and does cheat: but in another sense I m ready to believe my very self–
That every cheat s inspired, and every lie
Quick with a germ of truth.
You ask perhaps
Why I should condescend to trick at all
If I know a way without it? This is why!
There s a strange secret sweet self-sacrifice
In any desecration of ones soul
To a worthy end,–is nt it Herodotus 330 (I wish I could read Latin!) who describes
The single gift o the lands virginity,
Demanded in those old Egyptian rites,
(I ve but a hazy notion–help me, sir!)
For one purpose in the world, one day in a life,
One hour in a day–thereafter, purity,
And a veil thrown oer the past for evermore!
Well, now, they understood a many things
Down by Nile city, or wherever it was!
I ve always vowed, after the minutes lie, 340
And the end s gain,–truth should be mine henceforth.
This goes to the root o the matter, sir,–this plain
Plump fact: accept it and unlock with it
The wards of many a puzzle!
Or, finally,
Why should I set so fine a gloss on things?
What need I care? I cheat in self-defence,
And there s my answer to a world of cheats!
Cheat? To be sure, sir! Whats the world worth else?
Who takes it as he finds, and thanks his stars?
Dont it want trimming, turning, furbishing up 1350

And polishing over? Your so-styled great men,
Do they accept one truth as truth is found,
    Or try their skill at tinkering? Whats your world 5
Here are you born, who are, I ll say at once,
Of the luckiest kind, whether in head and heart,
Body and soul, or all that helps them both.
Well, now, look back: what faculty of yours
Came to its full, had ample justice done
By growing when rain fell, biding its time,
Solidifying growth when earth was dead, 1360
    Spiring up, broadening wide, in seasons due?
Never! You shot up and frost nipped you off,
Settled to sleep when sunshine bade you sprout;
One faculty thwarted its fellow: at the end,
All you boast is " I had proved a topping tree
In other climes "–yet this was the right clime
Had you foreknown the seasons. Young, youve force
Wasted like well-streams: old,–oh, then indeed,
Behold a labyrinth of hydraulic pipes 137
    Through which you d play off wondrous waterwork;
Only, no water s left to feed their play.
Young,–you ve a hope, an aim, a love: its tossed
And crossed and lost: you struggle on, some spark
Shut in your heart against the puffs around,
Through cold and pain; these in due time subside,
Now then for ages triumph, the hoarded light
You mean to loose on the altered face of things,–
Up with it on the tripod! Its extinct.
Spend your lifes remnant asking, which was best,
Light smothered up that never peeped forth once, 13 80
Or the cold cresset with full leave to shine?
Well, accept this too,–seek the fruit of it
Not in enjoyment, proved a dream on earth,
But knowledge, useful for a second chance,
Another life,–you ve lost this world–you ve
gained Its knowledge for the next. What knowledge, sir,
Except that you know nothing? Nay, you doubt
Whether twere better have made you man or brute,
If aught be true, if good and evil clash.
No foul, no fair, no inside, no outside, 1390
    There s your world!
    Give it me! I slap it brisk
    With harlequins pasteboard sceptre: whats it now?
Changed like a rock-flat, rough with rusty weed,
At first wash-over o the returning wave!

All the dry dead impracticable stuff
Starts into life and light again; this world
Pervaded by the influx from the next.
I cheat, and whats the happy consequence?
You find full justice straightway dealt you out,
Each want supplied, each ignorance set at ease, 1400
Each folly fooled. No life-long labor now
As the price of worse than nothing! No mere film
Holding you chained in iron, as it seems,
Against the outstretch of your very arms
And legs i the sunshine moralists forbid!
What would you have? Just speak and, there, you see!
You re supplemented, made a whole at last,
Bacon advises, Shakespeare writes you songs,
And Mary Queen of Scots embraces you.
Thus it goes on, not quite like life perhaps, 1410
    But so near, that the very difference piques,
Shows that een better than this best will be–
This passing entertainment in a hut
Whose bare walls take your taste since, one stage more,
And you arrive at the palace: all half real,
And you, to suit it, less than real beside,
In a dream, lethargic kind of death in life,
    That helps the interchange of natures, flesh
    Transfused by souls, and such souls! Oh, t is choice!
    And if at whiles the bubble, blown too thin, 1420
    Seem nigh on bursting,–if you nearly see
    The real world through the false,–what do you see?
    Is the old so ruined? You find you re in a flock
    O the youthful, earnest, passionate–genius, beauty,
    Rank and wealth also, if you care for these:
    And all depose their natural rights, hail you, (Thats me, sir) as their mate and
yoke-fellow,
    Participate in Sludgehood–nay, grow mine, I veritably possess them–banish doubt,
    And reticence and modesty alike! 1430
    Why, heres the Golden Age, old Paradise
    Or new Utopia! Heres true life indeed,
    And the world well won now, mine for the first time!
    And all this might be, may be, and with good help
    Of a little lying shall be: so, Sludge lies!
    Why, he s at worst your poet who sings how Greeks
    That never were, in Troy which never was,
    Did this or the other impossible great thing!
    Hes Lowell–its a world (you smile applause),
    Of his own invention–wondrous Longfellow, 1440

Surprising Hawthorne! Sludge does more than they,
And acts the books they write: the more his praise!
But why do I mount to poets? Take plain prose–
Dealers in common sense, set these at work,
What can they do without their helpful lies?
Each states the law and fact and face o the thing
Just as he d have them, finds what he thinks fit,
Is blind to what missuits him, just records
What makes his case out, quite ignores the rest.
Its a History of the World, the Lizard Age, 1450
The Early Indians, the Old Country War,
Jerome Napoleon, whatsoever you please,
All as the author wants it. Such a scribe
You pay and praise for putting life in stones,
Fire into fog, making the past your world.
There s plenty of " How did you contrive to grasp
The thread which led you through this labyrinth?
How build such solid fabric out of air?
How on so slight foundation found this tale,
Biography, narrative?" or, in other words, 1460
"How many lies did it require to make
The portly truth you here present us with?"
"Oh," quoth the penman, purring at your praise,
"T is fancy all; no particle of fact: I was poor and threadbare when I wrote that
book
Bliss in the Golden City. I, at Thebes?
We writers paint out of our heads, you see!"
"–Ah, the more wonderful the gift in you,
The more creativeness and godlike craft!"
But I, do I present you with my piece, I470 It s " What, Sludge? When my sainted
mother spoke
The verses Lady Jane Grey last composed
About the rosy bower in the seventh heaven
Where she and Queen Elizabeth keep house,–
You made the raps? T was your invention that?
Cur, slave and devil! "–eight fingers and two thumbs
Stuck in my throat!
Well, if the marks seem gone, Tis because stiffish cock-tail, taken in time, Is better
for a bruise than arnica. There, sir! I bear no malice: tis nt in me. 1480 I know I acted
wrongly: still, I ve tried What I could say in my excuse,–to show
The devils not all devil. I dont pretend,
He s angel, much less such a gentleman
As you, sir! And I ve lost you, lost myself,
Lost all-l-l-l-.
No–are you in earnest, sir?

0 yours, sir, is an angels part! I know
What prejudice prompts, and what the common course
Men take to soothe their ruffled self-conceit:
Only you rise superior to it all! 1490
   No, sir, it dont hurt much; its speaking long
That makes me choke a little: the marks will go!
What? Twenty V-notes more, and outfit too,
And not a word to Greeley? One–one kiss
O the hand that saves me! You ll not let me speak, I well know, and I ve lost the right, too true!
But I must say, sir, if She hears (she does)
   Your sainted. Well, sir,–be it so! Thats, I think, My bed-room candle. Good-night!
Bl-l-less you, sir!
   R-r-r, you brute-beast and blackguard! Cowardly scamp! 1500 I only wish I dared burn down the house
And spoil your sniggering! Oh what, you re the man?
   You re satisfied at last? You ve found out Sludge?
We ll see that presently: my turn, sir, next!
I too can tell my story: brute,–do you hear?–
You throttled your sainted mother, that old hag,
In just such a fit of passion: no, it was.
To get this house of hers, and many a note
Like these. I ll pocket them, however. five,
   Ten, fifteen. ay, you gave her throat the twist, Or else you poisoned her! Confound the cuss! 1511 Where was my head? I ought to have prophesied He ll die in a year and join her: thats the way.
   I dont know where my head is: what had I done?
How did it all go? I said he poisoned her,
And hoped he d have grace given him to repent,
Whereon he picked this quarrel, bullied me
And called me cheat: I thrashed him,–who could help?
He howled for mercy, prayed me on his knees
To cut and run and save him from disgrace: 1520 I do so, and once off, he slanders me.
   An end of him! Begin elsewhere anew!
Boston s a hole, the herring-pond is wide,
V-notes are something, liberty still more.
Beside, is he the only fool in the world?
APPARENT FAILURE.
"We shall soon lose a celebrated building."
Paris Newspaper. l.
   No, for I ll save it! Seven years since, I passed through Paris, stopped a day
To see thev baptism of your Prince;

Saw, made my bow, and went my way:
Walking the heat and headache off, I took the Seine-side, you surmise,
Thought of the Congress, Gortschakoff,
    Cavours appeal and Buols replies,
So sauntered till–what met my eyes?
M. w.–18
    Only the Doric little Morgue! 10
The dead-house where you show your drowned: Petrarchs Vaucluse makes proud
the Sorgue,
    Your Morgue has made the Seine renowned. One pays ones debt in such a case; I
plucked up heart and entered,–stalked, Keeping a tolerable face
    Compared with some whose cheeks were chalked: Let them! No Briton s to be
balked!
    First came the silent gazers; next,
    A screen of glass, we re thankful for; 20
Last, the sights self, the sermons text,
    The three men who did most abhor Their life in Paris yesterday,
    So killed themselves: and now, enthroned
Each on his copper couch, they lay
    Fronting me, waiting to be owned.
I thought, and think, their sin s atoned.
    ni.
    Poor men, God made, and all for that!
    The reverence struck me; oer each head Religiously was hung its hat, 30
    Each coat dripped by the owners bed, Sacred from touch: each had his berth,
    His bounds, his proper place of rest, Who last night tenanted on earth
    Some arch, where twelve such slept abreast,–Unless the plain asphalt seemed best.
    How did it happen, my poor boy?
    You wanted to be Buonaparte And have the Tuileries for toy,
    And could not, so it broke your heart? 40 You, old one by his side, I judge,
    Were, red as blood, a socialist,
A leveller! Does the Empire grudge
    You ve gained what no Republic missed?
Be quiet, and unclench your fist!
    v 1.
    And this–why, he was red in vain,
    Or black,–poor fellow that is blue! What fancy was it turned your brain?
    Oh, women were the prize for you! Money gets women, cards and dice 50
    Get money, and ill-luck gets just The copper couch and one clear nice
    Cool squirt of water oer your bust, The right thing to extinguish lust!
    Its wiser being good than bad; Its safer being meek than fierce: Its fitter being sane
than mad.
    My own hope is, a sun will pierce The thickest cloud earth ever stretched;
    That, after Last, returns the First, 60
    Though a wide compass round be fetched;

That what began best, cant end worst, Nor what God blessed once, prove accurst.
EPILOGUE.

FlrST SPEAKER, as Davtd.

1.

On the first of the Feast of Feasts,
The Dedication Day,
When the Levites joined the Priests
At the Altar in robed array,
Gave signal to sound and say,– ii.

When the thousands, rear and van,
Swarming with one accord Became as a single man (Look, gesture, thought and word) In praising and thanking the Lord,–10 ill.

When the singers lift up their voice,
And the trumpets made endeavor,
Sounding, "In God rejoice! "
Saying, "In Him rejoice
Whose mercy endureth forever! "– iv.

Then the Temple filled with a cloud,
Even the House of the Lord; Porch bent and pillar bowed:
For the presence of the Lord, In the g)ory of His cloud, 20
Had filled the House of the Lord.

Second Speaker, as Renan.

Gone now! All gone across the dark so far,
Sharpening fast, shuddering ever, shutting still, Dwindling into the distance, dies that star
Which came, stood, opened once: We gazed our fill With upturned faces on as real a Face
That, stooping from grave music and mild fire, Took in our homage, made a visible place
Through many a depth of glory, gyre on gyre, For the dim human tribute. Was this true r 30
Could man indeed avail, mere praise of his, x To help by rapture Gods own rapture too,
Thrill with a hearts red tinge that pure pale bliss? Why did it end? Who failed to beat the breast,
And shriek, and throw the arms protesting wide. When a first shadow showed the star addressed Itself to motion, and on either side The rims contracted as the rays retired;
The music, like a fountains sickening pulse, Subsided on itself; awhile transpired 40
Some vestige of a Face no pangs convulse, No prayers retard; then even this was gone,
Lost in the night at last. We, lone and left Silent through centuries, ever and anon
Venture to probe again the vault bereft Of all now save the lesser lights, a mist
Of multitudinous points, yet suns, men say—And this leaps ruby, this lurks amethyst,

But where may hide what came and loved our clay? How shall the sage detect in yon expanse 50

The star which chose to stoop and stay for us?

Unroll the records! Hailed ye such advance Indeed, and did your hope evanish thus? Watchers of twilight, is the worst averred?

We shall not look up, know ourselves are seen, Speak, and be sure that we again are heard,

Acting or suffering, have the disks serene Reflect our life, absorb an earthly flame,

Nor doubt that, were mankind inert and numb, Its core had never crimsoned all the same, 60

Nor, missing ours, its music fallen dumb? Oh, dread succession to a dizzy post,

Sad sway of sceptre whose mere touch appalls, Ghastly dethronement, cursed by those the most

On whose repugnant brow the crown next falls!

THIRD SPEAKER.

1.

Witless alike of will and way divine,
How heavens high with earths low should intertwine!
Friends, I have seen through your eyes: now use
mine!

Take the least man of all mankind, as I;
Look at his head and heart, find how and why 70
He differs from his fellows utterly: ill.

Then, like me, watch when nature by degrees
Grows alive round him, as in Arctic seas
(They said of old) the instinctive water flees 1v.

Toward some elected point of central rock,
As though, for its sake only, roamed the flock
Of waves about the waste: awhile they mock

With radiance caught for the occasion,–hues
Of blackest hell now, now such reds and blues
As only heaven could fitly interfuse,–80 v1.

The mimic monarch of the whirlpool, king
O the current for a minute: then they wring
Up by the roots and oversweep the thing,

And hasten off, to play again elsewhere
The same part, choose another peak as bare,
They find and flatter, feast and finish there.

v111.

When you see what I tell you,–nature dance
About each man of us, retire, advance,
As though the pageants end were to enhance 89 1x.

His worth, and–once the life, his product, gained–
Roll away elsewhere, keep the strife sustained,
And show thus real, a thing the North but feigned–

When you acknowledge that one world could do
All the diverse work, old yet ever new,
Divide us, each from other, me from you,– x1.
Why, where s the need of Temple, when the walls O the world are that? What use
of swells and falls From Levites choir, Priests cries, and trumpet-calls?
xn.
That one Face, far from vanish, rather grows,
Or decomposes but to recompose, 100
Become my universe that feels and knows.
NOTES.
Men And Women.
Transcendentalism is a criticism, placed in the mouth of a poet, of another poet, whose manner of singing is prosaic, because it seeks to transcend (or penetrate beyond) phenomena, by divesting poetic expression of those concrete embodiments which enable it to appeal to the senses and imagination. Instead of bare abstractions being suited to the developed mind, it is the primitive mind, which, like Boehmes, has the merely metaphysical turn, and expects to discover the unincarnate absolute essence of things. The maturer mind craves the vitalizing method of the artist who, like the magician of Hal-berstadt, recreates things bodily in all their beautiful vivid wholeness. Yet the poet who sincerely holds so fragmentary a conception of art is himself a poem to the poet who holds the larger view. His boy-face singing to God above his ineffective harp-strings is a concrete image of this sort of poetic transcendentalism.

It is obvious that Browning uses the Halberstadt and not the Boehme method in presenting this embodiment of his subject. The supposition of certain commentators that Browning is here picturing his own artistic method as transcendental is a misconception of his characteristic theory of poetic art, as shown here and elsewhere.

line22. Boehme: Jacob, an " inspired " German shoemaker (1575-1624), who wrote "Aurora," "The Three Principles," etc., mystical commentaries on Biblical events. When twenty-five years old, says Hotham in " Mysterium Magnum," 1653, " he was surrounded by a divine Light and replenished with heavenly Knowledge. going abroad into the Fieldes to a Greene before Neys-Gate at Gorlitz and viewing the Herbes and Grass of the Fielde, in his inward light he saw into their Essences. and from that Fountain of Revelation wrote De Signatura Rerum," on the signatures of things, the " tough book" to which Browning refers.

37. Halberstadt: Johann Semeca, called Teutonicus, a canon of Halberstadt in Germany, who was interested in the unchurchly study of mediaeval science and reputed to be a magician, possessing the vegetable stone supposed to make plants grow at will, having the same power over organic life that the philosophers stone of the alchemists had over minerals, so that, like Albertus Magnus, another such mage of the Middle Ages, he could cause flowers to spring up in the midst of winter.

Bow It Strikes a Contemporary is a portrait of the Poet as the unpoetic gossiping public of his day sees him. It is humorously colored by the alien point of view of the speaker, who suspects without understanding either the greatness of the poets spiritual personality and mission, or the nature of his life, which is withdrawn from that of the commonalty, yet spent in clear-sighted universal sympathies and kindly mediation between Humanity and its God.

3. Valladolid: the royal city of the kings of Castile, before Philip II. moved the Court to Madrid, where Cervantes, Calderon, and Las Casas lived and Columbus died.

76. Titians: pictures by the Venetian, Tiziano Vecellio (1477-1576), glowing in color, presumably of large golden-haired women like his famous Venus.

90. Corregidor: the Spanish title for a magistrate j literally, a corrector, from corregir, to correct.

Artemis Prologizes represents the goddess Artemis awaiting the revival of the youth Hippolytus, whom she has carried to her woods and given to Asclepios to heal. It is a fragment meant to introduce an unwritten work and carry on the story related by Euripides in " Hippolytus," Tvhich see.

An Epistle gives the observations and opinions of Kar-shish, the Arab physician, writing to Abib, his master, upon meeting with Lazarus after he has been raised from the dead. Well versed in Eastern medical lore, he tries to explain the extraordinary phenomenon according to his knowledge. He attributes Lazarus version of the miracle to mania induced by trance, and the means used by the Nazarene physician to awaken him, and strengthens his view by describing the strange state of mind in which he finds Lazarus,–like a child with no appreciation of the relative values of things. Through his renewal of life he had caught a glimpse of it from the infinite point of view, and lives now only with the desire to please God. His sole active quality is a great love for all humanity; his impatience manifests itself only at sin and ignorance, and is quickly curbed. Karshish, not able to realize this new plane of vision in which had been revealed to Lazarus the equal worth of all things in the divine plan, is incapable of understanding Lazarus; but in spite of his attempt to make light of the case, he is deeply impressed by the character of Lazarus, and has besides a hardly acknowledged desire to believe in this revelation, told of by Lazarus, of God as Love. Professor Corson says of this poem: "It may be said to polarize the idea, so often presented in Brownings poetry, that doubt is a condition of the vitality of faith."

17. Snakestone: a name given to any substance used as a remedy for snake-bites; for example, some are of chalk, some of animal charcoal, and some of vegetable substances.

28. Vespasian: Neros general who marched against Palestine in 66, and was succeeded in the command, when he was proclaimed Emperor (70-79), by his son, Titus.

29. Black lynx: the Syrian lynx is distinguished by black ears.

43. Tertians: fevers, recurring every third day; hence the name.

44. Falling-sickness: epilepsy. Caesars disease (" Julius Caesar," i. 2, 258).

45. Therc s a spider here: "The habits of the aranead here described point very clearly to some one of the Wandering group, which stalk their prey in the open field or in divers lurking-places, and are distinguished by this habit from the other great group, known as the Sedentary spiders, because they sit or hang upon their webs and capture their prey by means of silken snares. The next line is not determinative of the species, for there is a great number of spiders any one of which might be described as Sprinkled with mottles on an ash-gray back. We have a little Saltigrade or Jumping

spider, known as the Zebra spider (Epiblemum icenicum), which is found in Europe, and I believe also in Syria. One often sees this species and its congeners upon the ledges of rocks, the edges of tombstones, the walls of buildings, and like situations, hunting their prey, which they secure by jumping upon it. So common is the Zebra spider, that I might think that Browning referred to it, if I were not in doubt whether he would express the stripes of white upon its ash-gray abdomen by the word mottles. However, there are other spiders belonging to the same tribe (Saltigrades) that really are mottled. There are also spiders known as the Lycosids or Wolf spiders or Ground spiders, which are often of an ash-gray color, and marked with little whitish spots after the manner of Brownings Syrian species. Perhaps the poet had one of these in mind; at least he accurately describes their manner of seeking prey. The next line is an interrupted one, Take five and drop them. Take five what? Five of these ash-gray mottled spiders? Certainly. But what can be meant by the expression drop them? This opens up to us a strange chapter in human superstition. It was long a prevalent idea that the spider ir various forms possessed some occult power of healing and men administered it internally or applied it externally as a cure for many diseases. Pliny gives a number of such remedies. A certain spider applied in a piece of cloth, or another one (a white spider with very elongated thin legs), beaten up in oil is said by this ancient writer upon Natural History to form an ointment for the eyes. Similarly, the thick pulp of a spiders body, mixed with the oil of roses, is used for the ears." Sir Matthew Lister, who was indeed the father of English araneology, is quoted in Dr. Jamess Medical Dictionary as using the distilled water of boiled black spiders as an excellent cure for wounds." (Dr. H. C. Mccook in Poet-lore, Nov., 1889.) 55. Gum-tragacanth: yielded by the leguminous shrub, Astragalus tragacantha.

60. Zoar: the only one that was spared of the five cities of the plain (Genesis xiv. 2).

108. Lazarus. fifty years of age: in The Academy, Sept. 16, 1896, Dr. Richard Garnett says: " Browning commits an oversight, it seems to me, in making Lazarus fifty years of age at the eve of the siege of Jerusalem, circa 68 A. D." The miracle is supposed to have been wrought about 33 A. D., and Lazarus would then have been only fifteen, although according to tradition he was thirty when he was raised from the dead, and lived only thirty years after. Upon this Prof. Charles B. Wright comments in Poet-lore, April, 1897: "I incline to think that the oversight is not Brownings. Let us stand by the tradition and the resulting age of sixty-five. Karshish is simply stating his professional judgment. Lazarus is given an age suited to his appearance–he seems a man of fifty. The years have touched him lightly since heaven opened to his soul. And that marvellous physical freshness deceives the very leech himself."

177. Greek fire: used by the Byzantine Greeks in warfare, first against the Saracens at the siege of Constantinople in 673 A. D. Therefore an anachronism in this poem. Liquid fire was, however, known to the ancients, as Assyrian bas-reliefs testify. Greek fire was made possibly of naphtha, saltpetre, and sulphur, and was thrown upon the enemy from copper tubes; or pledgets of tow were dipped in it and attached to arrows.

281. Blue-flowering borage: (Borago officinalis). The ancients deemed this plant one of the four " cordial flowers," for cheering the spirits; the others being the rose, violet, and alkanet. Pliny says it produces very exhilarating effects.

Johannes Agricola la Meditation presents the doctrine of predestination as it appears to a devout and poetic soul whose conviction of the truth of such a doctrine has the strength of a divine revelation. Those elected for Gods love can do nothing to weaken it, those not elected can do nothing to gain it, but it is not his to reason why j indeed, he could not praise a god whose ways he could understand or for whose love he had to bargain.

Johannes Agricola: (1492-1566), Luthers secretary, 1519, afterward in conflict with him, and author of the doctrine called by Luther antinomian, because it rejected the Law of the Old Testament as of no use under the Gospel dispensation. In a note accompanying the first publication of this poem, Browning quotes from " The Dictionary of All Religions" (1704): " They say that good works do not further, nor evil works hinder salvation; that the child of God cannot sin, that God never chastiseth him, that murder, drunkenness, etc., are sins in the wicked but not in him, that the child of grace being once assured of salvation, afterwards never doubteth. that God doth not love any man for his holiness, that sanctification is no evidence of justification." Though many antinomians taught thus, says George Willis Cooke in his " Browning Guide Book," it does not correctly represent the position of Agricola, who in reality held moral obligations to be incumbent upon the Christian, but for guidance in these he found in the New Testament all the principles and motives necessary.

Fictor Ignotns is a reverie characteristic of a monastic painter of the Renaissance who recognizes, in the genius of a youth whose pictures are praised, a gift akin to his own, but which he has never so exercised, spite of the joy such free human expression and recognition of his power would have given him, because he could not bear to submit his art to worldly contact. So he has chosen to sink his name in unknown service to the Church, and to devote his fancy to pure and beautiful but cold and monotonous repetitions of sacred themes. His gentle regret that his own pictures will moulder unvisited is half wonderment that the youth can endure the sullying of his work by secular fame.

67. Travertine: a white limestone, the name being a corruption of Tiburtinus, from Tibur, now Tivoli, near Rome, whence this stone comes.

Fra Lippo Idppt is a dramatic monologue which incidentally conveys the whole story of the occurrence the poem starts from–the seizure of Fra Lippo by the City Guards, past midnight, in an equivocal neighborhood–and the lively talk that arose thereupon; outlines the character and past life of the Florentine artist-monk (1412-1469) and the subordinate personalities of the group of officers; and makes all this contribute towards the presentation of Fra Lippo as a type of the more realistic and secular artist of the Renaissance who valued flesh, and protested against the ascetic spirit which strove to isolate the soul.

1. The Carmine: monastery of the Del Carmine friars.

17. Cosimo: demedici (1389-1464), Florentine statesman and patron of the arts.

23. Pilchards: a kind of fish.

53. Floiver o the broom: of the many varieties of folksongs in Italy that which furnished Browning with a model for Lippos songs is called a stornello. The name is variously derived. Some take it as merely short for ritornello , others derive it from a starno, to sing against each other, because the peasants sing them at their work, and

as one ends a song, another caps it with a fresh one, and so on. These starnelli consist of three lines. The first usually contains the name of a flower which sets the rhyme, and is five syllables long. Then the love theme is told in two lines of eleven syllables each, agreeing by rhyme, assonance, or repetition with the first. The first line may be looked upon as a burden set at the beginning instead of, as is more familiar to us, at the end. There are also stornelli formed of three lines of eleven syllables without any burden. Browning has made Lippos songs of only two lines, but he has strictly followed the rule of making the first line, containing the address to the flower, of five syllables. The Tuscany versions of two of the songs used by Browning are as follows:

"Flower of the pine!
Call me not ever happy heart again.
But call me heavy heart, O comrades mine."

"Flower of the broom I
Unwed thy mother keeps thee not to lose
That flower from the window of the room."

67. Saint Laurence: the church of San Lorenzo.

88. Aunt Lapaccia: by the death of Lippos father, says Vasari, he " was left a friendless orphan at the age of two. under the care of Mona Lapaccia, his aunt, who brought him up with very great difficulty till his eighth year, when, being no longer able to support the burden, she placed him in the Convent of the Carmelites."

121. The Eight: the magistrates of Florence.

130. Antiphonary: the Roman Service-Book, containing all that is sung in the choir—the antiphones, responses, etc.; it was compiled by Gregory the Great.

131. Joined legs and arms to the long music-notes: the musical notation of Lippos day was entirely different from ours, the notes being square and oblong and rather less suited for arms and legs than the present rounded notes.

139. Camaldolese: monks of Camaldoli.–Preaching Friars: the Dominicans.

189. Giotto: reviver of art in Italy, painter, sculptor, and architect (1166-1337).

196. Herodias: Matthew xiv. 6-n.

235. Brother Angelica: Fra Angelico, Giovanni da Fie-sole (1387-1455), flower of the monastic school of art, who was said to paint on his knees.

236. Brother Lorenzo: Lorenzo Monaco, of the same school.

276. Guidi: Tommaso Guidi, or Masaccio, nicknamed "Hulking Tom" (1401-1429). Vasari makes him Lippos predecessor. Browning followed the best knowledge of his time in making him, instead, Lippos pupil. Vasari is now thought to be right.

323. A Saint Laurence. at Praia: near Florence, where Lippi painted many saints. Vasari speaks of a Saint Stephen painted there in the same realistic manner as Brownings Saint Laurence, whose martyrdom of broiling to death on a gridiron affords Lippos powers a livelier effect. The legend of this saint makes his fortitude such that he bade his persecutors turn him over, as he was "done on one side."

346. Somethingin Sant Ambrogiifs: picture of the Virgin crowned with angels and saints, painted for Saint Ambrose Church, now at the Belle Arti in Florence. Vasari says by means of it he became known to Cosimo. Browning, on the other hand, crowns his poem with Lippos description of this picture as an expiation for his pranks.

354. Saint John: the Baptist; see reference to camel-hair, line 375 and Matthew iii. 4.

355. Saint Ambrose: (340-397), Archbishop of Milan. 358. Man of Vz: Job i. i.

377. lite perfeci opus: this one completed the work.

381. Hot cockles: an old-fashioned game.

Andrea del Sarto. This monologue reveals, beside the personalities of both Andrea and Lucrezia and the main incidents of their lives, the relations existing between Andreas character, his choice of a wife, and the peculiar quality of his art; the whole serving, also, to illustrate the picture on which the poem is based. The gray tone that silvers the picture pervades the poem with an air of M. w.—19 helpless, resigned melancholy, and sets forth the fatal quality of facile craftsmanship joined with a flaccid spirit.—Mr. John Kenyon, Mrs. Brownings cousin, asked Browning to get him a copy of the picture of Andrea and his wife in the Pitti Palace. Browning, being unable to find one, wrote this poem describing it, instead. Andrea (1486-1531), because his father was a tailor, was called del Sarto, also, il pittore senza errori, "the faultless painter."

2. Lucrezia: di Baccio del Fede, a cap-makers widow, says Vasari, who ensnared Andrea " before her husbands death, and who delighted in trapping the hearts of men."

1S. Fiesole: a hillside city on the Arno, three miles west of Florence.

93. Morello: the highest of the Apennine mountains north of Florence.

105. The Urbinate: Raphael Santi (1483-1520), so called because born at Urbino.

106. Vasari: painter and writer of the "Lives of the Most Excellent Italian Painters," which supplied Browning with material for this poem and for " Fra Lippo."

130. Agnolo: Michel Agnolo Buonarotti, painter, sculptor, and architect (1475-1564).

149. Francis: Francis I. of France (1494-1547), who invited Andrea to his Court at Fontainebleau, where he was loaded with gifts and honors, until, says Vasari, " came to him certain letters from Florence written to him by his wife. with bitter complaints," when, taking "the money which the king confided to him for the purchase of pictures and statues,. he set off. having sworn on the Gospels to return in a few months. Arrived in Florence, he lived joyously with his wife for some time, making presents to her father and sisters, but doing nothing for his own parents, who died in poverty and misery. When the period specified by the king had come. he found himself at the end not only of his own money but. of that of the king."

184. Agnolo. to Rafael: Angelos remark is given thus by Bocchi, "Bellezze di Firenze ": " There is a bit of a manikin in Florence who, if he chanced to be employed in great undertakings as you have happened to be, would compel you to look well about you."

210. Cue-oivls: the owls cry gives it its common name in various languages and countries; the peculiarity of its cry as to the predominant sound of oo or oiv naming the species. This Italian aulo is probably the Bubo, of the same family as our cat-owl. Buffbn gives its note, he-hoo, boo-hoo; hence the Latin name, Bubo.

241. Scudi: Italian coins.

261. The New Jerusalem: Revelation xxi. 15-17.

263. Leonard: Leonardo da Vinci (i 45 2-1519), painter, sculptor, architect, and engineer, who, together with Rafael and Agnolo, incarnates the genius of the Renaissance. He visited the same Court to which Andrea was invited, and was said to have died in the arms of Francis I.

The Bishop orders his Tomb. This half-delirious pleading of the dying prelate for a tomb which shall gratify his luxurious artistic tastes and personal rivalries, presents dramatically not merely the special scene of the worldly old bishops petulant struggle against his failing power, and his collapse, finally, beneath the will of his so-called nephews; it also illustrates a characteristic gross form of the Renaissance spirit encumbered with Pagan survivals, fleshly appetites, and selfish monopolizings which hampered its development.–"It is nearly all that I said of the Central Renaissance,–its worldliness, inconsistency, pride, hypocrisy, ignorance of itself, love of art, of luxury, and of good Latin–in thirty pages of the Stones of Venice, put into as many lines, Brownings being also the antecedent work" (Ruskin). The Church of St. Praxed is notable for the beauty of its stone-work and mosaics, one of its chapels being so extraordinarily rich that it was called Orto del Paradiso, or the Garden of Paradise; and so, although the bishop and his tomb there are imaginary, it supplies an appropriate setting for the poetic scene.

I. Vanity, saith the preacher: Ecclesiastes i. z.

21. Epistle-side: the right-hand side facing the altar, where the epistle is read by the priest acting as celebrant, the gospel being read from the other side t y the priest acting as assistant.

25. Basalt: trap-rock, leaden or black in color.

31. Onion stone: for the Italian cipollino, a kind of greenish-white marble splitting into coats like an onion, cipalla; hence so called.

41. Olive-frail: a basket made of rushes, used for packing olives.

42. Lapis lazuli: a bright blue stone.

46. Frascati: near Rome, on the Alban hills.

48. God the Father s globe: in the group of the Trinity adorning the altar of Saint Ignatius at the church of II Gesu in Rome.

SI. Weavers shuttle: Job vii. 6.

54. Antique-black: Nero antico. Browning gives the English equivalent for the name of this stone.

58. Tripod: the seat with three feet on which the priestess of Apollo sat to prophesy, an emblem of the Delphic oracle.–Thyrsus: the ivy-coiled staff or spear stuck in a pine-cone, symbol of Bacchic orgy. These, with the other Pagan tokens and pictures, mingle oddly but significantly with the references to the Saviour, Saint Praxed, and Moses. See also line M, where Saint Praxed is confused with the Saviour, in the mind of the dying priest. Saint Praxed, the virgin daughter of a Roman Senator and friend of Saint Paul, in whose honor the Bishops Church is named, is again brought forward in lines 73-75 in a queer capacity which pointedly illustrates the speaker and his time.

66. Travertine: see note " Pictor Ignotus," 67.

68. Jasper: a dark green stone with blood-red spots, susceptible of high polish.

77. fullys: Marcus Tullius Cicero (106-46 B. c.).

79. Ulpian: a Roman jurist (170-228 A. D.), belonging to the degenerate age of Roman literature.

99. Elucescebat: he was illustrious; formed from elu-cesco, an inceptive verb from eluceo: in post classic Latin.

102. Else I give the Pope my villas: perhaps a threat founded on the custom of Julius II. and other popes, according to Burckhardt, of enlarging their power " by making themselves heirs of the cardinals and clergy. Hence the splendor of the tombs of the prelates. a part of the plunder being in this way saved from the hands of the Pope."

108. A vizor and a Term: a mask, and a bust springing from a square pillar, representing the Roman god Terminus, who presided over boundaries.

Bishop Blougrams Apology is made over the wine after dinner to defend himself from the criticisms of a doubting young literary man, who despises him because he considers that he cannot be true to his convictions in conforming to the doctrines of the Catholic Church. He builds up his defence from the proposition that the prob-, lem of life is not to conceive ideals which cannot be realized, but to find what is and make it as fair as possible. The bishop admits his unbelief, but being free to choose either belief or unbelief, since neither can be proved wholly true, chooses belief as his guiding principle, because he finds it the best for making his own life and that of others happy and comfortable in this world. Once having chosen faith on this ground, the more absolute the form of faith, the more potent the results; besides, the bishop has that desire of domination in his nature, which the authorization of the Church makes safer for him. To Gigadibs objection that were his nature nobler, he would not count, this success, he replies he is as God made him, and can but make the best of himself as he is. To the objection that he addresses himself to grosser estimators than he ought, he replies that all the world is interested in the fact that a man of his sense and learning, too, still believes at this late hour. He points out the impossibility of his following an ideal like Napoleons, for, conceding the merest chance that doubt may be wrong, and judgment to follow this life, he would not dare to slaughter men as Napoleon had for such slight ends. As for Shakespeares ideal, he cant write plays like his if he wanted to, but he has realized things in his life which Shakespeare only imagined, and which he presumes Shakespeare would not have scorned to have realized in his life, judging from his fulfilled ambition to be a gentleman of property at Stratford. He admits, however, that enthusiasm in belief, such as Luthers, would be far preferable to his own way of living, and after this, enthusiasm in unbelief, which he might have if it were not for that paguy chance that doubt may be wrong. Gigadibs interposes that the risk is as great for cool indifference as for bold doubt. Blou-gram disputes that point by declaring that doubts prove faith, and that mans free will preferring to have faith true to having doubt true tips the balance in favor of faith, and shows that mans instinct or aspiration is toward belief; that unquestioning belief, such as that of the Past, has no moral effect on man, but faith which knows itself through doubt is a moral spur. Thus the arguments from expediency, instinct, and consciousness, all bear on the side of faith, and convince the bishop that it is safer to keep his faith intact from his doubts. He then proves that Gigadibs, with all his assumption of superiority in his frankness of unbelief, is in about the same position as himself, since the moral law which he follows has no surer foundation than the religious law the bishop follows, both founded upon instinct. The bishop closes as he began, with the consciousness that rewards for his way of living are of a substantial nature, while Gigadibs has nothing to show for his frankness, and does not hesitate to say that Gigadibs will consider his conversation with the bishop the greatest honor ever conferred upon him. The poet adds some lines, somewhat apologetic for the bishop, intimating that his arguments were suited to the calibre of his critic, and that with a profounder critic he would have made a more serious defence. Speaking of a review of this poem by Cardinal Wiseman (1802-1865). Browning says in a letter to a friend, printed in Poet-lore, May, 1896: "The most curious notice I ever had was from Cardinal Wiseman on Blougram –/. e., himself. It was in the Rambler, a Catholic journal of those days, and certified to be his by Father Prout, who said nobody else would have dared put it in." This review praises the poem for its " fertility of illustration and felicity of argument," and says that "though utterly mistaken in the very groundwork of religion, though starting from the most unworthy notions of the work of a Catholic bishop, and defending a self-indulgence every honest man must feel to be disgraceful, it is yet in its way triumphant."

6. Brother Pugin: (1810-1852), an eminent English architect, who, becoming a Roman Catholic, designed many structures for that Church.

34. Corpus Christi Day: Thursday after Trinity Sunday, when the Feast of the Sacrament of the Altar is celebrated.

45. Che: what.

54. Count D Orsay: (17 9 8-18 5 2), a clever Frenchman, distinguished as a man of fashion, and for his drawings of horses.

113. Parmas pride, the Jerome. Correggio. the Modenese: the picture of Saint Jerome in the Ducal Academy at Parma, by Correggio, who was born in the territory of Modena, Italy.

184. A chorus-ending from Euripides: the Greek dramatist, Euripides (480 B.-406 B. c.), frequently ended his choruses with this thought–sometimes with slight variations in expression: " The Gods perform many things contrary to our expectations, and those things which we looked for are not accomplished; but God hath brought to pass things unthought of."

316. Peters . or rather, Hildebrands: the claim of Hildebrand, Pope Gregory VII. (1073-io85)fortemporal power and authority exceeding Saint Peters, the founder of the Roman Church.

411. Schelling: the German philosopher (1775-1854).

472. Austrian marriage: the marriage of Marie Louise, daughter of the Emperor of Austria, to Napoleon I.

475. Austerlitz.: fought with success by Napoleon, in 1805, against the coalition of Austria, Russia, and England, and resulting in the alliance mentioned with Austria and fresh overtures to the Papal power and the old French nobility.

514. Trimmest house in Stratford: New Place, a manT sion in the heart of the town, built for Sir Hugh Clopton, and known for two centuries as his " great house," bought with nearly an acre of ground by Shakespeare, in 1597.

516. Giulio Romano: Italian painter (1492-1546), referred to in " Winters Tale," v. ii. 105.–Doivland: English musician, praised for his lute-playing in a sonnet. in "The Passionate Pilgrim," attributed to Shakespeare.

519. " Pandulph" etc.: quotation from " King John," Hi. i. 138.

568. Luther: Martin (1483-1546), whose enthusiasm reformed the Church.

577. Strauss: (1808-1874), one of the Tubingen philosophers, author of a Rationalistic " Life of Jesus."

626. " What think ye etc.: Matthew xxii. 4.2.

664. Ichors ovr the place: ichor = serum, which exudes where the skin is broken, coats the hurt, and facilitates its healing.

667. Snakeneath Michaels foot: Rafaels picture in the Louvre of Saint Michael slaying the dragon.

703. Brother Newman: John Henry (1801-1890), leader of the Tractarian movement at Oxford, which approached the doctrines of the Roman Church. The last (goth) tract was entirely written by him. The Bishop of Oxford was called upon to stop the series, and in 1845 Dr. Newman entered the Romish Church.

715. King Bomba: means King Puffcheek, King Liar, a sobriquet given to Ferdinand II., late king of the Two Sicilies.–Lazzaroni: Naples beggars, so called from the Lazarus of the Parable, Luke xvi. xo.

716. Antonelli: Cardinal, secretary of Pope Pius IX.

728. Naples liquefaction: the supposed miracle of the liquefaction of the blood of Saint Januarius the Martyr. A small quantity of it is preserved in a crystal reliquary in the great church at Naples, and when brought into the presence of the head of the saint, it melts.

732. Decrassify: make less crass or gross. 744. Fichte: (1762-1814), celebrated German metaphysician, who defined God as the " moral order of the universe."

877. "Pastor est tui Dominus": the Lord is your shepherd.

915. Anacreon: G reek lyric poet of the sixth century B. c.

972. In partibus Episcopus, etc.: "In countries where the Roman Catholic faith is not regularly established, as it was not in England before the time of Cardinal Wiseman, there were no bishops of sees in the kingdom itself, but they took their titles from heathen lands."

Cleon expresses the approach of Greek thought at the time of Christ towards the idea of immortality as made known by Cleon, a Greek poet writing in reply to a Greek patron whose princely gifts and letter asking comment on the philosophical significance of death have just reached him. The important conclusions reached by Cleon in his answer are that the composite mind is greater than the muni.-of the past, because it is capable of accomplishing much in many lines of activity, and of sympathizing with each of those simple great minds that had reached the highest possible perfection " at one point." It is, indeed, the necessary next step in development, though all classes of mind fit into the perfected mosaic of life, no one achievement blotting out any other. This soul and mind development he deduces from the physical development he sees about him. But since with the growth of human consciousness and the increase of knowledge comes greater capability to the soul for joy while the failure of physical powers shuts off the possibility of realizing joy, it would have been better had man been left with nothing higher than mere sense like the brutes. Dismissing the idea of immortality through ones works as unsatisfactory to the individual, he finally concludes that a long and happy life is all there is to be hoped for, since, had the future life which he has sometimes dared to hope for been possible, Zeus would long before have revealed it. He dismisses the preaching of one Paulus as untenable.

"As certain also of your own poets have said ": this motto hints that Pauls speech at Athens (Acts xvii. 22-28) suggests and justifies Brownings conception of such Greek poets as Cleon seeking " the Lord, if haply they might feel after him." Pauls quotation, "For we are also his offspring," is from the " Phoenomena " by Ara-tus, a Greek poet of his own town of Tarsus.

I. Sprinkled isles: probably the Sporades, so named because they were scattered, and in opposition to the Cyclades, which formed a circle around Delos.

Si. Phar;: light-house. The French authority, Allard, says that though there is no mention in classical writings of any light-house in Greece proper, it is probable that there was one at the port of Athens as well as at othei points in Greece. There were certainly several along both shores of the Hellespont, besides the famous father of all light-houses, on the island of Pharos, near Alexandria. Hence the French name for light-house, phare.

S3. Pcecile: the portico at Athens painted with battle pictures by Polygnotus the Thasian.

60. Combined the moods: in Greek music the scales were called moods or modes, and were subject to great variation in the arrangement of tones and semitones.

83. Rhomb. lozenge. trapezoid: all four-sided forms, but differing as to the parallel arrangement of their sides and the obliquity of their angles.

140. Terpander: musician of Lesbos (about 650 B. c.), who added three strings to the four-stringed Greek lyre.

141. Phidias: the Athenian sculptor (about 430 B. c.)–and his friend: Pericles, ruler of Athens (444-429 B. C.). Plutarch speaks of their friendship in his Life of Pericles.

304. Sappho: poet of Lesbos, supreme among lyricists (about 600 B. c.). Only fragments of her verse remain.

305. JEschylus: oldest of the three great Athenian dramatists (525-472 B. c.).

3 0. Paulus; we have heard his fame: Pauls mission to the Gentiles carried him to many of the islands in the Egean Sea as well as to Athens and Corinth (Acts xiii.-xxi.).

Rude! to the Lady of Tripoli: Rudel symbolizes his love as the aspiration of the sunflower that longs only to become like the sun, so losing a flowers true grace, while the sun does not even perceive the flower. He imagines himself as a pilgrim revealing to the Lady of Tripoli by means of this symbol the entire sinking of self in his love for her. Even mens praise of his songs is no more to him than the bees which bask on a sunflower are to it.

Rudel was a Proven9al troubadour, and lived in the twelfth century. The Crusaders, returning from the East, spread abroad wonderful reports of the beauty, learning, and wit of the Countess of Tripoli, a small duchy on the Mediterranean, north of Palestine. Rudel, although never having seen her, fell in love with her and composed songs in honor of her beauty, and finally set out to the East in pilgrims garb. On his way he was taken ill, but lived to reach the port of Tripoli. The countess, being told of his arrival, went on board the vessel. When Rudel heard she was coming, he revived, said she had restored him to life by her coming, and that he was willing to die, having seen her. He died in her arms; she gave him a rich and honorable burial in a sepulchre of porphyry on which were engraved verses in Arabic.

One Word More is the dedication to Elizabeth Barrett Browning which was appended to " Men and Women as first published when it contained fifty poems since distributed under other titles.

The poet, recalling how Rafael when he would all-express his love, wrote sonnets to the loved one, and hoi Dante prepared to paint an angel for Beatrice, draws the conclusion that there is no artist but longs to give expression to his supreme love in some other art than his own which would be the medium of a spontaneous, natural outburst of feeling in a way impossible in the familiar forms of his own art. Thus he would gain a mans joy and miss the artists sorrow, for, like the miracles of Moses, the work of the artist is subject to the cold criticism of the world, which expects him nevertheless always to be the artist, and has no sympathy for him as a man. Since there is no other art but poetry in which it is possible for Browning to express himself, he will at least drop his accustomed dramatic form and speak in his own person; though it be poor, let it stand as a symbol for all-expression. Yet does she not know him, for he has shown her his soul-side as one might imagine the moon showing another side to a mortal lover, which would remain forever as much a mystery to the outside world as the vision seen by Moses, etc. Similarly, he has admired the side his moon of poets has shown the whole world in her poetry, but he blesses himself with the thought of the other side which he alone has seen.

5. Century of sonnets: Rafael is known to have written four love sonnets on the back of sketches for his wall painting, the " Disputa," which are still preserved in collections, one of them in the British Museum. The Italian text of these sonnets with English translations are given in Wolzogens Life of him translated by F. E. Bunnett. Did he ever write a hundred? It is supposed that the lost book once owned by Guido Reni, apparently the one referred to in stanza iv., was a book of drawings. Perhaps these also bore sonnets on their backs, or Browning guessed they did.

10. Who that one: Margarita, a girl Rafael met and loved in Rome, two portraits of whom exist,—one in the Bar-berini Palace, Rome; the other in the Pitti, in Florence. They resemble the Sistine and other Madonnas by Rafael.

21. Madonnas, etc.-" San Sisto," now in Dresden " Foligno," in the Vatican, Rome; the one in Florence is called "del Granduca," and represents her appearing in a vision; the one in the Louvre, called " La Belle Jardiniere," is seated in a garden among lilies.

32. Dante once, etc.: " On that day," writes Dante, "Vita Nuova," xxxv., " which fulfilled the year since my lady had been made of the citizens of eternal life, remembering of her as I sat alone, I betook myself to draw the resemblance of an angel upon certain tablets." That this lady was Beatrice Portinari, as Browning supposes, Xantes devotion to her, in both "The New Life" and " The Divine Comedy," should leave no doubt. Yet the literalness of Mr. W. M. Rossetti makes him obtuse here, as he and other commentators seem to be in their understanding of Browning throughout this stanza. Browning evidently contrasts Dantes tenderness here towards Beatrice with

the remorselessness of his pen in the " Inferno " (see Cantos 32 and 33), where he stigmatized his enemies as if using their very flesh for his parchment, so that ever after in the eyes of all Florence they seemed to bear the marks of the poets hate of their wickedness. It was people of this sort, grandees of the town, Browning fancies, who again " hinder loving," breaking in upon the poet and seizing him unawares forsooth at this intimate moment of loving artistry. " Chancing to turn my head," Dante continues, "I perceived that some were standing beside me to whom I should have given courteous greeting, and that they were observing what I did: also I learned afterwards that they had been there a while before I perceived them." The tender moment was over. He stopped the painting, simply saying, "Another was with me."

74. He who smites the rock: Moses, whose experience in smiting the rock for water (Exodus xvii. 1-7; Numbers xx. 2-i i) is likened to the sorrow of the artist, serving a reckless world.

97. Sinai-foreheaft-. brilliance: Exodus xix. 9, 16; xxxiv. 30.

101. Jethro" s daughter: Moses wife, Zipporah (Exodus ii. 16, 21).

102. Ethiopian bondslave: Numbers xii. i.

122. Liberal hand: the free hand of the fresco-painter cramped to do the exquisite little designs fit for the missal marge = margin of a Prayer-book.

1SO. Samminiato: San Miniato, a church in Florence.

161. Turn a neiu side, etc.: the side turned away from the earth which our world never sees.

163. Zoroaster: (589-513 B. c.), foqnder of the Persian religion, and worshipper of light, whose habit it was to observe the heavens from his terrace.

164. Galileo: (1564-1642), constructor ofthe first telescope, leading him to discover that the Milky Way was an assemblage of starry worlds, and the earth a planet revolving on its axis and about an orbit, for which opinion lie was tried and condemned. When forced to retire from his professorship at Padua, he continued his observations from his own house in Florence.

164. Dumb to Homer, dumb to Keats: Homer celebrates the moon in the " Hymn to Diana " (see Shelleys translation), and makes Artemis upbraid her brother Phoebus when he claims that it is not meet for gods to concern themselves with mortals (Iliad, xxi. 470). Keats, in " Endymion," sings of her love for a mortal.

174. Moses, Aaron, Nadab and Abihu, etc.: Exodus xxiv. i, 10.

In A Balcony.

In a Balcony presents in three dramatic scenes a crisis in the lives of three human beings, ending tragically for two of them. The dramatic motive is the conflict between Norberts truthful and Constances dissembling policy. Constance, winning her way, loses all she thought to have gained and more, while, had Norberts straightforward course been followed, all would have been gained for both. She tries to convince Norbert that should he ask her hand of the queen now, not only will his request not be granted, but his own future prospects will probably be ruined; for being in high favor with the queen on account of his services, he might aspire to ask anything of her even to sharing the crown, but when she discovers all was done for the sake of winning Constance and not primarily for her, the revulsion of feeling will lead to her refusing. Rather than this, Constance would have their love remain unannounced; but Norbert will not consent to anything less than a frank avowal to all the world of his love, and is ready to rely on the justice of the queen to grant him the reward he chooses. Against his better judgment, he finally submits to follow Constances advice so far as to flatter the queen by insinuating that he asks for Constance because she is as near as he dare approach to the queen. When Constance learns that the queen has mistaken Norberts dissembling for an avowal of love to herself, that she is overwhelmed with joy, and how great her sufferings have been through the starving of her affections, with sympathies roused and with fears for the consequences if the queen finds out the mistake, she tries to force Norbert, whose character she still fails fully to comprehend, into actually giving himself to the queen. Norbert now shows himself the champion of truth at any cost, but too late. The queen is undeceived, but cannot forgive the deception. Constance, at last, learns to know Norbert as he really is, and her love reaches a height worthy of his.

130. Rubens: (1577-1640), the greatest of the Flemish school of painters.

Dramat1s Persons.

James Lees Wife. A cycle of love-lyrics, each representing a scene in the growth of a husbands estrangement as reflected in the mood of the constant wife. In I., which represents her as having turned to look oui upon the world, descrying in the face of nature a change omi nous to her of a change in their love, the mood is one of vague dread and forecast. In II., seated by the fireside, whose security and cheer kindle sinister suggestions of wreck by sea and land, the mood is one of poignant foreboding. In III., the outer world again calling her attention to the stormy and decrepit aspects of the waning year, the mood is one of remonstrance against the overpowering of the light of the inner life by the law of change which masters the external world. In IV., the home being left behind, the walk and talk along the beach reveal husband and wife on the brink of alienation. Alike irksome to him are her loving idealization and criticism of him, and the mood which here leads her to anatomize his love is one of clear recognition of the estrangement. In V., on the cliff, left alone and aloft, her mood is one of brooding over the meaning of love, finding appropriate images for her thoughts and feelings in dry turf and cold rock, dreary in spite of sunshine, but which the cricket and butterfly visit with color, even as love with its resplendent grace dowers the low mind with a sudden winged glory. In VI., turning for distraction to a book, she reads a fanciful poem of the wind as a voice of human woes. Her impatience with the young poet for his easy assumption of defeat by imagination instead of experience, leads her to put her own actual experience into imaginative shape, transitoriness, typified in the flitting beauty of the dawn, making its perpetual call upon the spiritual faculty of man, and urging him onward ceaselessly. Then recognizing this insight into the use of change as a step farther on, her mood turns again to the contemplation of the human piteousness of perpetual change. In VII., at the seas edge, among its rocks, the mood that finds expression is one of spiritual aspiration as the fruit of suffering. The autumn of the " brown old earth" diffusing cheer, though weighted with experience, seems to her fancy the embodiment of her insight that the love which is disappointed of its satisfaction on the natural plane of life must seek through that disappointment a finer spiritual fruition. In VIII., beside the drawing-board, pursuing in art the impulse she has just received to seek the significance of love on a higher impersonal plane, the hand whose beauty she is learning, through her faulty drawing, to love becomes to her one of Gods many exemplifications of love in skill or in power. Her perception of its beauty as beyond the human power, even of a Da Vinci to outvie, leads her to understand a Da Vincis interest in the actual as well as in the beautiful. The crude peasant hand in its structure and uses, showing Gods power, is as worthy of study as the perfect hand that shows Gods skill. The mood expressed is one of rapid insight through analogies of art and experience, which imply that her bemoaning her love for lack of the ideal perfection she craved is like her scorn of the peasant hand for its lack of the beauty of the cast. The use that survives the beauty, and the use that survives the failure of her ideal, remain. In IX., on deck, taking her way in the world apart from her husband, the estrangement fully grown to the separation she accepts, the final mood is one of utter belief in the power of love. Had his love been as supreme as hers no fault in look or thought would have mattered.

Gold Hair. A quizzical story playing with the pious naivetes of a guide-book legend. It tells how a reputed girl-saint of good family in Brittany valued the gold of this life spite of heaven and the grave, and, managing to hide her money in her beautiful gold hair before she died, remained in mens praise as a model of sanctity, and was only detected as a miser years afterwards when her skull was found in her coffin wedged in with her dear gold coins. The sophistical moral suggested is that such a marvellous and damning mixture of good and evil in the human heart as this story lays bare warrants the doctrine of Original Sin, and supplies a reason for sticking to the Christian faith, despite Bishop Colenso and the " Essays and Reviews."

1t. ilix: like flax.

M. w–20 96. O cor humanum, etc.: probably refers to Lucretius ii. 14–" O miseras hominum mentes, O pectora caeca!"–O wretched mind of man, O blind breast I heart, "cor humanum," being substituted in the poets memory for mind, " mentes hominum."

90. I. ouis-d or: a French gold coin.

128. Thirty pieces. Potters Field: Matthew xxvii.

3. 5-7- 143. Essays and Revietus: a collection of seven dissertations by Dr. Temple of Rugby, Professor Jowett of Oxford, and other English churchmen, on theological topics, all bearing on the advantage to religion and morality derivable from a freer scrutiny ot the Bible as to the character of its facts, and the nature of its authority as a sacred book. It was a shock to many, and it excited much discussion, initiating in England what is now known as the Higher Criticism of the Bible.

145. Coienso: Bishop of Natal, South Africa–whose examination of the Bible was instigated by the questions of a Zulu native–published in 1862 the first volume of his work on the Pentateuch, which added fuel to the debate stirred up by the " Essays and Reviews."

The Worst of It is addressed mentally by a husband to a wife who has been false to him after having given him a years perfect happiness. Love of her has been so much to him that stanch apology for her rights of choice, and loyal resentment of the imputation of evil she will suffer in the world through having broken his bonds, contend with his own pain, and his secret fear that her womanhood must sustain some real taint, without in the least marring the quality of his own fidelity or altering his obedient renunciation of any right over her.

Dis AUter VIsum. A womans arraignment of a mans worldly-wise decision against yielding to the impulse to express the love he felt for her. Her keen recollection of their last meeting, and her ironical reproach of him, because their present meeting reveals each entangled in a degrading companionship, find outlet in the shape of an undercurrent of thought addressed to him under cover of an apparently light manner, suited to a casual meeting of friends. The situation before and after the ten dividing years that have passed is made clear; and not less so her conclusion, that his wise caution was unwise and cowardly from the larger point of view, thwarting to their soul-development thenceforth, and involving two others, moreover, in their spiritual blight. The double title emphasizes the moral motive of the poem: Dis Ati-ter Visum, " The gods see otherwise," words used by Virgil,. ffineid, ii. 579, after describing the last vain resistance of the Greeks by the Trojans.–Le Byron de noajours: "The modern Byron," that is, the lover who excites passion, but does not indulge love.

36. Schumann: Robert, musical composer and critic (1810-1856).

38. Ingres: Jean August, painter (1780-1867).

40. Heine: Heinrich, lyrical poet (1800-1856).

42. Votive frigate: the model of a vessel hanging in the church, the pious (votive) offering, presumably, of one whom the saints had aided to make a safe voyage.

58. Sure of the Fortieth spare Arm-chair sure of being elected to fill the first vacancy in membership of the forty of the French Academy.

Too Late presents a series of moods of a man who first realizes the full force of his love when the woman he loved is dead. He blames himself now for not having been more determined in his suit. He waited to tell his love until she should sufficiently encourage him with a glance; when she marries some one else, he blames no one, but calmly thinks that Time will give her to him. Either his love will reach out toward her round the obstacle of her husband, or else a miracle will sweep the obstruction entirely away. Now Edith is dead there is no hope. It is not worth while to vent his rage on the past, nor upon the husband, whom he represents as a person very inferior to himself, a poet, who rhymed rubbish that nobody read–and incapable of loving Edith.

All that is left to him is to get what satisfaction he can by living with his back to theworld, kneeling in the imagined presence of Edith, and perfecting in spirit the courtship once planned.

93. (ltktl: Daniel v. 27.

138. Summum jus: utmost justice.

A6t Vogler (after he lias been extemporizing upon the musical instrument of his invention). The musician rises into a state of exaltation through the wonder of his own musical gift, the outcome of which seems to him more entirely creative than that of any other art, because the form is evolved from the subjective consciousness and not imitated from nature, as it is, more or less in the other arts. While they are obedient to laws, the composers inspiration is a revelation of the divine will, and being such is eternal in its essence. From this he reasons that all good is of the same nature, and, though only partial now, is destined to persist and form a perfect whole in the future. Evil is simply the discord that enhances the beauty of the coming concord, and is destined to be resolved in it, is, indeed, the evidence in its aspect of failure that perfection is assured in the future.—AM Vogler: George Joseph Vogler, born

VViirzburg, Bavaria, June 15, 1749; educated for the church, but his musical talent, which showed itself at an early age, was also developed; ordained priest in Rome, 1773, and opened a school of music in Mannheim, 1775. At Stockholm, he founded a second school of music, and became famous for his performances on an instrument which he had invented, called the Orchestrion, a compact organ, in which four keyboards of five octaves each, and a pedal board of thirty-six keys, with swell complete, were packed into a cube of nine feet; travelled all over Europe with his organ, visited London 1790, his performances being received with enthusiasm; opened a third school of music at Darmstadt, where Weber and Meyerbeer became his pupils. Here he died May 6, 1814. His " Missa Pas-toricia" is performed every Christmas at the Hof Ka pelle, Vienna. (See Groves " Dictionary of Music and Musicians.") 3. Solomon willed: Jewish and Moslem legends gave Solomon sovereignty over the demons and powers of nature which he owed to the possession of a seal on which the "most great name of God was engraved" (Lane, "Arabian Nights ").

7. Ineffable Name: the unspeakable name of God. Mysterious names of the Deity occur in other religions besides the Jewish.

23. Romes dome: it has been customary to illuminate the dome of Saint Peters on Easter Sunday and other important festivals.

34. Protoplast: the thing first modelled from which copies are imitated.

52. Out of three sounds he frame, not a fourth sound, but a star, etc.: if you were to mix three colors together, the result would be a fourth color in which the individuality of the first three colors would be sunk; but if you mix three sounds together in a chord, the result will not be a fourth sound, but a wonderful harmony of all three, partaking of the individuality of each, and this is done by combining tones chosen from natures chaos of sounds through the creative power of the artist.

91. Common chord: consists of the fundamental, with a major (four semitones), or minor (three semitones) third, and a perfect fifth (seven semitones) over it.

93. Ninth: if major, contains an octave and two semitones; if minor, an octave and one semitone. These last lines of the poem, stripped of their symbolic meaning, may be taken as an exact explanation of a simple harmonic modulation. Suppose Abt Vogler, when he "feels for the common chord," to have struck the chord of C major in its first inversion, i. e. the third, E, in the bass, the fifth, G, at the top; now, " sliding by semitones," that is, playing in succession chords with the upper note a semitone lower, he would come to the chord A, E, C, which is the (minor) tonic chord of the scale of

A, the relative minor of C, and so he would thus " sink to the minor." Now he blunts the fifth of this chord E, to Eb which thus becomes a minor ninth over the root D, the whole chord being D, F, A, C, Eb, and, as he explains, he stands on alien ground because he has modulated away from the key of C, but, instead of following this dominant by its natural solution, its own tonic, which would be G, B, D, he treats it as if it were what is called a supertonic harmony. So, after pausing on this chord to survey awhile the heights he rolled from into the deep, he suddenly modulates back to C. He has dared and done, his resting-place is found–the C major of this life. This is the progression:–

"C major of " Sliding by semitones." " alien ground." this Life."

Rabbi Ben Ezra gives expression to a religious philosophy which recognizes the perfectness of the divine plan in which love plays an equal part with power. Therefore, doubts and rebuffs are welcomed as the divine means for perfecting the souls growth and shaping it for the glorification of the divine. The very failure of man in the flesh showing his infinite possibilities of growth removes him forever from the brute, perfect on its plane, and gives assurance both of God, and of mans tendency God-wards, from which follows the certainty of God and the enduringness of the human soul. Old age is joyously accepted as the vantage ground from which life can be viewed and the truth in regard to its struggles discerned.

Rabbi Ben Ezra, or Ibn Ezra, was a medioeval Jewish writer and thinker, born in Toledo, near the end of the eleventh century. His real name is said to be Abraham ben Meir ben Ezra. He was poor but studied hard and travelled in Africa, the Holy Land, Persia, India, Italy, France, and England; but during all his wanderings he kept busy writing, and gained much fame as a theologian, philosopher, physician, astronomer, mathematician, and poet. Dr. Berdoe quotes Mr. A. J. Campbell to the effect that the distinctive features of the Rabbi of the poem and the philosophy put into his mouth are drawn from the writings of the real Rabbi. Dr. M. Friedlander has written five volumes of exposition on the writings of Ibn Ezra, published for the Society of Hebrew Literature by Triibner and Co. (Died 1167 or 1168.) 151. Potters wheel: borrowed from Isaiah lxiv. 8, and Jeremiah xviii. 2-6.

A Death In the Desert is a supposed MS. account of Saint Johns dying testimony to the truth of the revelation of God made man through Christ. Johns own spiritual faith transcends the idea of evidence as dependent upon witness or memory of signs and wonders. He has been nourished on such external evidence to the end that his faith now rests upon internal evidence,–has become one with the desires and aspirations of his soul. Foreseeing future scrutiny of the superficial truth of fact, he meets these doubts by declaring that there must be development in the nature of the evidence which shall appeal to developing man; and that mans progress is dependent on his finding a developing internal warrant for faith in Absolute Love and Power, the good for man of proof, consisting merely in its capacity to educe his faith, not to enable him to dispense with the need of it. So, when man can perceive will and love in man, before assumed to be altogether Gods, instead of requiring conviction from the sort of proof that satisfied less developed man, let him exert his faith in the essential truth, acknowledging its action as a result of old processes outgrown because assimilated, and not disproved because in essence true. Pamphylax, Xanthus, Valeus, Theotypas, narrative and gloss are all imagined by Browning; the Revelation and Gospel of Saint John being the main sources feeding the inspiration of the poem.

6. Terebinth: the turpentine tree.

23. The decree: some decree ordering the persecution of the Christians, perhaps Domitians.

SO. Ball ofnard: spikenard, giving an aromatic odor.

122. Head ivool-iuhite, etc.: Revelation i. 14, 15.

279. Prometheus: the Titan who stole fire from Olym-pos and brought it to man, defying Zeus, who had refused it. schylus founded his " Prometheus Bound " upon

the myth; and possibly in the two other parts of his Trilogy which have not come down to us, his satyrs may have touched it in gay wonder, as Browning imagines.

329. This Ebion, this Cerinthus: Ebion is said to have been a pupil of Cerinthus, but may not have been a real person. Cerinthus was a contemporary of John, or nearly so, who held the Ebionite heresy that the Christ part only resided in Jesus, who was merely human, and that this divine part was not crucified, having flown away before.

Caliban upon Setebos gives the ruminations of a typical undeveloped mind as to the nature of God, which is influenced by his observations of the capriciousness of nature, his fear of its threatening aspects, his hatred of his nasters cruelty to him, and his own undeveloped nature. Yet even at this low stage of development a reaching toward something better is evidenced in Calibans supposition that behind Setebos is a power which he calls the Quiet, indifferent to the affairs of man, but so far superior to Setebos as not to be actively antagonistic to man. Browning has taken Shakespeares Caliban as a fit subject out of which to evolve the sort of anthropomorphic reasoning he wished to portray. Shakespeare possibly got his hint for Caliban from an old book of travels, "Purchas his Pilgrimage," in which a strange brute-man is described (see also Dr. Furness Variorum " Tempest ").–Thou thougktest, etc.: Psalm l. ji.

4. While he kicks: the third person used by Caliban is characteristic of an early phase in language development.

24. Setebos: in Edens " History of Travayle " there is a description of giants that inhabited Patagonia, two of whom were captured by Captain Magellan, and finding themselves caught " cryed upon theyre greate deuyll Setebos to helpe them."

Confessions. A dying man confessing to a priest refuses to be overcome by a sense of the worlds badness, but dwells instead upon the sweetness of love as he tells of his stolen interviews with a girl he loved, illustrating with his medicine bottles and the curtain, which from their arrangement call up a vision in all its details of the scene where the lovers used to meet.

May and Death-A natural outbreak of irritation at the return of May, with its renewed joys and poignant memories of old associations cut short by Death, the first pang of it, starting the wish that all Springs joys had died with the friend, then softening, for the sake of other such pairs of friends, to the longing to reserve as sacred to the dead merely one little plant whose red-splashed leaf seems to betoken his own bleeding sorrow. The poem was a personal utterance on the death of a cousin, Charles Silverthorne.

13. One plant: the Spotted Persicaria or Polygonum Persicaria, whose leaves have purple stains varying in size and brightness according to the nature of the soil where it grows.

Deaf and Dumb translates into speech the impression received from a group of statuary, which is that obstructions only serve to emphasize more clearly the soul of beauty and love. The obstruction of the prism reveals the inner beauty of a ray of light; so the obstruction of the senses by deafness and dumbness seems to impress more clearly the beauty of the soul upon the expression nd reveal it in the eyes. The lines were written in 1862 for a group exhibited at the International Exhibition of that year, by Woolner, of Constance and Arthur, the deaf and dumb children of Sir Thomas Fairbairn.

prosjtfce, meaning "look forward," anticipates Death as the climax and fruition of Life,–tiie best and last occasion for the assertion of the spirits mastery,–the gateway to the rapture of the Souls reunion with its supplementary Soul.

Eurydice to Orpheus gives speech to the yearning expressed in Eurydices face, in the picture, which tempts them both to let the past go and to defy the future for the sake of the instants satisfaction of their love. Orpheus descending to Hades so worked upon Persephone, Queen of the Dead, by the magic of his music, that she gave him his wife Eurydice on condition that he should not turn to look at her till they reached the upper world, else he would "all his long toils forfeit" for that look.

Youth and Art. In this half-humorous soliloquy a woman regrets the foolishness that made herself and a young artist choose worldly ease and comfort instead of confessing to each other their love and casting in their lot together, thus gaining the true happiness that only once was within their grasp.

8. Gibson: John (1790-1866), sculptor, well known by his " Tinted Venus."

1Z. Grisi: Giulietta (born in Milan, 1812), a celebrated opera singer.

31. E in alt: E in the upper part of the scale, high E.

32. Chromatic scale: a scale which proceeds by halftones.

58. Bals-par: dress balls.

60. An R. A.: Royal Academician.

A Face. The poet, in sketching how he would like to have the portrait of a certain beautiful woman painted, gives a vivid likeness of her, though his descriptions are all indirect.

3. Tuscans early art: the early Tuscan painters verr still under the influence of the Byzantine school of painting, one of the marked features of which was the constant use of gold backgrounds. Cimabue, who was the first of the Tuscans to break away from the conventions of the Byzantine school, frequently used gold backgrounds.

14. Correggio loves to mass, etc.: this is a true bit of criticism upon Correggios style, which is especially remarkable for its chiaroscuro. " He knew how to anatomize light and shade in endless gradation." His angels, grouped in brilliant depths of sky, might well wonder at the solitary head on the pale gold ground.

A Likeness, in giving two instances of the unsympathetic regard which the uninitiated will bestow upon a likeness deeply cherished by its owner, and a third instance in which a friend being too appreciative, the possessor of the likeness feels it no longer peculiarly his own, and, half pleased, half vexed, would as soon toss it to his friend as only a duplicate after all, illustrates: first, how the person to whose sympathies an object has especially appealed, is secretly grieved by others lack of appreciation; and second, the irritation aroused through the loss of the sense of peculiar possession occasioned by the full appreciation of another.

18. Tipton Slasher: an English boxer.

22. Rarey: the famous horse-tamer, whose method of subduing the most vicious brutes consisted in firmness and gentleness.

23. Sayers: the English prize-fighting champion.

54. Marc Antonio: an engraver.

55. Festina lente: hasten slowly.

6i. Volpato: an eminent designer and engraver, born at Bassano in 1738; died 1803.

Mr. Sludge, " the Medium " is a humorous monologue conveying an American mediums defence to his patron who has caught him in cheating, followed by a short soliloquy conveying his unequivocal self-exposure. The whole presents dramatically the conditions and nature both of spiritualism and the belief in spiritualism current in the

middle part of the nineteenth century, illustrating the credulity of the public and the self-deception of the medium. Hawthorne, in his " French and Italian Notebooks," June 9, 1858, writes: "Browning and his wife had both been present at a spiritual session held by Mr. Home the American medium, David D. Home, and had seen and felt the unearthly hands, one of which had placed a laurel wreath on Mrs. Brownings head. Brown ing, however, avowed his belief that these hands were affixed to the feet of Mr. Home, who lay extended in his chair, with his legs stretched far under the table. The marvellousness. melted strangely away in his hearty gripe, and at the sharp touch of his logic."

.168. Parson: Richard (1759-1808), the celebrated scholar, professor of Greek and librarian of the London Institution.

345. Hymn in G, with a natural F, etc.: impossible music, of course, since the scale of G requires F sharp, and a piece set in consecutive fourths would be cacophony.

678. Rakab: Joshua ii. 1-24; vi. 25.

788. Pasiphae: wife of Minos, and, according to the Greek myth, enamoured of a bull.

921. Charless Wain: the constellation of the Great Bear.

1140. Bridgeijuater book: the Bridgewater treatises were written to meet the thesis set by the Earl of Bridgewater, "On the Power, Wisdom, and Goodness of God as manifested in Creation," for which purpose he bequeathed j8, ooo, in 1829, to the Royal Society.

Apparent Failure saves the Morgue in a double sense; for it was written to preserve the famous little building from destruction, and it seeks to make its gloomy purpose less hopeless, retrieving three poor wretches whose death and doom seemed sealed there from the imputation of utter failure.

1. Seven years since: in the summer of 1856 Browning was in Paris.

3. Baptism of your Prince: Louis Napoleon, only child of Napoleon III. and Empress Eugenie, bom March 16, 1856.

1. The Congress: the Paris Congress of the European Powers on Italys unity and freedom, Prince Gortschakoff representing Russia, Count Cavour, then prime minister of Piedmont, speaking for Italy, Count Buol, Austrian foreign minister, 1852-1859, objecting.

12. Petrarchs Vaucluse: a fountain in Vaucluse, in southern France, the source of the Sorgue. In the village of Vaucluse Petrarch lived for a time.

Epilogue. First Speaker, as David, gives symbolically the point of view of one who believes in special revelation of religious truths. Second Speaker, as Renan, shows disillusionment as to special revelation along with regret for the lost ideal and hopelessness in consequence of it. Third Speaker, the poet, restores the lost ideal, not through the reinstating of a special revelation, but through the recognition of the revelation that comes to every human being in feeling and knowledge.

1. " On the first of the Feast of Feasts ": refers to the dedication of Solomons Temple, i Kings viii. and ix.; 2 Chronicles v. and vi.–Renan, born at Treguier, Cotes-du-Nord, France, 1823. Distinguished for his "Life of Christ," from which he banished all supernatural elements.

This book should be returned to the Library on or before the last date stamped below.

A fine is incurred by retaining it beyond the specified time.

Please return promptly.

J. UW H3

; .

s U ;

." ".-.-

Lightning Source UK Ltd.
Milton Keynes UK
UKOW041830240912

199553UK00001B/391/P